COLD WAR STORIES: TRAITOR IN BLUE

FRANK JAMES SCHRENK

FRANK JAMES SCHRENK

For Uncle Frank
KIA November 1944

CHAPTER 1
Hurtgen Forest, Germany

Sergeant Frank Dunn was a squad leader in the 28th Infantry Division. He landed on Normandy beach in July 1944, marched down the Champs-Elysees in Paris the following August and fought his way across France to the German border. He received the Bronze Star medal for charging a German machine gun nest that had pinned down the squad when he was a Private First Class. His squad leader had been killed and Frank decided to take charge since he was the oldest soldier in the squad. Being oldest was probably not a good reason to take charge when he thought about it, but at the time, it seemed like a good idea. He was also wounded during this battle and received the Purple Heart. After being treated for his wound, Frank returned to duty and was promoted to sergeant which was how he became a squad leader in Company A of the 110th Infantry Regiment, 28th Infantry Division.

The 28th Infantry Division was the first of the allied armies to reach German soil. About a week later Frank's squad was dug in at the edge of a small town called Simonskall in the Hurtgen Forest during the coldest November in recent German history. It was snowing again and so cold that the water in their canteens kept freezing into a slushy mix. The roads however were a muddy quagmire that bogged down the trucks and tanks. Frank wondered how the air could be so cold and yet the roads stayed muddy. Simonskall was located at the bottom of a long valley along the Kall creek and surrounded by steep hills. The squad was dug in on the hill on the far side of the valley. Germans occupied the top of the hill and their artillery made life miserable for the Americans.

"Sarge, the Looie wants you back at headquarters" one of his men said as he crawled up to Frank's foxhole. The 'Looie' was Lieutenant Duncan. Frank turned to the soldier and looking at his dirty, bearded face, struggled to remember the soldier's name. There had been so many replacements over the last four months that he had difficulty remembered the names of the new guys. He also knew that there was a high probability that they would be either killed or wounded soon so didn't want to befriend any of them. He lost several friends since they arrived in Normandy and he decided to put off making any new friends until this damn war was over. The latest rumors were that the war would be over by Christmas. He hoped so, it would be good to get back to Philly, suck down some suds with his buddies and tell war stories.

As he crawled out of his foxhole, he remembered the man's name and said, "Roger, Private Ardmore. Pass the word to the rest of the squad reminding them to keep low and awake. The cold makes you want to sleep and before you know it, you have frostbite or worse, like a German trying to kill you." Although this advice was well known, Frank made it a point to repeat it over and over again to his men.

Lieutenant Duncan had set up his headquarters in a captured German bunker that once served as a medical aid station.

When Frank got there, the other three squad leaders, Sergeants McGarvey, Sullivan and Nelson, were squatting against one wall and drinking hot coffee. He leaned his Thompson submachine gun against the wall of the bunker and opened the canvas bag on his web belt containing his canteen. He separated the canteen from the metal cup that it sat in and poured some coffee into it. The coffee did little to warm him up, but every little bit helped. He asked a sergeant if he could arrange to run some coffee up to his squad who were sitting in their muddy foxholes. The Looie was on the radio so Frank quietly asked the other squad leaders how they were holding up. They shrugged their shoulders. The Germans were pouring artillery onto the entire regiment and they were taking a lot of causalities.

When Lieutenant Duncan got off the radio, he turned to the squad leaders and said, "The 112th regiment is being driven back by the Germans from Schmidt, the objective town." The 109th and the 110th regiments had the mission to protect the flanks of the 112th. "We have been ordered to hold our position until relieved. Make sure your men have dry socks and plenty of food and water."

As the squad leaders were leaving the bunker and crossing the lane back to their positions, an artillery barrage came raining down on them. Frank, McGarvey and Sullivan dove to the ground. Sergeant Nelson ran to a foxhole and hunkered down. The artillery splintered the trees in the forest and one round landed near the three sergeants. Sergeant McGarvey felt the ground rise under him and it stunned him. He heard a ringing in his ears and felt like throwing up. Through the ringing in his ears, he heard Sergeant Sullivan screaming in pain and saw Frank lying about three feet from him. He managed to steady himself and crawled over to Frank. Frank was hit in the head and did not move. McGarvey checked his pulse and found none. Sergeant Frank Dunn's spirit was leaving his body.

Frank's spirit was looking down at his body and felt sad that he wouldn't live to see his sister's baby. He was sure it was a boy and he had so much to share with him.

CHAPTER 2
Philadelphia, Pennsylvania

The telegram delivered to Frank's mother on December 1, 1944 stated:

THE SECRETARY OF WAR DESIRES ME TO EXPRESS HIS DEEP REGRET THAT YOUR SON SERGEANT FRANK DUNN WAS KILLED IN ACTION ON TEN NOVEMBER IN GERMANY.

No other details were received.

Sometime later, a card was received that stated:

GENERAL MARSHALL EXTENDS HIS DEEP SYMPATHY IN YOUR BEREAVEMENT. YOUR SON FOUGHT VALIANTLY IN A SUPREME HOUR OF HIS COUNTRY'S NEED. HIS MEMORY WILL LIVE IN THE GRATEFUL HEART OF OUR NATION.

The family was rocked. Lawrence Logan was Frank's brother-in-law and tried to enlist with Frank after the Japanese attack on Pearl Harbor in December 1941 but was turned down due to his age. Lawrence had married Mary Dunn, Frank's sister, in June 1941. Three years later, she was pregnant with their first child who they had planned to name Lawrence if it was a boy. They decided to change that to Frank in honor of his uncle. In January 1945, Frank was born. Lawrence and Mary Logan focused their attention on baby Frank and learned to deal with the grief of losing his uncle. They lived in a row house in Philadelphia and although they didn't have a lot of money, neither Frank nor his sister Marie (who was born eighteen months later)-noticed any hardships. They had enough to eat and good clothes to wear.

Frank was constantly reminded of his Uncle Frank because his mother kept his picture hanging in the living room. The picture was done professionally, and his Uncle Frank was in his uniform with the red Keystone prominently shown on his upper arm. The Germans called the 28th Division the 'Bloody Bucket' Division because of the resemblance between the keystone and a bucket. When Frank would look at the picture, he felt like his uncle was looking after him.

When Frank was nearing graduation from high school, he didn't have any plans for a job or college, so he and two friends put in job applications everywhere they thought might hire them. One of them was with the City of Philadelphia as an engineering aide to a surveyor. After hearing no responses from any of the applications, he spent the summer outside working for a dollar an hour at a restaurant in downtown Philly dishing out water ice in wax impregnated paper cups to hot, weary shoppers. When fall came, they moved him inside to man the soda fountain. In October, he received a letter from the City of Philadelphia offering him the job as an Engineering Aide I. It was almost five months after submitting the application. He had almost forgotten about it but to his delight it was a fifty percent jump in pay - $1.50 an hour! He grabbed it!

He reported to the survey office in northeast Philly. Everyone in the survey office was older than him but he was not surprised. He was assigned to a team of four and was treated as low man on the totem pole, which of course, he was. His team chief suggested he spend some time learning how to operate the theodolite, or running the gun in surveyor slang, which they used to measure vertical angles with a small telescope. He picked up the nuances of running the gun and after passing a test of his proficiency, was given a raise and designated Engineering Aide II.

Frank bought a car and started banking some money. He dated several girls and found one he really liked. Barb Neary lived a couple blocks from him. Barb was a cutie, about as tall as his mother, who topped out at five feet. Frank and Barb had been dating for over a year when he received a notice from the draft board to report for his physical examination. The rated result was a '1-A'; which meant he could be drafted soon.

You have an opportunity to learn a trade if you volunteer for the Air Force or Navy.

Frank was not surprised that this thought sounded like a voice in his head. He had been aware of it for a long time and imagined it was the voice of his Uncle Frank, so he decided that he did not want to be drafted into the Army. It meant a longer enlistment to volunteer to go into the Air Force or the Navy, but he deferred to the voice in his head. He went to the Air Force recruitment office and took the test to determine his aptitude. He planned to take the test for the Navy if he didn't score well. He was pleased that he scored high on the Air Force test and after being assured that he would receive training in the electronics field, he signed up. He didn't bother taking the

Navy test since he got what he wanted from the Air Force. His parents had apprehensions about him going into the military but glad it was the Air Force rather than the Army.

San Antonio, Texas

Frank started Basic Training at Lackland Air Force Base (AFB), TX in May 1965. Arriving recruits from Philadelphia were kept together in what was called a Flight. There were several Flights in a Training Squadron. They were greeted by Staff Sergeant (SSGT) Harley. Harley looked to be about 50 years old and was built like a fireplug – a bit on the short side but burly. He didn't smile when he looked over the recruits and looked somewhat disgusted at what he saw.

SSGT Harley roared at them, "I am your Technical Instructor for the next six weeks and I will make airmen out of you sissy civilians. I was a Ranger in the Army during World War II and stormed the cliffs at Normandy. I am from Philadelphia and will be extra tough on you guys from Philly. Are there any questions?" Nobody said a word.

Basic wasn't as tough as Frank expected from the greeting by SSGT Harley. It consisted of a lot of marching around, attendance at class to learn about Air Force rank, Air Force rules and the many ways you could screw up and be sent to the stockade. The most physical part was doing exercises each day in sandy soil. Near the end of Basic training, they went through a confidence course a couple times. This consisted of things like climbing over hurtles, ascending cliffs with ropes and crossing a wide creek on a rope ladder. Weapons training consisted of shooting a 30 caliber M-1 carbine at a target. They were issued 70 rounds, ten for practice and 60 for qualifying. If you hit the silhouette target with all 60 qualifying rounds, you were awarded a small arms expert marksman ribbon. Frank got all sixty and was authorized to wear the ribbon on his dress blue uniform. However, he didn't really feel like a small arms expert.

Basic trainees were required to pull four-hour stints of guard duty as part of the training. Why anyone would want to break into a trainee barracks was lost on Frank. When Frank's turn came, he was bored and sleepy but that changed when he was approached in the middle of the night by the Deputy Tech Instructor, Airman First Class (A1C) Graham of his Flight.

Be careful – don't argue with him. Do what he says and document it.

Frank was shocked to hear the voice in his head again. A1C Graham told him to wake up four airmen who he named and told them to put on civilian clothes. He took the four trainees out of the barracks. Graham told Frank, "Don't tell anyone, except your replacement on guard duty, that we are on a night detail."

Frank didn't know what a night detail meant but was afraid to ask. Soon after Graham and the trainees left, Airmen Mike Morrison showed up to replace Frank for his shift. Frank told Mike, "Graham has taken four guys from the barracks on a night detail and they had not returned. Graham told me they would be back by first light. I wrote down exactly what happened and the times in case something goes wrong." Mike was nervous but agreed with Frank that it was a good idea to write down what happened.

Unknown to Frank and Mike, Graham's 'night detail' was to go have a good time in Mexico. However, Graham's plan to have them back by morning went awry when one of the basic trainees claimed a girl had stolen his wallet. The Mexican police were called and the five of them were detained in Mexico.

The next morning, SSGT Harley stormed into the barracks and ordered all the trainees to fall out and stand in formation. The trainees were asleep at the time and hurriedly put on their fatigues while SSGT Harley was screaming at them, "Fall out NOW and forget about squaring away your area."

When they were all standing at attention, SSGT Harley took roll and asked, "Who was on guard duty when A1C Graham stopped by the barracks last night?"

Tell him what happened and show him your notes!

Frank raised his hand and Mike raised his also. "You two stay here and the rest of you go back into the barracks and prepare for today's training."

SSGT Harley motioned for them to follow him into his office. He told them that Graham and the four trainees were in jail in Mexico. He asked them what had happened when they were on guard duty.

Frank pulled out his notes and told SSGT Harley, "Deputy Tech Instructor Graham showed up during the night and took four airmen trainees out of the barracks for a night detail. They were supposed to return in the morning." Harley took the notes and told them to join the rest of the flight for the days training.

Mike and Frank were both concerned that they would be held responsible. However, they were not punished but heard that the four trainees had two additional weeks of basic training added to their training as punishment and A1C Graham was sent to the stockade. Frank never heard any more about it but was grateful the voice in his head warned him to be careful and document what happened.

Biloxi, Mississippi

After basic training, the graduating Flight was promoted from Airman Basic to Airman Third Class (A3C). Frank and several other recruits, including Mike Morrison received orders to report to Kessler AFB, MS for electronics training. Frank and Mike became close friends since the Mexico incident. Mike was from Maryland and had worked at Safeway grocery store before joining the Air Force. He was a few inches taller and about as thin as Frank. After his enlistment was up, Mike planned to go back home, marry his girlfriend and be a Safeway manager after being discharged from the Air Force. Mike's plan kind of paralleled the plans Frank had but he had not made the decision to leave after his enlistment was up or stay for twenty years or more.

Upon arriving at Keesler AFB on an Air Force chartered bus from Lackland in July 1965, Frank stepped off the air-conditioned bus and almost gagged. The heat was stifling, and the humidity was so thick you could see it in the air. Stepping out of the thick air, sergeants from the various training squadrons were calling out names of the airmen and placing them in separate clusters outside the bus. Frank and Mike found out they were in the same squadron and were assigned a room shared with two other airmen. One was from Tennessee and the other from North Carolina. The Basic Electronics course did not start for two weeks, so the four of them were put on kitchen patrol, or KP. They rose in the morning at 0400, reported for KP duty at 0500 and left after dinner at 1900. It was hot, exhausting duty and they were glad when class started. Frank really enjoyed the classes and helped Mike, when he asked.

Their Squadron Commander addressed the troops one cloudy and windy morning. "Today we have an evacuation order from the Base Commander. Hurricane Betsy is bearing down and will hit somewhere between New Orleans and Biloxi. It is predicted to make landfall on 11 Sep. That means we can expect very high winds and possible flooding. Keesler will probably be on the side of the hurricane where the winds and rain will be the worst. Tonight, we are going to march across base and take shelter in a cinder block class building in the Triangle Area. Pack your rain gear, an extra set of boots, fatigues, socks and underwear in case we must stay for an extended period. C-rations and water are being stockpiled there for us for 3 days, if needed. I expect you all to move out sharply and orderly. There is no need to panic."

You are not in danger.

Frank was stunned by this thought. It was more a premonition than a thought and he had no idea where it came from. He did not have time to ponder it though as the squadron was dismissed to go back to their barracks and pack. Their roommate from Tennessee was nervous and seemed to be on the verge of panic. Frank, Mike and the other roommate had all been through hurricanes before, being from the East coast and kind of took them in stride. "How can you guys be so calm? A hurricane is coming, and we could be killed!"

Mike said, "Calm down. Hurricanes are mostly wind and rain. The building we are going to is on high ground and made of cinder block. We will be fine and the only thing we should be concerned about is how much debris we will be picking up after the storm. Our barracks, however, are made of wood and will probably sustain significant damage."

They joined the rest of the squadron and marched to the Triangle Area. Hurricane Betsy made landfall near New Orleans instead of Biloxi and didn't cause much damage to the barracks buildings. A few shingles came off the roof, but no flooding damage.

Later, Mike and Frank took a walk on the beach since they were warned not to go there. Telling them not to go was like waving a red flag in front of a bull. The beach was full of airmen. Alligators and snakes were reported to be sucked from the surrounding swamps and bayous and dumped on the beach.

Mike said, "I don't see anything but swamp grass."

Just as he said that, a snake slithered out from the grass and headed for the Gulf of Mexico. They watched the snake as it went into the water with his head up and swam away looking back at them.

"Whoa," said Mike "did you see that. I bet it's a cottonmouth."

Frank heard that snakes tended to group together and said, "Where there's one, there's probably more."

They started looking at the swamp grass and wondered if it concealed more snakes or maybe an alligator.

"OK. Fun time is over. Anyone for a beer at the White House?" Frank said. The White House was the nearest watering hole from the East gate of Keesler.

Mike agreed.

CHAPTER 3
Langley, Virginia

In 1961, the Director of Central Intelligence, or DCI, looked at the two men sitting in his office and said, "The President has approved our proposed experiment." The Deputy Director of Intelligence (DDI) smiled broadly but the Deputy Director of Operations (DDO) just nodded. The DDO was not a fan of the proposed, now approved, experiment. The Central Intelligence Agency (CIA) had been 'borrowing' men from the various Services, especially Special Forces types who were experienced, to conduct covert operations. This new experiment was to recruit men who were inexperienced, some were still teenagers, into what was called the Joint Program and train them in the use of subterfuge rather than brute force to thwart Soviet plots. They would be provided physical and firearms training, but the focus would be on observation and reporting. Screening tests had been administered to seniors in high school but were disguised as aptitude tests. The Army jumped the gun by offering commissions to graduating seniors who excelled in the screening test which raised eyebrows in the CIA. The CIA saw this as an attempt to scarf up the cream of the crop before they could be recruited into the Joint Program. The Army felt justified in doing this as events in Vietnam were heating up and they needed young men to fill the ranks of the Army Security Agency. The Army backed off when the Chairman of the Joint Chiefs of Staff made it clear that the President wanted a Joint Program between the Department of Defense (DOD) and the CIA. By 1965, the program had recruited several Service members with mixed results. Some became stressed to the point of extreme depression and were undergoing therapy. Others excelled and were invited to join the CIA as training officers for new recruits. Stricter criteria were established to minimize recruiting people who were not cut out for the type of life expected of them.

Biloxi, Mississippi

Frank had just completed the Basic Electronics course at Kessler AFB, which was about the halfway point of his approximate eleven-month training. He was looking forward to taking two weeks leave that was allowed before he entered the next half of the course. The next half was called 'Sets'. This training consisted of troubleshooting and repairing the different types of communication equipment that they may encounter at their next assigned duty station.

Frank had purchased plane tickets and was preparing to catch an Air Force shuttle bus to the New Orleans airport and fly home to see his parents and girlfriend. His flight home was scheduled to leave the next day and he was surprised when his buddy Mike came by and said the squadron commander wanted to see him before he left. Frank asked Mike if he knew what it was about, but Mike just shrugged his shoulders. Frank hurried to the commander's office and was told to go into the office. Frank's commander, First Lieutenant (1LT) Owens, introduced him to a civilian named Harry Wexford and then left the room and closed the door. Frank looked at the closed door then turned to the civilian who was about 5 foot 10 inches tall and looked to be physically fit. His complexion was a bit sallow and reminded Frank of someone who had recently recovered from an illness. The civilian said, "Don't worry about remembering my name, it's not my real name and not important at this time." Frank didn't respond to this statement and was at a loss as to what to expect.

"My organization has been interested in you for some time. Do you remember getting a letter from the Army Security Agency when you were a senior in high school?"

"Yes."

"And what did you think of it?"

Frank said, "I was surprised that they were offering me a commission. I asked my parents and friends what they thought, and all said they thought it was a mistake since the Army only offered commissions to college graduates. I threw it away."

"Well, I'm glad you did. By the way, all the seniors in your class responded as you did. However, do you recall taking an aptitude test before graduating from high school?"

"Vaguely."

"It was sponsored by the Government and given to students who attended both public and private high schools, which included the Catholic high school you attended. It was an experiment that was designed to see who might have the potential to work for the Government in specific areas. So you are wondering why am I telling you all this you."

"Yes."

"Frank, you have shown an aptitude, among other things, for understanding situations given the briefest of details and for adapting into radically different environments. Generally, people can do one or the other quite well, but not both. That's what brought you to our attention."

"I am assuming you are trying to recruit me for something, correct?"

"I see you understand the situation," the civilian said, smiling. "You are getting ready to go on leave back home and I would like you to think about an additional course to the 'Sets' part of your training. You will receive what we call 'special training' to collect information, process it and report your analysis. You will continue as a radio repairman student when you return from leave. Upon graduation, you will be ordered to your next duty station and you will perform two roles – one as a radio repairman and the other working for us. You will be provided additional compensation and you will have to volunteer for this additional training. At no time while you are on leave will you disclose any reference to this meeting. In two weeks, after you return from leave, I would like to meet with you again for your answer. Please do not feel pressured to say yes. Think about it and if you do not want to volunteer, we will not do anything to impact your chosen career in the Air Force. But remember, this meeting is between you and me.

It is not to be mentioned to anyone else, ever, OK?"

"Yes, I understand and will think about it over the next two weeks."

Frank departed from the airport in New Orleans for home the following day and was so distracted thinking about the meeting he just had that he almost missed his flight home.

"Get it together," he said to himself. He was afraid to say yes but equally afraid to say no because this may be an opportunity for advancement and would probably be exciting. He was a little reluctant recalling what he had heard since entering the Air Force, 'Never volunteer for anything but leave.' He ran the pros and cons through his head during the flight home and pretty much made up his mind to say yes. He wondered if it would be dangerous and decided that that would be even more exciting but scary at the same time. He wondered if he was going to be sent to Vietnam. That would be logical since the war was starting to heat up by the day.

When opportunity knocks, answer the door.

Frank looked around to see who said that, but he wasn't near anyone. He realized the voice, or was it a thought, came from inside his head. He boarded the four-engine prop plane and slept most of the way home.

Philadelphia, Pennsylvania

When he entered the terminal after departing the plane in Philadelphia, he heard a high-pitched scream. "Oh my God,"

Barb kept repeating. "I love your uniform. You must keep it on the whole time you are home."

"I don't think so," Frank said laughing. He hugged Barb and his mom and shook his dad's hand. They came to the airport to pick him up and they hadn't told him beforehand. His mom worked at a 5 & 10 cent store, in charge of the hosiery counter, and Saturday was one of her big days. Besides, it had only been a little over seven months since he had last seen them. But they were here, and everyone was happy to be together again.

They drove home in his dad's 1960 Ford that he bought brand new. It was the first car he bought brand new and he babied it. It seemed that he washed it every weekend, when it wasn't raining. As soon as they walked in the door to their house, his mom started cooking dinner. She made his favorite roast beef dinner with mashed potatoes, cucumbers mixed in oil and vinegar and her delicious coleslaw.

After dinner, Frank asked if he could borrow his dad's car. His dad didn't like anyone driving his car, but he had sold Frank's 1955 Chevy after Frank joined the Air Force so grudgingly approved. Frank and Barb took off to see a movie at a drive-in theater. They snuggled under a blanket with the heater keeping them cozy. They didn't see much of the movie as they kissed and groped one another. They never made love before and Frank was thinking that tonight might be the night.

"Stop," cried Barb. "I want to but made up my mind to wait until I'm married." Frank stopped and although disappointed, knew that Barb would be miserable if they did make love and he later changed his mind about getting married. It wasn't like they were engaged, and he still had over three years left to his enlistment. She was a senior in high school and neither one wanted to marry until she graduated, and he got out of the Air Force or decided to make it a career. He still hadn't decided if he wanted to be a lifer or to only serve his current enlistment.

Frank moved away from her and after they settled down a bit, he asked, "Would you be proud of me if I went to Vietnam?"

Barb's mouth dropped open and said, "No and don't you dare volunteer to go there. I would be worried sick the whole time."

Frank said, "I might not have a choice. The Air Force sends people where they are needed."

Barb started crying and Frank was sorry he brought it up. Frank wondered how he would break it to Barb if he did get orders for Vietnam. Since he didn't have any control over it, he pushed it to the back of his mind, and would deal with it later. Getting sent to Vietnam after tech school had a high probability. He was waiting for the voice in his head to provide advise but he heard only silence.

The rest of his two-week leave was spent going out with Barb every night, looking up his friends from the neighborhood during the day and relating his experience to them of Air Force life. Of course, that only consisted of basic training and half of tech school, so was short and kind of boring. He made no mention of the secret meeting he had at Keesler.

Frank's mom, sister and Barb went to the downtown Philly department stores looking for a farewell present for him. He and dad were home alone watching television. Frank turned to his dad and said, "Have you ever had thoughts just pop up in your head and you wondered where they came from."

His dad looked away from the television and smiling said, "Yeah, I think everyone does. Why do you ask? Are you having a thought now?"

"Not now but I had an issue come up while in basic training when some guys were pulled out of the barracks in the middle of the night by the assistant technical instructor when I was on guard duty. I didn't know how to respond to this situation and a thought, like a voice, came into my head to let it go but document it. It turned out it wasn't approved by the technical instructor and they all got arrested in Mexico. Me and the guy who came on duty after me were questioned about it and when I showed my notes, we were told we did the right thing."

"Wow, that's bizarre. About the voice though, it reminds me of a story my father told me about a voice telling him to stop working in the coal mines and find something else to do. That voice was his brother, who was killed in the mines about a year before. My father was so spooked that he opened a candy store and never went back in the mines."

Frank was surprised to hear that story. His dad looked at him and reluctantly said, "Maybe what you are hearing is your Uncle Frank's voice providing advice. When he heard your mom was pregnant, he wrote to me that he had a lot of experience he wanted to share with you. He was adamant about being a mentor to you."

Frank thought about that for a minute and said, "But Dad, I never heard his voice. He died before I was born."

His dad looked very serious and said, "Well, it's a thought. Just the same, I think it would be best if we kept this conversation to ourselves."

CHAPTER 4
Biloxi, Mississippi

Frank flew back to Keesler AFB and pondered about what his father had said. He took the bus from New Orleans to Keesler and signed into the squadron indicating he was back from leave. He was shocked when he was told by the airman on duty that they did not have a bunk for him.

"So, what do I do now?"

The disinterested airman in admin said, "Talk to the Master Sergeant."

Frank knocked on the office door of Master Sergeant O'Neill who shouted, "Come!"

"Airman Frank Logan reporting for duty but I understand there is no place for me to bunk."

"Yep, your timing sucks. The squadron has received more students than expected and is filled up, but there is an option. There is a bunk in a room with three Vietnamese foreign students. I can't force you to take this bunk, but your next phase of training would be delayed until a bunk opened. This may not be until the current class graduates."

When Frank had finished basic training, he knew that an inordinate number of guys had enlisted in the Air Force because of the buildup in Vietnam. Lackland AFB did not have room to house everyone, so was putting them up at hotels in San Antonio to await the next available basic training course. Keesler AFB was experiencing the same buildup. Frank thought, 'That could mean six months of KP!'

Don't even think about passing this up. It could be a test as part of the recruiting process.

"In that case, I'll take it," Frank said.

"OK. Go to Building 1907, Room 2A. I have alerted them that you may be moving in for a while. You know that students drop out on occasion and as soon as a bunk becomes available, you can move. See the airman out front and he will tell you where we stored your stuff while you were on leave."

Frank picked up his stuff and went to Building 1907, Room 2A. The three Vietnamese students introduced themselves as Hong, Phu and Duck. He noted that Hong was the serious one and seemed to be the dominant one of the three, Phu was a bit arrogant and not so friendly, and Duck was chatty and friendly. He couldn't help but think-that being put in this room was a result of the meeting he had before he went on leave.

The admin airman knocked on the door and said the squadron commander wanted to see him. Frank followed the airman back to the admin building and when he was ushered into the commander's office, he saw the civilian he met with before going on leave. As before, 1LT Owens left the room and closed the door.

"Well, have you decided?" asked the civilian.

"Yes. I will do it."

"Good. To give you a little background, my name is Chuck Whelan, not Harry Wexford, and I work for the CIA." He reached into his jacket and produced an ID which showed a picture of Chuck under the words *The United States of America Central Intelligence Agency*. "The CIA is leading a Joint Program which includes the Air Force, the other Services and several intelligence organizations. You are now on a special team that we will train and introduce you to other members as necessary. While at Keesler and when you graduate from the radio repairmen course, you will operate as a normal airman until we order to perform other duties. You will receive generic training initially and toward the end, it will be more specific when we decide where you will be assigned after graduation. The way we are going to train you will be in addition to your 'Sets' course. You will be on B-shift for 'Sets' but will be trained by us in the morning." Course training at Keesler was divided into A, B and C shifts. A-shift attended class in the morning, B in the afternoon and C in the evening.

Frank asked, "Is bunking with three Vietnamese part of the training?"

Chuck smiled, "Yes, but they do not know about the special training you will be given and since they are all on A-shift, there will be no conflict with your schedule of training. As of now, you will probably get orders for Vietnam after graduation, so any language skills you might pick up will be useful.

Do you have any other questions?"

"Yes, about a million but I am in information overload now. How do I get in touch with you if I have questions later?"

Chuck said, "I will be one of your trainers and any questions can be addressed by me during your special training. I will accompany you to Building 2505 on Monday at 0830. We will provide you with a schedule of events for the next ten weeks. No written material will leave Building 2505 so that means no homework." He smiled a kind of Cheshire cat smile and said, "Good Luck!" Frank was told by Chuck that in addition to learning how to collect, process and analyze information, he was to be provided weapons training and self-defense courses. The duration of the special training would be four hours a day, five days a week and parallel the 'Sets' course of ten weeks and five hours a day. He wondered if he could keep his roommates and friends in the dark for the whole ten weeks.

CHAPTER 5
Biloxi, Mississippi

Chuck Whelan was one of the first recruits in the Joint Program and now worked for the CIA to recruit promising candidates. Chuck was only three years older than Frank but felt a lot older. He was in training to be an Army supply clerk when first recruited and took part in several counter-intelligence missions. After a mission in Vietnam a year ago, Chuck had arrived early to a meeting with his team members in a bar in Saigon. As he entered the bar, he was shot through his right lung by a 20 year-old-man who looked like a 12-year-old kid. It was surmised later that he was a Viet Cong soldier who must have thought Chuck was coming for him. The bullet propelled him into a wall which accounted for him being able to remain upright for a while. He pulled his side arm from his holster and fired several rounds into the man who had shot him as he slid down the wall. He remembered his team members rushing into the bar and heard a lot of screaming before he passed out. He woke briefly as he was delicately laid in the back seat of a taxi and rushed to the hospital on the Ton Son Nhut Air Base. It was fortunate that he was in Saigon as the wound would probably have been fatal if they were still in the boonies of the Mekong Delta. After he was stabilized, he was flown to Walter Reed hospital in Washington D.C. He was there for several months recuperating and going through physical therapy. It was determined that his operational days were on hold until he fully recovered, and the CIA offered him the recruitment and training position for the Joint Program. On Monday, Chuck met Frank at his barracks, and they walked to Building 2505, which looked like a small barn. It was painted the same pale green as all the rest of the wooden buildings on Keesler but was surrounded by a chain link fence with barbed wire on top. A keypad was located on the entry gate and a buzzer next to it. Chuck entered a code into the keypad and the gate swung open.

Chuck said, "When you report in for training, ring the buzzer and look into the camera above the door. The guard will let you in." Frank was surprised to see his prior roommate Mike Morrison who had been in the same Basic Electronics course. That was before they completed it, went on leave and he had been roomed with the Vietnamese. He didn't know the other ten airmen in the class.

Frank asked Mike, "So how did you get involved in these special classes?"

"I had a meeting with a guy named Chuck Whelan who made me an offer that I couldn't refuse," he said laughing.

Frank laughed, "I guess we can now at least talk to each other about our recruitment."

Chuck Whelan took them aside and said, "Yes you can as long as you keep it to yourselves. Neither of you know anyone else in the class and I want you to keep it that way." Frank and Mike looked at each other, not sure what to say to that.

Chuck asked everyone to take a seat. The room they were in was small but had a conference table with five seats on each side. Chuck stood at the end of the table and addressed the class. "I don't encourage any of you to be too social with each other for the next ten weeks and don't share conversations about this experience with nobody else and I mean NOBODY!" He shouted the last word.

Frank was thinking that 'don't' and 'nobody' was a double negative but with the word 'nobody' being repeated might mean it wasn't. He smiled to himself. Chuck looked at him "Did I say something funny, Airman Dumb?" Frank said "Sir, its Logan," then saw the smile on Chuck's face and they all started laughing.

"Seriously though, you know you all must keep mum about this, right?"

In unison, they said, "Yes Sir!"

Chuck said to them, "All right, before we get started, go down the hall to the second door on the left and you will be provided with school supplies and instruction books."

Frank was glad that Mike Morrison had also been recruited by Chuck Whelan, and he could talk to him about what they thought of Chuck and the training they would be undertaking. Frank had a special bond with Mike since they were both involved in the Mexico incident during Basic.

Frank asked Mike, "Do you think any of the other guys we came with from Lackland are also in special classes?"

Mike said, "I'm not sure. We both have seen some of them downtown and around the base but since none of us could talk about our meetings with Chuck, who knows?"

They picked up their supplies and returned to the room where Chuck was writing a course outline on the blackboard. They were to be trained on various ways of collecting information, tying bits of data into a coherent picture, looking for patterns and anomalies, using many types of communications, marking drop points and other covert techniques.

Chuck introduced them to Soaring Eagle Milligan. Soaring Eagle was a full blood Sioux Indian who would teach them basic karate techniques, including how to fall, how to make various fists, delivering punches with maximum force, identification of pressure points on the body and where lethal blows should be administered. Soaring Eagle also taught them offensive and defensive techniques with an assortment of knives which included the Ka-bar and stiletto. He provided small arms training with the M1 carbine, M-14, M-16 and AK-47 rifles, the Ithaca 37 pump action shotgun as well as the .45 caliber M1911, the 9mm Browning High Power, the .38 caliber Smith and Wesson Model 10 and 12, and the .22 long rifle High Standard pistols, with and without suppressors. Frank felt that now he really was a small arms expert.

Soaring Eagle was on the operations side of the CIA as opposed to the intelligence side of the CIA where Chuck was assigned. Usually operations and intelligence were run separately but in the Joint Program, they were wedded at the hip. Soaring Eagle was six feet tall, muscular and very agile. He grew up on an Indian reservation and was an avid hunter who kept his and other poor families supplied with meat. He became very familiar with weapons and provided maintenance to the tribe's hunters. Prior to joining the CIA, he had been trained as a sniper in the United States Marine Corps. His face usually had a frown on it which he attributed to his tribes' genetics. Soaring Eagle was 26 years old and detested being pulled from operating in the field to train totally inexperienced airmen. He had spent the last five years on the operational side of a counterintelligence team and was told that he would return to his old job with the proviso that it would include at least one of the graduates from the 'special training' program.

Frank and Mike were not permitted to take any of the school supplies and instruction books from Building 2505 at the end of the morning special class. They returned to the barracks to get ready for the march to 'Sets' class with the rest of B-shift. Each day, they marched past a reviewing stand on the way to class in mass formation to the various student halls around the base where the classes were held. Mass formation was 8 men across and usually 9 men deep, but it varied depending on the squadron size.

Mike said, "Man this is dumb. Why don't they just let us straggle to class rather than march past a reviewing stand?"

Frank laughed, "You're in the Air Force now and Air Force officers need to get a little air and some sun on the reviewing stand, so their skin isn't so white that their Army officer buddies chuckle at them."

Mike smiled, "Yeah but they could do that down on the beach. It's only a few blocks away."

"Don't give them any ideas. The next thing you know, they will have us marching in the sand."

They both laughed.

Frank returned from 'Sets' class and went back to his room in the barracks. His three roommates were sitting around doing homework. Frank was still a little uncomfortable with them, afraid he would inadvertently say something that they might take the wrong way.

"Hey guys," Frank said, "How was class?"

Duck responded with a chuckle, "I like going downtown instead of class."

Hong chastised him saying "You should be grateful for such an opportunity. You could be dodging bullets at home instead of learning technology being made available to us by America to help our country defeat our enemies."

Frank thought, 'Whoa, where did that come from.'

Frank saw Duck shrug his shoulders and go back to his homework. He then looked at Phu who had a snarky smile on his face.

Frank got to learn some of the quirks and customs of his three Vietnamese roommates. He also learned some words and phrases. Hong wasn't very talkative, and Frank had the feeling that Hong wanted Frank moved out of the room. He constantly asked if Frank heard that any bunks opened up. Phu had a negative attitude and Frank felt that he hated being in America. He even wondered if Phu might sympathize with the Viet Cong who were fighting the South Vietnam government. Duck on the other hand was a real party person. He went to downtown Biloxi on a regular basis and would have flunked out of class, but the Air Force did not fail foreign students. They had once failed a student from the Middle East and upon return to his native country, he was summarily executed since he embarrassed his country. The Air Force did not want a repeat of this incident.

Frank sat on his bunk and opened the schematics of the communication set that he was being taught how to repair. The Air Force still had a lot of systems using vacuum tube technology. Solid state technology was being used in most commercial systems but not so much in military systems. He heard from his instructors that the technology in military systems always lagged the technology in commercial systems because of the acquisition process used by the military which went through rigorous reviews before getting approval. Proponents of new systems had to convince Air Force generals that the system could not only perform better than the current ones but had to postulate how safety, maintenance, sustainment, environmental survivability, reliability, etc. would be addressed. Then the Air Force had to convince Congress to fund the system amid competition from other Air Force systems like airplanes which trumped most funding decisions. It was a painful process and by the time they contracted for the new system and obtained delivery, the technology in it was close to being obsolete.

Frank smiled as he recalled a quote from Niccolo Machiavelli (1469-1527). "It must be remembered that there is nothing more difficult to plan, more doubtful of success nor more dangerous to manage than the creation of a new system. For the initiator has the enmity of all who profit by the preservation of the old institution and merely lukewarm defenders in those who would gain by the new one."

Duck interrupted Frank's musing, "Do you want to go downtown?"

Frank had never been downtown with Duck but heard many stories of his partying. "Sure, why not? I'm going to take a quick shower first and change into civvies." Hong and Phu just sneered at the two of us and went back to their homework.

Be careful. This guy is a loose cannon.

Frank was stunned to hear the voice again. He thought about backing out of going downtown but wanted to see if the stories about Duck were true. Besides, he would be careful.

As he and Duck were leaving the base, Frank said, "Do you want to go to the White House?" The White House was a small hotel with a quiet bar located a couple blocks from the Keesler rear gate and had a view of the Gulf of Mexico.

"No, let's go to the Dew Drop Inn."

"You know that the Dew Drop Inn is off limits, right?"

Duck said, "Yeah but I go there all the time. No Air Police patrols ever check it out."

Frank had never been there, "OK, why not?"

As soon as they walked in the door of the Dew Drop Inn, the din of conversation stopped and all they could hear was the jukebox. "Damn gook," someone said. Frank looked over in the direction of the comment and saw four guys sitting at a table. They were locals and obviously did not like foreigners.

"What are you looking at?" one of locals spit out in a slurred voice.

Before Frank could answer, Duck started off in their direction but two girls sitting at the bar slid off their stools and took Duck's arms.

One girl said to the one of the four locals "Leave them alone, you Redneck. Duck is our friend and so is the guy he is with! What's your name, Honey?" she asked Frank and laughed uproariously.

Before Frank could answer, one of the girls asked Duck, "Can you buy me a drink, Duckie?" Duck laughed and said, "Sure, what are you having?"

"The usual, Duckie." Duck turned to the bartender and said, "Two champagne cocktails for the girls and I'll have a rice wine. What are you drinking Frank?"

Before Frank could answer, the bartender said, "I told you before; we don't carry any damn rice wine!"

Duck said, "OK, I'll have a Jax. How about you Frank?"

"Yeah, Jax is good for me." Jax beer was from a brewery in New Orleans and was a favorite in this part of the south.

The girls led Frank and Duck to a table near the back door. "Let's party Duckie!"

Frank looked around the bar and most patrons were staring at them, but a few started talking among themselves again. Frank stopped looking around the bar when he got to the table with the four rednecks. They stared back and one of them gave him the finger. Frank ignored him and looked at the back door to see if it was locked. It didn't look like it was.

Duck looked at the four locals and said, "Bring it on!"

The bartender came over with the drinks and leaned down to Frank "You might want to get your friend out of here before things get ugly."

Frank couldn't agree more, "Duck, let's do some bar hopping after this drink."

Duck was clearly enjoying the attention he was getting from the girls and said, "Maybe later." He turned to one of the girls and said, "Do you want to dance?"

"Sure Duckie. Do you have some money for the juke box, so I can play our favorite song? Oh, and can you buy us another drink?"

Frank saw what Duck obviously didn't or maybe he didn't care that the girls were fleecing him. The four locals were getting pissed and it was only a matter of time before things did get ugly.

Frank said to the girls, "We have to be going but thanks for the company."

One of the girls said, "Duckie ain't afraid. He knows karate, and nobody messes with him."

Just then, one of the four locals staggered over to the table and said, "I'm going to kick your little karate ass, gook." He grabbed Duck by the front of his shirt and lifted him out of his seat and slammed him against the wall. The girls screamed and jumped back out of the way. Duck's arms were flailing and if he knew karate, he was really hiding it. Frank, on the other hand, did know karate and yelling eee-ya as he was taught, struck out with a straight punch to the locals left kidney since he was behind him as the local had Duck pinned against the wall. The local dropped Duck who rolled in a ball on the floor. The local grabbed his back and sat down on the floor.

One of the other locals jumped up from their table and started across the floor to Frank. Frank assumed a karate position awaiting his foe when the guy stopped halfway across the room and said, "You better pick up your gook friend and get the hell out of here."

Frank picked up a smiling Duck and pushed the bar on the back door. Thankfully it opened, and he half dragged Duck down an alley to the street. He saw a taxi, hailed it down and they jumped in as Frank saw police cars from Biloxi and the Air Police heading for the Dew Drop Inn.

"Man, that was great!" Duck said. "Usually the bartender steps in and saves my ass."

Frank looked at Duck in awe. "You mean this happened before?"

"Yeah but usually the locals are afraid of me a little since they think I know karate. This is the first time someone actually attacked me. The bartender tells them to back down and if he thinks there may be real trouble, he calls me a taxi."

"Well, I don't think they still believe you know karate and if I were you, I'd stick to the bars airmen usually frequent." Frank thought that airmen might even want to mess with Duck though. Frank shook his head and swore he was never going downtown with Duck again. If he had been arrested, he thought for sure Chuck would drop him from the program. Belatedly, he remembered the warning from the voice in his head.

"He handled that well" said Chuck to Soaring Eagle. They had followed Frank and Duck to see what kind of trouble they might get into. They were disguised in their best red neck regalia and blended in with the crowd.

Soaring Eagle smiled and said, "Good thing that Duck gave us a heads up so we could see how Frank could handle himself in a real world situation. He only had to deliver one punch at the big guy and he dropped him like a rock. He must have paid attention to what I taught him."

Chuck smiled back and said, "Not only that, he had the good sense to get away from the scene too. I think he shows promise to do field work."

"Do you think we should tell him that Duck is one of ours?"

Chuck thought about it for a second and said, "No, he doesn't have the need to know, at least not yet."

They both knew that the current crop of recruits at Keesler would probably be assigned to units in Vietnam and Duck may be teamed up with Frank in a future operation.

CHAPTER 6
Biloxi, Mississippi

When Frank and Mike went to the morning class on collection, processing and reporting techniques, they were surprised to see Chuck Whelan sitting with an Air Force officer who they had not seen before. Frank was expecting something like this would be happening soon since he was approaching graduation from the radio repairmen course.

The Air Force officer sitting next to Chuck addressed the class, "You are going to be reviewed individually instead of your normal training routine." Frank looked around at his classmates and they were obviously as clueless as he was.

Chuck said, "OK. Let's start with Frank." They went to an office and after Frank entered, Chuck closed the door. Frank was nervous and expected to hear that his assignment was to be Vietnam. He knew that Barb would be upset but he was kind of looking forward to Vietnam. He didn't know why America was involved in what looked like a civil war. His main reason for wanting to go is that he wanted to experience what it might have been like for his Uncle Frank.

War is not what you think. It's ugly and you may find yourself doing things that you could never imagine yourself doing. Be very careful what you ask for, you may get it.

The Officer interrupted the voice in his head. "I heard that you guys are doing well in 'Sets' and the special training we have been providing. I think it's time we have a discussion on your assignment after graduation. Have you heard about Operation FRELOC?"

Frank hesitated for a minute. Was this a code word for an operation in Vietnam? "No, I haven't heard of Operation FRELOC."

"It stands for Fast Relocation. You may have heard that President Charles de Gaulle of France made the announcement that France is demanding that all foreign headquarters and installations be removed from France by 1967. The Air Force organization that has been charged with removing the installations is the Ground Electronics Engineering Installation Agency, or GEEIA, pronounced gee-ah, as it is commonly known. You and several other graduates in your radio repairman course will receive orders to report to GEEIA at Ramstein AB in Germany, but they will not be cleared to know about your special training. You will be provided additional details on your special role when you arrive in Germany. Do you have any specific questions?"

Frank was flabbergasted. He looked at the officer to see if he could detect a smile indicating that he was pulling Frank's chain about going to Germany and not Vietnam. He remembered meeting some GEEIA guys who were undergoing additional training at Keesler and they said they loved being in GEEIA. Lots of travel and exciting work. He became aware of the officer staring at him, obviously waiting for a reply. Frank said, "I thought I was going to get orders for Vietnam, but Germany sounds good. Are the rest of the guys in special training going to Germany also?"

"No decision has been made yet on their assignments. I'm sure they will tell you when they find out."

Too bad, Frank thought. He said, "I'm not clear on what my role will be but can wait until I get to Ramstein for more details. Who should I say you are if asked by whoever meets me at Ramstein?"

The Officer smiled, "No one will know me there. Your contact in GEEIA will be Technical Sergeant (TSGT) Billy Black. He will contact you a couple days after your arrival. As you know, you will have four weeks leave before departing for Ramstein. Please remember not to mention this meeting to anyone while on leave."

"Can I share the information on my orders to Germany with the other guys and my family?"

"Yes. Having orders for GEEIA in Germany is not a secret. In fact, having those orders will not attract any attention from our adversaries. You will be flying under the radar, so to speak."

Frank went back to the room and Chuck asked Mike to join him in the other office. After Mike and Chuck left, his classmates asked "Well, tell us what he said."

Frank said, "Chuck told me I'm going to a GEEIA squadron in Germany." They looked at each other and one of them said,

"Really. That's a choice assignment. I wonder where we're going." Frank didn't want to tell them that no decision had been made yet since they would find out soon enough.

After Chuck had talked to Mike, they left Building 2505. Mike was kind of down in the mouth since he was told that no decision had been made on his assignment. Frank was wondering why it was decided to send him to Germany since he had spent the last ten weeks bunked with Vietnamese troops but now was not going to Vietnam. He was relieved since Barb would be pleased and he would not be apologizing to her during the four weeks he was on leave before departing for Germany. She would not be happy though that he was not being stationed at a base close to Philly, like McGuire or Dover. He had been provided a 'dream sheet' which asked for his input on where he would like to be assigned. He put down McGuire or Dover. He was asked if he wanted to be stationed overseas and he checked no. When asked if he was to be stationed overseas, where were his first choices. He put down England and Bermuda. So, of course, he was being sent to Germany.

A few days later, Mike came to Frank's room and said, "Let's take a walk. Frank's Vietnamese roommates said hello to Mike, wondering what was up. After they left the barracks, Mike said, "Got my orders. I am going to Goodfellow AFB in San Angelo, TX for further training in the Air Force Security Service. The rest of the class got their orders too. They are all going to the GEEIA squadron in the Philippines with frequent TDY to Vietnam."

Frank was wondering why Mike had been singled out to go for

additional training. "Do you know where you will be going after San Angelo?"

"No but I am going to request Germany. Maybe we could meet somewhere and catch up."

"Sounds good," Frank said. He wondered if his and Mike's path would ever cross again after they left Keesler.

Mike said, "Some of the guys in the class are headed for the White House for a couple beers after our graduation today. They want to get together for what may be the last time we all see each other."

Frank and Mike saw some of their class sitting at the bar in the White House. They climbed up on a bar stool, ordered some beers and talked about some of the funny things that happened to them over the time they spent at Keesler. They were happy for Frank getting orders for Germany but were a little jealous. After a few beers, one of them said, "Let's take a walk along the beach for maybe the last time. A guy in their class named Gary must have had a few more beers than the rest of them because he was slurring his words and walked a bit unsteady. Just before they left the White House, Gary picked up two of the White House beer glasses and put them in his coat pocket. "A souvenir of our good times together."

They walked along the beach and Gary pointed to the islands off the coast of Biloxi. "Let's swim out to Ship Island," and he took off. They all laughed and followed him down to the water. He took his shoes off and waded in the Gulf up to his ankles. He noticed a large pipe that probably was a drain for a storm sewer leading out to the Gulf and climbed up on it. He walked about 50 feet along it and slipped off into the Gulf. They all laughed as he struggled in the water, then he stood up and the water was only up to his knees. He started walking a little further and the water was very shallow. He stopped and turned around and said, "I think I broke my souvenirs." He came back soaked and sure enough, he broke the glasses. Mike helped him get the broken glass out of his pockets and miraculously, neither one got cut.

Mike said, "Let's get him back to the base to get some dry clothes." They started back and ran into a couple of the guys in their barracks leaving the gate as they were walking into Keesler.

One of them said, "You guys are going the wrong way. There is a beauty pageant going on at the Holiday Inn tonight. They are choosing Miss Mississippi from contestants from all over the state."

Gary said, "Let's go!" Frank said, "Why don't you change out of your wet clothes first?" Then Mike said to Frank, "Why don't we go down to the Holiday Inn after Gary changes clothes?"

Frank and Mike walked back to their barracks and were waiting for Gary to change but when it seemed to be taking too long, they decided to check on him. He was passed out in his bunk. They laughed and left him there. They headed back out the Keesler gate and walked back to Highway 90 and turned east toward the Holiday Inn.

The Holiday Inn was crowded with men in tuxedos or suits and ladies in evening gowns. Mike said, "I think we might be a little under dressed." Both laughed since they were wearing chinos and golf shirts. Frank said, "Maybe we ought to split before being asked to leave."

As they started to leave, the crowd split and moved to the sides of the corridor they were standing in. Beautiful young girls in evening gowns waltzed down the corridor of the hotel. One of the girls had trouble with her high heels and almost twisted her ankle, bumping into Frank, who stopped her from falling. The girl was a little embarrassed and said, "I hate high heels." They both laughed and when two of the bouncers approached, the girl said, "I'm alright. I just tripped, and this boy saved me." The two bouncers looked at Frank while Frank was thinking 'Boy!'

He told the girl, "I'm in the Air Force and stationed at Keesler AFB." The girl looked at him, "I guess calling you boy wasn't cool. Sorry. I am Miss Hattiesburg and greatly appreciate you coming to my rescue. If you forgive me, I would like to invite you and your friend to attend the judging?"

Frank looked at Mike and shrugged his shoulders but didn't get a response. "That would be great, but we aren't really dressed for it."

She smiled and said, "Not to worry, I don't think anybody will be looking at you guys." She turned to one of the bouncers, "Please give two complimentary tickets to my friends in the Air Force." She winked at Frank and said, "Let's get together after the judging."

Frank and Mike entered the auditorium and the bouncers dragged two folding chairs in and set them against the wall, far from the stage. Frank could hardly make out Miss Hattiesburg from this distance, but the announcer solved this problem by calling out each girl who responded by doing a little curtsey.

Mike whispered to Frank, "Do you think there will be a swimsuit judging?"

Frank smiled and said, "That would be great."

However, there was no swimsuit judging. This part of the judging was apparently to announce the winner of Miss Mississippi and the runners up. Miss Hattiesburg didn't make the cut. After the judging, the girls were swamped by friends and family and Miss Hattiesburg looked at them and shrugged her shoulders indicating that she would not be joining them.

Mike teased Frank all the way back to the base. "I bet you thought you were going to score with her, right?" Frank said, "No, I have a girl friend at home and Miss Hattiesburg was only being friendly." Mike laughed and said, "Right and you wouldn't have tried to get in her pants." Frank said, "Absolutely not!" Mike only laughed harder and said, "Wait until Gary hears what he missed!"

Frank said farewell to his friends at Keesler a couple days later and caught the bus to the airport in New Orleans. He was looking forward to his four weeks leave. He had already written to his parents and Barb that he had orders for Germany but didn't go into a lot of detail. They had not responded but might be waiting to see him in person to share their feelings.

CHAPTER 7
Philadelphia, Pennsylvania

When he landed in Philadelphia International Airport, he was surprised to see that only his Dad had shown up to meet him. Before he had a chance to ask, his dad laughed and said, "Your mom and Barb had to work, so I am the official greeter." Frank didn't know how he felt about Barb not showing up. He told himself not to be disappointed but couldn't help himself. He thought he was being selfish, and the world shouldn't be expected to stop just because he was coming home. He pushed his disappointment to the back of his mind.

On the drive home, his dad went on about Frank getting orders for Germany and implored him to be careful. Frank thought that his dad feared that he might lose a son as well as a brother-in-law to the Germans. Frank tried to tell him it was fortuitous for him to be assigned to Germany and not Vietnam. His father looked at him and shook his head up and down in agreement. Frank thought he put his dad's mind at ease.

His mom and Barb were still at work and his dad was busying himself in the kitchen. He decided to lay on the living room floor with a big pillow behind his head and watch TV. He dozed off and woke up when his mom and Barb returned from work. Frank forgot about his disappointment when Barb gave him a big hug and kiss. His mom was smiling from ear to ear and asked if he was hungry. That was her favorite question when she was happy to see someone. His mom and Barb went into the kitchen and clanging pots, prepared dinner. They all sat down for another great dinner and he was peppered with questions about Germany.

A couple of days later, his mom came to him looking a little scared.

"I was straightening out some of your things and inadvertently saw your secret orders."

At first, he thought she was talking about his special training, but he didn't have anything in his things that would give her a clue.

"Secret orders? I don't have any secret orders." She showed him his travel orders and pointed to the word secret.

He laughed, "Mom, that is only my clearance level. There is nothing secret about it."

She was not convinced. "Then why would they put such a thing where anyone can see it?"

"Don't worry. It's not really secret." She looked at him and it was clear she didn't believe him.

She looked serious, "You wouldn't tell me if it was secret even if it was."

He just laughed, "Really, it's not secret."

She said, "OK." However, she did not go through his things

again for the rest of the time that he was on leave.

One day Barb said, "Let's take a ride down the shore." It was mid-April and still chilly, but she wanted to go anyway. He borrowed his dad's car and they headed for Wildwood, NJ. The beach was empty and the breeze off the ocean was downright cold. They drove down to Cape May and stopped in what probably was the only restaurant open this time of year and they had hot chocolate.

Barb said, "I am really going to miss you. Can you get leave to come home after a while?"

"Getting leave may not be so much of a problem as getting the money to buy a plane ticket."

"How much are we talking about?" She said

"I'm not sure but I think it's about $500."

"Wow! My dad only makes about $7,000 a year. Do people really pay that much for a plane ticket?"

"Yeah and my dad makes less than yours. Maybe I can save up and fly back home in a year or so."

She was upset, "You will meet somebody there and forget about me."

"I don't think so. We will write to each other and send pictures, like the ones you sent me from the beach when I was at Keesler," He said.

"Yes. I remember you put my picture up in your locker next to Franny's!" She said rather harshly.

Franny is her friend who is really built and when my friends saw her, they insisted I hang her picture up in my locker.

"Guilty as charged but I was coerced!"

She laughed, "Sure you were." They had this conversation several times after he inadvertently sent a photo to her of his barracks room which showed his open locker and the pictures she sent him.

On the way back to Philly, they stopped at Olga's diner at the traffic circle of routes 70 & 73. Olga's had good food and great desserts. They pigged out and went home just as it was getting dark.

Frank had a lot of time on his hands while on leave. His mother, father, sister and girlfriend all had jobs, so he only got to see them at night. He decided to head to the library and see if there were books on why he was hearing a voice in his head. He read one that talked about people who seemed to have multiple personalities, but it wasn't quite what he was experiencing. He didn't jump from one personality to another.

He read another that postulated a spirit or soul that existed in a material body that sounded a lot like what he was taught as a Catholic. It also mentioned that spirits may be angels and that there were good and bad angels. Another talked about spirits being reincarnated in another body upon the death of the one they occupied. His Uncle Frank was killed about three months before he was born but the theories were that his spirit or soul was there when he was conceived. Since it was all theories and no one really knew, he began to think it was possible that somehow, his Uncle Frank's spirit was the source of the voice but didn't think it was not the dominant spirit in his body.

He kept looking and found a book that said spirits do not retain the memory of the past human life it occupied. He also said that according to St. Thomas Aquinas in his book "Summa Theologica", spirits have no matter. The author said that is the reason they occupy humans so to experience physical things and interact with the environment. He thought it sounded analogous to the way a computer was made to operate. The four basics of a computer: input unit, memory storage unit, central processing unit and an output unit. The spirit could be the central processing unit and the body provided the other three units. The book went on to postulate that a body usually had several spirits in it that competed for control. As in nature, an alpha spirit eventually took control but was tempted by the other spirits to deviate from the norm established by the alpha spirit and could account for deviant behavior. It went on to discuss the biblical description of angels bearing children with female humans. Since that didn't jibe with the "Summa Theologica" belief that spirits do not have matter, the author believed there was no physical interaction between the angels and the female human, but a spiritual one where the embryos were the host for the spirits. He also proposed that spirits could traverse the universe and wherever organic life existed, they could repeat the process on that world. It goes on to say that as worlds come and go over time eternal, the spirits will depart the old world and find another world. That seemed a little farfetched but would explain a lot.

He left the library thinking that he still didn't really know what was happening to him but was grateful for the advice he was getting from the voice in his head.

When his leave was up, Frank's parents and Barb went him to the Philadelphia International Airport to catch his flight to Germany. It was a very tearful event and he was getting butterflies thinking about spending the next three years in Germany.

When he boarded, he found he was sitting next to an Air Force Master Sergeant who said, "Where are you being assigned?"

Frank told him, "I'm going to Germany. Ramstein AB...in a GEEIA squadron.'

"A what squadron?"

"It's an engineering and installation squadron."

"Never heard of it." Then he turned from Frank, put his seat back and closed his eyes.

Frank changed planes at National Airport in Washington DC. As he headed to the gate for his connection flight to Charleston, SC, he saw A2C Gerhardt Schultz who was in his 'Sets' and the Joint Program training class. They stopped in a coffee shop and it turned out Gerhardt had orders for GEEIA also.

Frank said, "I thought you had orders for the Philippines."

"I did but they were changed when I was on leave. I am delighted since I speak German and was not happy with my previous orders."

When they got to Charleston, they found an Air Force shuttle bus going to Charleston AFB where they boarded the Military Airlift Command flight to Rhein-Main AB in Frankfurt, Germany.

CHAPTER 8
Ramstein, Germany

Upon arrival in Germany, Frank and Gerhardt spent the night in a transit barracks at Rhein-Main. The next morning, they were directed to a shuttle bus that would take them to Ramstein AB. Gerhardt was five foot ten inches tall and was broad chested. His complexion had a red shade to it like a lot of Germans and looked like he was blushing all the time. He told Frank he was born in Germany, but his family left there in 1954 and settled outside Philadelphia in a suburban tract called Levittown. He learned to speak English in grammar school in Germany and after being in America for the last ten years or so, had virtually no German accent. Frank had heard of Levittown but never went there. His dad used to take Frank with him almost every weekend to collect cinder blocks that his dad used to build a wall behind their house separating the house from the back alley. The cinder blocks were all different colors and were at building sites where his dad laid gas pipes for the Philadelphia Gas Works. He swore it wasn't stealing since they were left over from the houses going up and "would be thrown away anyway." Frank aided and abetted this *liberation* of the errant cinder blocks. He and his dad never went to Levittown though.

In addition to Frank and Gerhardt, there were three other guys going to GEEIA but the majority of those on the bus were assigned to other squadrons at Ramstein. After the shuttle bus driver looked at their orders, he said, "I can drop you GEEIA troops off at the transit barracks and inform the GEEIA squadron that you arrived at Ramstein. Is that alright?"

"That works for me." Frank said. The other GEEIA guys concurred.

The scenery on the ride from Rhein-Main AB to Ramstein AB started out as flat plains of farmer's fields, then many rows of grape vines to the right and left as far as the eye could see. The grape vines faded as the shuttle started up a hill and the terrain turned hilly for the rest of the trip to Ramstein. The GEEIA Squadron was one of the guest units at Ramstein AB and reported to the European GEEIA region in Wiesbaden, Germany who in turn reported to Headquarters GEEIA at Griffiss AFB, NY.

They were assigned rooms in the transit barracks and saw the enlisted man's club across the street. They unpacked their gear, then walked over to the club and had a couple beers to relax from the trip. After two days in the transit barracks, the intercom system belted out in a loud voice, "Attention GEEIA troops. Time to pack up and move out of the transit barracks and into the GEEIA barracks. They met a staff sergeant in the lobby who directed Frank and the rest of the GEEIA troops to a blue bus that was parked out front to transport them to the GEEIA barracks on the north side of Ramstein". The drive from the transit barracks to the GEEIA Squadron took about ten minutes.

The GEEIA First Sergeant, Senior Master Sergeant (SMS) Oliver met the bus and rattled off a role call to be sure everyone was accounted for and he assigned each to a room. Frank was assigned a room with two other radio repairmen. After getting settled in and unpacked, all the new arrivals were called down to the orderly room.

SMS Oliver said, "You will be given a tour of the facilities at Ramstein AB and assigned a sponsor. A2C Logan, Schultz and Young will accompany SSGT Jordan, your sponsor, who will provide the transportation for a tour of the base and the amenities available to you while stationed here." Frank introduced himself to Dick Young and already knew Gerhardt Schultz.

SSGT Jordan showed them to his car, "We will be together for about 2 or 3 days and I will try to answer any questions you may have. If you ask me a question I can't answer, I will find someone who can, OK?"

"Yes sir!" came the reply from all of them, sounding a bit like a chorus.

"Don't call me sir. I am not an officer, so you can call me Tom or SSGT Jordan, as you wish."

Tom Jordan led them out to his car, and they took off to tour Ramstein AB. Tom pointed out the PX, the dining facility, the bank, etc. He said, "Do you guys mind if we make a little detour to the town of Ramstein. I need to see a mechanic about my car acting up." They all nodded OK.

They all got out of the car when they got to the auto repair shop and Tom tried explaining what the car was doing wrong. The mechanic was German and did not speak very good English.

Tom was struggling to be understood when Gerhardt told him, "I speak German and can translate between you guys if you want."

Tom breathed a sigh of relief. "Please, if you don't mind." Dick and Frank felt like they were at a tennis match moving their heads from the mechanic to Gerhardt to Tom and back again. At one point, Gerhardt told Tom in German what the mechanic said in German. Tom said, "Huh?"

Everyone laughed, and Gerhardt was a bit embarrassed at his mistake. From then on, he got the translations right and Tom got his car fixed. The car only needed plugs, points and a carburetor tune up and they were on our way.

One of the stops was at the Consolidated Base Personnel Office (CBPO) to drop their hand carried personnel file off. Before leaving the states, they were told to bring their birth certificates from home to apply for a passport. However, to everyone's surprise, Gerhardt had swastikas in the four corners of his birth certificate! He was born in Germany during World War II. His passport processing stopped dead.

The clerk asked him, "Do you have any relatives living in East Germany?"

Gerhardt said, "I don't know but can ask my parents."

The clerk said, "I am going to request another background check before we proceed. Also, I am going to see if the interim secret clearance you were granted is still valid."

Tom told Gerhardt, "I think we should go back and see SMS Oliver to find out what needs to be done."

Tom took them back to the GEEIA barracks and came out saying, "Gerhardt will not be accompanying us anymore. SMS Oliver said he will look into this but decided that Gerhardt should stay around the barracks until this incident is resolved."

Frank saw Gerhardt later and asked, "So what are you going to do?"

"Write my parents to find out if they know if we have any relatives in East Germany. I was born here but we immigrated to the states right after World War II when I was just a little kid. My immediate family all immigrated to the states either before or right after the war. Germany was in chaos, especially what they now call East Germany, before the Berlin Wall went up but I don't remember them mentioning where our relatives might be living now."

"Well, good luck and I hope it all works out."

CHAPTER 9
Ramstein, Germany

Frank was quickly picking up the routine and lexicon of the GEEIA squadron; for example, 'TDY' meant Temporary Duty and applied to travelling for work away from Ramstein and being 'in station' meant that you were not TDY. GEEIA troops traveled all over Europe, the Middle East and Africa installing new equipment at some sites and disassembling and packing up decommissioned equipment at other sites.

All personnel were required to convene each morning at the GEEIA warehouse for announcements and instructions at 0800 and again at 1600 while in station. Things were a bit lax for troops in station. By convening at 0800, this gave the troops in the barracks time to have breakfast in the morning and to walk across the base to the GEEIA warehouse. Being released at 1600 gave them time to walk back to the dining facility for dinner if they wanted to eat there.

The GEEIA warehouse was situated next to a railroad track spur where equipment was delivered for check out prior to installation. An inventory was taken to be sure they had the necessary hardware to complete the installation. Most of the time, the equipment was delivered directly to the site where the installation was to be performed. The warehouse was also used to repair equipment and train on it prior to installation.

The workload was so intense that there was usually no time to train on the equipment and contractors from the equipment manufacturer would accompany teams to the installation site and perform any repair and tuning unique to that piece of equipment.

"A2C Logan," cried Technical Sergeant (TSGT) Billy Black, "Glad to finally meet you. I would have been in touch earlier but was TDY to Wiesbaden for the last couple of days. Let's go grab a cup of coffee and I will bring you up to speed on the team and our mission."

Frank was surprised that TSGT Black talked to him as an equal since he was his supervisor. Black was about the same height as Frank but a little thinner. He had a deep southern accent and some words out of his mouth took a second to digest before being understood. Frank slipped off the stool he had been sitting on at one of the work benches and followed TSGT Black out of the warehouse to Black's 1965 Ford Falcon.

"I had my car shipped over from the states because I had just bought it new before getting orders to Germany. However, in hindsight, I should have sold it or stored it and bought a German car when I got here. Maintenance cost an arm and a leg here, but I must admit, they do a thorough job."

They drove across the base to a windowless building with a fence and concertina wire on the top. "This is a SCIF or Secure Compartmented Information Facility." TSGT Black explained "Have you been in one before?"

"No, I don't think so. The building we trained in at Kessler had a cipher lock on the door and one on the fence around it."

TSGT Black said "It may have been one but this one is where we are briefed on our 'extra mission' when we go on a GEEIA mission. You have been cleared at the Top Secret level but your orders will only say Secret since GEEIA only requires the lower clearance. I heard that A2C Schultz ran into a snag at CBPO when he showed them his birth certificate. He will be the fourth man on our team with you and SSGT Bakersfield."

Frank was taking this all in but not quite understanding the implications. "Do you know anything more about Gerhardt's, excuse me A2C Schultz, predicament?"

"Yes, SMS Oliver got it straightened out with the security folks who issue clearances. I don't know what he told them because my experience with them is that security folks move cautiously, or should I say, slower than shit! I didn't expect that they would resolve his case for a year or more."

TSGT Black said "By the way, you can call me Billy when we are alone or with the rest of the team, but Air Force protocol expects you to use my rank when we are in the company of other NCOs. To give you a little background on me, I am originally from Georgia, served as an instructor at Keesler after graduation, then spent a tour in Indochina, returned to Keesler for additional training, then got orders for GEEIA. I thought I was going to have a stateside tour but the Air Force thought different. I am married and have one son. SSGT Don Bakersfield is married with six kids, may God have mercy on him, whose wife is truly a saint, because Don is like having a seventh kid."

Frank laughed as Billy continued, "Don spent his entire career in the states, first as an instructor at Keesler for seven years, then a stint at Goodfellow AFB in San Angelo, before getting orders for GEEIA. Don and I were supposed to be the vanguard at GEEIA to conduct our special mission while participating in Operation FRELOC, which I understand you have been briefed on, right?"

"Yes, but not recently or in detail, so you may have to bring me up to date. I don't understand why France would want to withdraw from NATO. It seems to me that they would want to ally with the other NATO nations after what happened to France in World War II. I was told that the details of Operation FRELOC would be made known to me when I arrived at GEEIA, but you are the only contact I was provided and today is the first time I met you."

"Well, to begin with, France didn't withdraw from NATO but withdrew its contribution of men, officers and enlisted, to the NATO Command but still maintains coordination on NATO plans. They think the U.S. is riding roughshod over the other NATO nations by imposing its nuclear strategy on NATO, and France does not want to sign up to it. The implication for us is that not only does NATO headquarters have to move from Paris to Brussels, but all foreign military installations must be moved out of France. It turns out that the other GEEIA teams have been working overtime. Most of the sites are well on their way to being dismantled and some relocated, or their equipment being reallocated somewhere else. President de Gaulle, in his infinite wisdom" said Billy sarcastically, "did not expect us to be moved out until late in 1967. He said he would pay the U.S. ten cents on the dollar for our sites if we were out by the end of 1966. Since GEEIA is probably going to complete the relocation by the end of 1966, de Gaulle must figure out how he is going to pay us given their economic issues. It puts him in a real bind but that's his problem. It also brings me to what our new mission will be now that significant participation by us in Operation FRELOC is OBE or Overcome by Events. The short answer is that I have no idea what our new mission will be. We are in 'hurry up and wait' mode."

About a week later, Billy told Frank, Don and Gerhardt "The powers in charge have informed me that our new mission has not been decided yet. They are awaiting analysis of some intelligence that has just been collected. So, I have asked our section lead if he would permit us to get some training on the equipment that has been piling up in the warehouse from the sites in France. He said, 'Why not, most of that equipment is trash anyway and will probably go to the PDO, or Property Disposal Office'. So, is either one of you familiar with the 'jerk27'?"

Frank knew that 'jerk27' was the acronym for the GRC-27. "Yes, the 'jerk27' communications system was covered in one of the classes Gerhardt I had in 'Sets' at Keesler. It is a UHF system with really noisy blower fans, as I recall."

"Great. I have the manual and schematic for it and I found a dummy load to put on the output side, so we don't broadcast into the air and piss off the air traffic controllers at Ramstein."

Since Billy nor Don had not worked on this piece of gear before, it fell to Frank and Gerhardt who tried to tune the jerk27 with little luck. It was equipped with three crystal-controlled oscillators containing 38 crystals each. It could produce over 1700 frequencies in the 225-400 Mega Hertz range.

They reported back to Billy that they were having trouble tuning the jerl27. Billy said, "Maybe we should try changing the preset capacitors in the tuner."

Frank and Gerhardt looked at Billy to see if he was serious and obviously, he was. Gerhardt said, "The manual says don't mess with the tuner. It is factory preset and should be returned to the manufacturer if a malfunction is suspected."

Billy looked irritated, "Nothing else we are doing seems to work, and this crap is going to PDO anyway, so let's do it!"

They did and completely screwed it up. Billy said, "Well, it was worth a try. Let's get another one from storage and play with it." Frank said, "Billy, you know this is a depot level maintenance job that we are trying, and we don't have the necessary test equipment to do it right." Billy said, "Yeah, but we have nothing better to do until we get an assignment."

When Frank got back to the barracks, A2C Ray Burnside stuck his head in the door and asked Frank if he wanted to go out and drink a couple beers. Ray shared a room down the hall with two other guys. Frank thought that was a great idea after spending all day on the frustrating task Billy gave them.

Not a good idea.

Frank heard the voice in his head and thought about saying no. Ray yelled, "Hurry up, the guys are waiting downstairs." Frank shrugged his shoulders and said, "Coming."

CHAPTER 10
Ramstein, Germany

Sitting in the Capri bar with his friend Reinhart Uhler, Hans Glick ordered them another beer with their early dinner. *"Zwei Bier bitte,"* he said. Beer was priced fairly, one German Mark for a large glass, or the American equivalent of twenty-five cents. That was why the local bars were full of American airmen most nights but also had mostly German patrons during the daytime. Hans hated the airmen ever since one had got his onetime sweetheart, Heidi, pregnant and abandoned her. Hans was a short, thin and pale man who did not look like the type that would attract the beautiful red-haired Heidi. She was a bar maid at the Capri bar and fell in love with one of the airmen from GEEIA who promised to take her back with him to America. However, when his tour of duty was completed, the airman went back to America without Heidi. He promised her that he would send for her and their unborn child as soon as he got settled in the United States. He wrote to her a couple times, then all correspondence stopped.

Hans turned to Reinhart, "I'm glad it's all Germans in here during the day. Every time I think of poor Heidi being used by that rotten American, I get really angry."

Reinhart nodded, "It's a shame you can't do something to get even with them."

"Yeah, but how? I depend on them for my livelihood, so I must pretend to like them."

Hans and Heidi had known each other since they were children. Both of their fathers had fought in the German Army during the war and died for their country. The war was over for twenty years and Hans had never really known his father. His mother showed him pictures of his father in his uniform holding little Hans when he was born. He was not ready to accept the inevitable that Americans were here to stay, but at the same time felt he had to move on with his life. Hans drove a taxi and regularly entered the American air base at Ramstein to pick up airmen to take them downtown to the many bars nearby and return them off to their barracks when they had enough or too much to drink. Several airmen had their own cars and that cut into his income, but the drunken airmen gave such lavish tips that he made a decent living. When Heidi got pregnant, his mother told Hans to stop seeing her, or she would disown him. Hans knew that the whole town disowned Heidi as they thought every German girl who screwed American airmen and were stupid enough to get pregnant deserved it. Hans was torn between his love for Heidi and his disgust at what she had done. He had talked to her, but she flip-flopped between mourning for her lost American and hatred for him getting her pregnant and abandoning her. She was not responsive to Hans and it was clear to him that she was lost to him forever.

Bringing Hans out of his thoughts of Heidi, Reinhart said, "I'm sure you will think of something." Reinhart was physically the opposite of Hans. He was tall and overweight but had the confidence of a politician. He despised Hans but was under orders to befriend him and try to recruit him to the cause of the Neo-Nazis. He had suggested to Hans that he should install one of the new battery powered tape recorders in the back seat of his taxi, but Hans had almost panicked at the suggestion. Reinhart had met Hans at a meeting of a group of German veterans who espoused the expulsion of foreign armies on German soil. They permitted Hans to join the group since his father died in the war. The group met once a week and after hearing speeches from likeminded Germans, proceeded to drink a lot beer and boisterously proclaim what they planned to do to remove the foreigners from Germany. However, they never got around to executing their plans.

"Have you given any more thought about putting a hidden tape recorder in your back seat?"

Hans looked at him and said, "What if the Air Police at Ramstein want to search my taxi?"

"I can assure you it will be completely hidden behind a false wall in your trunk. My mechanic has experience in placing them and has done it on many taxi's at other locations throughout Germany." Reinhart looked at Hans reaction and could tell he was not going to commit to recording his passenger's conversations, so said, "I know you may be insulted but I could arrange for some compensation for your trouble. I will ask for say, 100 Marks for each tape that we remove from your trunk."

Hans thought about how his mother was struggling to balance the money that he brought in to maintain the house, buy food and pay taxes. They barely had enough money to get by and new clothes were a luxury that only came once a year at Christmas.

That night, Hans had just dropped off some airmen at Ramstein AB when he received a call for a pickup at one of the bars in Landstuhl. He left Ramstein AB at the gate that led to a part of the old *autobahn* the Americans had turned into a runway after the war and had eventually evolved into Ramstein AB. He drove along the old *autobahn* and exited to the road between the town of Ramstein and Landstuhl. He turned left toward Landstuhl and as he approached the Italian restaurant on the right side of the road, he noticed a multicolored old Volkswagen coming the other way. It was the same one he had seen earlier at the Capri bar. He knew it belonged to an airman who was probably driving back to Ramstein from Landstuhl after a night of drinking and trying to get some German girl to spread her legs for him. He thought about what Reinhart said earlier and he decided to swerve to the left in front of the approaching Volkswagen to see the reaction. To his surprise, he saw the Volkswagen leave the road and drop down into a farmer's field. He saw the faces of several of the occupants looking back at his Mercedes taxi and hoped they didn't recognize him. He didn't see the Volkswagen drive into the drainage ditch as he kept going to Landstuhl.

CHAPTER 11
Landstuhl Army Hospital, Germany

Frank didn't know where he was. He was lying on his back and seeing flashes of light through his closed eyelids. As he slowly regained consciousness, he opened his eyes and saw the flashes of light were overhead neon lights and he was being rolled down a hallway on some type of gurney. He heard the clicking of wheels rolling over a tile floor and he tried to sit up. He was gently pushed back down and heard a voice for the first time since he awoke.

"You have been in an auto accident and are now in Landstuhl Army Hospital. Please remain still."

The gurney came to a stop and several people were hovering over him.

He heard someone say, "Do you wear contact lenses?"

It seemed like an odd thing to say, but Frank replied "Yes."

He felt his head being turned sideways and someone expertly removed his contact lenses. He then heard someone say, "Did you give him anesthesia?" The reply was, "No, his alcohol content is a little too high, so we are going to have to sew him up without any anesthesia but will numb the area." Frank felt his hair being tugged as he slowly drifted off into unconsciousness again.

When Frank woke up, he felt a little nauseous and was surprised to see that he was in a bed with sides. He looked around and realized that he was in a hospital ward. It smelled of alcohol and other not so pleasant aromas that he couldn't readily identify. He counted seven other patients in the ward. Most of them were either asleep or unconscious. He started to recall someone telling him he was in an auto accident. He remembered that after a night of bar hopping with his buddies in Ramstein and Landstuhl, Germany, he was returning to Ramstein Air Base (AB) in an old Volkswagen driven by A2C Bob Gray. There were three other guys in the car, A2C George Otter, A2C Johnny Holbrook and A2C Ray Burnside.

Bob Gray had yelled, "Look at that idiot!" Frank saw a car coming down the middle of the road which forced their car into a farmer's field to avoid it. Frank leaned forward and looked back at the car that had run them off the road. That was the last thing he remembered until he was rolling down the corridor of the hospital. He wondered how the other guys were doing and started to sit up in the bed but felt an excruciating pain in his back. He closed his eyes until the pain subsided.

"Are you in pain?" Frank opened his eyes and saw a man dressed in white. "I am nurse Rudy and will be taking care of you, at least until the night nurse comes on duty."

Frank was surprised to see a male nurse. He didn't know men could be nurses. He wasn't sure what he thought about male nurses but told him, "My back hurts when I try to sit up."

The nurse said he would check with the doctor to determine

if a pain reliever could be administered. When he left, Frank had the terrifying thought that he might be paralyzed. Recalling a *Doctor Kildare* scene that he saw on television where the patient was asked to move his toes to determine if he had a severed spine. Frank quickly wiggled his toes and laid his head back on the pillow in relief. He almost laughed out loud. It was then that he became aware of the huge bandage on his head and remembered the comment about sewing him up. Then he wondered if he had any brain damage and laughing to himself, he wondered if anyone would notice.

Rudy the nurse came back with a doctor. Dr. Friedman was an Army Colonel who had seen many young soldiers and airmen who were hurt in 'accidents' that may have been precipitated by vengeance from Germans. He was a Lieutenant at the end of World War II and was now nearing retirement. He had seen the result of many disgruntled Germans who suffered during the war but also had suffered from mistreatment by the American, British, French and especially the Soviet Union victors of the war who had their own score to settle. Germany was a tinder box of hatred for many years but was now settling down to acceptance of the fact that Germany was going to be occupied for many years to come.

Dr. Freidman was looking at the chart hanging at the end of the bed, "So how are you feeling?"

Frank said, "I am having a sharp pain when I try sitting up."

The doctor nodded, "You may have a spinal injury. You also have a laceration on the back of your head that required seventeen stitches to close." Dr. Freidman asked Frank to move his toes and then to draw his legs up. He could do it, but it really hurt. He prodded around Frank's back and turned to the nurse, "Looks like a bad sprain but just in case, schedule an x-ray to see if the laceration had nicked his spine."

The doctor started to examine him further and when he touched his elbow, Frank nearly jumped out of the bed which caused a sharp jab of pain in his back again. Dr. Friedman then told the nurse, "Add an x-ray of the left elbow also."

Dr. Friedman administered a mild sedative and Frank drifted off to sleep.

Frank was awakened by the male nurse, "Time to go down for some x-rays." He had no idea how long he had been asleep. He was helped from the bed into a wheelchair by the nurse and an orderly. It was very painful whenever they touched his elbow and moved his back. It was then that Frank noticed a scrape on the front of his left foot where it met the leg and thought, "I wonder what else is screwed up." As they lowered him into the wheelchair, Frank felt the cold seat on his bare bottom. He told Rudy, "I think the gown I have on is ripped."

Rudy and the orderly looked at each other and started laughing. "That's the way they are made so we can get at you whenever we want to."

Frank tried pushing the gown around his butt but that just made his back hurt again, so he stopped and settled in for the ride. As they were rolling down the hall, Frank started feeling a bit better though.

Outside the x-ray room, he spotted Johnny Holbrook. He asked Johnny, "Hey man, do you know what happened to the rest of the guys in the car?" Johnny was almost incoherent, and his one eye was a translucent red. He mumbled, "Don't know" and stopped talking. Johnny was wheeled into the x-ray room and was gone when Frank finished his turn.

When the orderly wheeled him back into his room, Frank was pleasantly surprised to see Ray Burnside waiting there, "Wow, glad to see you."

Ray smiled, "Yeah, you too. You were unconscious the last time I was here. How are you feeling?"

"My back and elbow hurt but the head seems fine despite the huge bandage. How long was I out?"

Ray laughed, "About two days." Frank noticed Ray's right hand was bandaged, "What happened to your hand?"

Ray said, "I put my hands up to my head when the car started rolling, then the side window shattered, and I sustained several cuts that required stitches, hence the bandage on my hand. Do you remember any of that?"

"I remember that we were run off the road by a Mercedes driving down the middle of the road and our car dropping down into a farmer's field. I also remember looking for a way back up to the road, but my mind is a blank until I was being rolled down the corridor of the hospital."

Ray said, "When we got into the farmer's field, we were all

looking back to the road when Bob's car went into a huge concrete drainage ditch and rolled over several times. Johnny was in the front passenger seat and would have been ejected if not wearing his seat belt, but the door flew open and slammed back into him each time the car turned over." Frank remembered sitting in the middle of the back seat between George and Ray.

Ray continued to say, "When the car came to a stop, I was surprised to see you outside the car walking around and babbling. When we climbed out of the car, we had to keep sitting you down. Johnny was unconscious and when the ambulance came, he was considered the most critical. No one noticed your head bleeding because your jacket was black, and the blood didn't show up well in the dark. When the emergency responders noticed the blood, they transported you after Johnny. Bob broke his wrist because he had his hand through the steering wheel and got caught between the wheel and the turn signal lever. George Otter was helping Johnny and you into the ambulance when one of the emergency guys noticed that George was bleeding from his belly. It turned out that he had a punctured stomach that they surmise happened when he flew forward and landed on the gear shift on the floor. The plastic covering on the gear shift was missing but luckily, he only grazed the gear shift, so it is not too deep a puncture. I think you went through the windshield and took out the rearview mirror with your head."

After Ray left, Frank was thinking that he could have been killed and so could everyone else in the car. He started thinking about how much he would tell his parents and girlfriend. They would be glad to hear he was healing but would not want to hear that he had been drunk on his ass. Then he thought that being drunk is probably what saved all of them. He smiled at his cockeyed rational for getting drunk. He decided he would downplay the extent of his injuries and not mention that he was drunk.

Two days later Dr. Friedman came into the ward and told Frank, "The x-rays are all normal. You were lucky. A quarter inch deeper in the gash at the back of your head and you would have probably been paralyzed."

Frank gulped, "I kind of thought that might have been the case but I pushed it to the back of my mind."

Dr. Friedman came by a couple days later and told Frank, "I am going to release you back to your squadron today. Do you have transportation, or would you like me to arrange it?"

"My friends from Ramstein said they will pick me up, but thanks."

After Frank contacted Ray Burnside to pick him up, nurse Rudy showed up with a wheelchair. Frank very delicately lowered himself from the bed and into the chair, "I could probably walk but thanks for the ride."

"Hospital policy" said nurse Rudy.

Ray and another airman met him at the entrance to Landstuhl Army Hospital. "Frank, this is Pat Fry. I promised him that you would buy him some beers if he would pick you up and drive us back to Ramstein."

Pat laughed, "Not true but if you are well enough for a beer or two, I wouldn't refuse."

Ray said, "Let's stop for a beer at the Capri to celebrate your release and to show off your white turban."

Frank laughed and said, "OK, but only one beer." Ray and Don laughed at that idea.

Ray was a street-smart New Yorker who had a hot temper with people he didn't know but would give the shirt off his back for his friends. He had the swarthy complexion of an Italian, moderately tall and thin as a rail. He was married but his wife did not accompany him to Germany, so he was living in the barracks like most of the guys in the squadron. He had an expensive stereo system that he guarded like a pit bull and heaven help anyone who touched it without his permission.

Frank didn't know Pat that well. Pat was taller than Frank but like Frank, he was thin and wiry. Ray and Pat were inside plant guys. GEEIA was subdivided into teams with expertise in the engineering and installation of ground communications, navigation systems, outside plant (tower erection, etc.), inside plant (wiring runs, etc.) and radar.

They drove to the town of Ramstein and pulled into the Capri parking lot. Frank was in the front seat and had trouble getting out of the car, so Ray helped him, "Painful, huh?"

"Not too bad, more like a stiff back but don't touch my left elbow. That smarts a lot."

The Capri was not busy, being early afternoon when most of the airman were still on base. Ray and Pat set Frank down at a table, then went to play on the *fussball* machine. One of the bar girls, called Yutta, came to sit with him. "What happened to your head?" she said in English with a heavy German accent. Frank laughed, "Car wreck."

"Were you in the wreck with Ray?"

"Yeah, they just picked me up from the hospital."

"Let me get you a beer and I won't ask for a Cognac and coke, at least not this time." She smiled and went behind the bar to pour him a beer.

Frank and Yutta talked for about an hour. The beer was not going down well, and he thought he should have had something to eat before drinking beer. He began to feel a little nauseous and asked Ray and Pat to take him back to the barracks. He laid down on his bunk, grateful that his roommates weren't there and took a nap.

When Frank woke up from his nap, he felt a lot better so contacted Billy and said, "Hi Sarge. I'm out of the hospital and feel OK considering what happened."

"That's great. What .... that was my wife. She insists that you join us for dinner. Are you up for that?"

"You bet. It seems like forever since I had a home cooked

dinner."

"I'll be there in ten minutes to pick you up." Billy lived in the Ramstein AB housing area and his family occupied an apartment in a drab looking building. Billy had a young son who asked a million questions about the auto accident that Frank couldn't answer because he didn't recall details, so paraphrased what Ray told him happened.

After dinner, Billy and Frank were left alone and Billy asked, "Was it bad?"

"Not really, I don't remember much until I woke up in the hospital. I told your son what one of the other guys told me."

Billy laughed, "I think he likes you."

Billy was from Macon, Georgia. He was about 30 years old and was thinner that Frank but a couple inches taller. He and Frank swapped stories about life in Macon and Philadelphia. Life couldn't have been more different growing up in the south as compared to the north. Frank starting to get tired and asked Billy for a ride back to the barracks.

Billy dropped Frank off at the front of his barracks. His room was on the second floor of the barracks and his furniture, like that of each of his two roommates, was a bunk, a dresser and a large closet. The closet was not built-in because German law counted a built-in closet as another room and taxes were based on the number of rooms in a house. The closet was called a *Schrank* in German which made Frank wonder if his ancestors were closet builders. There was also a long desk with a chair that he and his roommates shared.

He laid down in his bunk and tried to get some sleep. The pain in his back kept nagging him so he took a pill that Dr. Friedman had prescribed him for pain. He slept until morning and woke up hungry. His two roommates were still asleep, so he quietly put on his fatigue uniform and as he was putting his boots on, he felt pain in the scrape on his ankle but tried to ignore it. He left the room and after gingerly going down the steps, headed for the restaurant next to the dining facility. He only ate the dining facility food when they had something good to offer, like steak or pork chops. Breakfast wasn't the forte of the dining facility. The eggs were runny, the bacon hardly cooked and the coffee burnt. The restaurant however had great coffee and made a mouthwatering ham and cheese omelet at a reasonable cost.

After breakfast he returned to the barracks and saw that his roommates must have headed to work but he was excused from work to rest for a few days. He decided to write his parents and Barb a letter explaining about the auto accident and assuring them that he was well on the road to recovery. He knew that his parents were concerned for his safety in Germany because of what happened to his Uncle Frank. That made him think about the voice in his head warning him about going downtown the night he was in the accident. He was sure it was the spirit of his Uncle Frank advising him. He decided not to ignore the voice anymore.

CHAPTER 12
Ramstein, Germany

The morning after Hans saw the Volkswagen leave the road, he heard that it crashed, and all the passengers injured. At first, he wished they were all killed but then got scared that the *Polizei* would know it was him from the descriptions provided by the airmen in the car. He couldn't remember if his taxi light was on when he swerved in front of them and thought that if it was, there was a good chance the *Polizei* could check all the calls and maybe figure out it was him. He didn't drive his taxi for the next couple days telling his mother that he wasn't feeling well. He really wasn't feeling well since he had a nagging belly ache that he attributed to his nerves being shot. He heard from other taxi drivers that the airmen were all drunk and couldn't identify the car that drove them off the road except that they thought it was a Mercedes which was one of the most popular cars in Germany. From this, he surmised that he did not have his taxi light on, or they would surely have known it was a taxi. He breathed a sigh of relief but made a point to eavesdrop on future conversations that his airmen customers had, to determine if they heard any updates to the investigation. The airmen usually talked to each other while totally ignoring the taxi driver thinking that he didn't speak much English.

He met Reinhart and told him what he had done. Reinhart

laughed, "I told you that you would think of some way to get even. When are you going to run another one off the road?"

Hans got nervous, "I don't think I will ever do it again. What if I get caught by the *Polizei?*"

Reinhart thought for a moment. "You are my friend, so I will start drinking in bars frequented by Americans and call you when I see one really drunk and driving. Most of the airmen take taxis so it shouldn't be hard to pick out the *dummkopts* who drink and drive."

"I don't know, let me think about it."

"Remember Heidi. There will surely be more German girls in her same predicament. Think of it as protecting the *Vaterland* in a way."

Hans got up to leave and said, "I will think about it."

"Think about what we talked about the recorder also. I know I can get you at least 100 marks a tape."

Hans smiled but said nothing.

After Hans left, Reinhart waited a few minutes and walked to a phone booth near the Capri. He dialed a number and speaking in German said, "I think he bought into it. We'll see if he has the guts. I'll keep on him until he does."

Ivan Kraskov smiled and said, "*Gute Arbeit.* Keep me posted." Kraskov was an assistant to the deputy of the chief clerk in the Soviet embassy. A position of such low importance that

that he hoped his real role of a KGB agent, or *Komitet Gosudarstveenoy Besopasnosti*, the Soviet external intelligence agency, would not be detected. He spoke fluent German with a Austrian accent and the man named Reinhart thought he was an East German spy. Kraskov was fifty-five years old and served in the Soviet army as an intelligence analyst during the World War II. He was recruited by the KGB and ran several operations in West Germany since being assigned to the Soviet embassy. He was of medium height with a beer belly and had little hair remaining on his head. He looked like a typical German.

CHAPTER 13
Bremen, Germany

There was a lot of animosity still prevalent by all Germans, East and West, from their mistreatment by the Soviet Union after World War II. Soviet soldiers extracted vengeance on Germans, particularly women, who were often raped in front of their husbands and children. Men were sent to forced labor camps or executed on a wholesale basis. This was considered payback from Operation Barbarossa, the German invasion of the Soviet Union in 1941 and the subsequent mistreatment of the Soviet civilians by German soldiers from 1941 through 1944.

Oleg Pavlov, however, was a Russian who was in Germany throughout World War II. His grandfather had immigrated to Germany after World War I and had opened a pastry shop in Bremen. Oleg's father had assumed ownership of the pastry shop after the death of Oleg's grandfather. During the war, Oleg's father was constantly harassed by German authorities and fellow citizens, who accused him of being a communist and a spy. His father was neither and professed his innocence whenever confronted. He somehow managed to avoid being sent to a German concentration camp but aged considerably during the war. The British and U.S. bombed Bremen continuously and inadvertently destroyed his father's pastry shop. Then, Oleg's father was killed in a British – German crossfire in

April 1945 during the last days of the battle to finally capture Bremen. Oleg was eight years old and witnessed the whole thing.

After the war, Germany was partitioned into American, British, French and the Soviet Union Sectors. In 1955, Oleg's mother passed away and he decided to leave Bremen. He crossed the border between the British and the Soviet Union Sectors. He was arrested by the East German *Volks Polizie*, called *Vopos*, and charged as a West German spy. He was interrogated and mildly tortured, if any torture can be considered mild, but managed to come to the attention of a Soviet KGB official.

Oleg convinced the KGB official that he wanted to help the Soviet Union in any way he could to avenge his father's treatment by the Germans and his death by the British. His flawless Bremen accent was seen as a valuable asset to the KGB official who endorsed Oleg to the Soviet intelligence agency in Moscow. They in turn brought him back to the Soviet Union for more intense interrogation and were convinced that he was telling the truth. They decided to provide training and indoctrination into intelligence work while keeping surveillance on him in the event he was really a West German spy. While in training, he joined the communist party, which impressed the KGB, and was offered the opportunity to return to West Germany to collect intelligence.

Oleg Pavlov, now 28 years old, was sitting in a Mercedes panel van about four kilometers from Hulseberg, Germany. The marking on the van said *Environmental Monitoring and*

Analysis and listed an address in Hamburg, Germany. There actually was an office there but was a front and manned by Germans who really thought they were associated with Environmental Analysis. The office was actually a cutout for one of the Soviet Union's illegal activities in West Germany.

Oleg was tasked with collecting signal traffic from the American Air Force Communications Squadron located at a German artillery range, near Hulseberg. The Soviet Union did not trust their reluctant ally, East Germany, with this mission.

Oleg would collect the signals, record and encode them. The recordings were then dropped off at the office in Bremen, who, thinking the data was being sent to a lab for analysis, forwarded the data, via a courier. In actuality, the encoded data was being sent to a secure site for analysis on the East Germany border with West Germany. The mission was not really time sensitive since the purpose was to determine the methodology NATO used when conducting command and control of artillery. The Soviet Union was planning to send conflicting commands using the same protocols as NATO to confuse and disrupt operations in the event of a breakout of war between NATO forces and the Warsaw Pact.

Oleg would drive around to different locations, as remote as possible, but with line of sight to the Hulseberg installation. If confronted by authorities, he would explain that he was collecting environmental data for the West German government and had fake documentation to back up his explanation. He positioned phony environmental sensors around the van to make it appear he really was collecting environmental data. The equipment in the van was configured to look innocent enough to fool a policeman. However, in order to get line of sight from as far away from Hulseberg as possible, and still get a satisfactory signal, he had to have an intercepting antenna as high as possible. He solved this problem by looping a rope onto a high branch of a tree some distance away from the van and hoisting an antenna on one end of the line and pulling it up the tree. He would bury the cable from the van to the base of the tree, so it would be hard to find if someone was looking for it. He would then check the strength of the intercepted signal and if adequate, would start recording over a band of frequencies known to be used by NATO.

CHAPTER 14
Ramstein, Germany

Billy Black came into the warehouse with a big smile on his face and told Gerhardt, Don and Frank, "We have a mission. We are going on a TDY trip to an Air Force Communications Squadron located on a German artillery range in northern Germany near Hulseberg."

He asked Frank, "Do you think you recovered enough from the auto accident to make this trip?"

Frank really wasn't up for it but said, "You bet!"

They talked about what equipment they would need to complete the job. When they were satisfied, the four of them piled into Billy's Ford Falcon and went to the SCIF for the secret mission brief which was the real reason they were selected for this job.

SMS Oliver, the GEEIA First Sergeant, conducted the briefing. "This trip may be helpful in finding out more information on what the Soviet Union and East Germany may be up to. The intelligence group at Langley suspect the comm site, called Detachment 5, even though they are located well back from East Germany, might be having their signals intercepted. The Soviets continually monitor the methodology used by NATO and West Germany, in this case, for directing and executing artillery strikes. The GEEIA engineering team is planning an experiment on a new electronics box that supposedly identifies the forensics of the intercepting systems used by the Soviet Union. Although you won't be privy on how the box works your team will provide a plausible cover story not related to the experiment. Your orders will read that you are only conducting an annual verification of the calibration of the existing communications systems at Detachment 5. You will be accompanied by Horst Keller, a vetted German with a Top Secret clearance from the research and engineering team who will conduct the experiment. Are there any questions?"

Billy said, "Who is our point of contact at Detachment 5 and when do we leave?"

SMS Oliver said, "Your point of contact is the Commander of Detachment 5, MAJ Jim Best. You may also encounter LTC Miles Garson, the Commander of the Air Force Communications Squadron located in Wiesbaden. MAJ Best reports to LTC Garson, who routinely visits Detachment 5. Both are cleared for your mission and will help you distract the other men of Detachment 5 while Horst is conducting the experiment. You can schedule a power wagon from the motor pool on Monday, which gives you five days to load up the necessary equipment and check it out."

Frank's back was still aching when he sat in certain positions, and he occasionally got nauseous from the pain, but he wanted to go on this trip. It was to be his first TDY and he wanted to show that he could contribute to the team's mission. He volunteered to get the power wagon out of the motor pool.

A power wagon is a four-wheel drive truck build by Dodge. The GEEIA version had a standard gear shift, called a 'stick', and four doors. It could easily carry five passengers. It had a locking metal canopy over the bed of the truck to protect toolboxes, suitcases, and equipment. It was painted blue and had the GEEIA logo on the two front doors.

Billy asked, "Can you drive a stick?"

Frank had learned how to drive a stick when he was on the survey team in Philly so responded, "Yes, I learned before I came in the Air Force."

"Do you have a Government license?"

"Uh... no I don't. Doesn't my civilian license count?"

"No, but there's no time to schedule the written test and qualifying drive before we leave for Hulseberg. I'll put you in to qualify on several trucks after we get back. Don can check out the power wagon from the motor pool."

On the day of departure, Frank accompanied Don to the motor pool. They drove back to the barracks to pick up Frank's luggage, then met up with Gerhardt, Billy and Horst. Billy decided to drive so Don slid over to the passenger side of the truck while Frank got in the back with Gerhardt and Horst. Frank winced in pain, feeling every bump in the road. He kept it to himself. They were only on the *autobahn* for a half hour when Billy noticed Frank was uncomfortable.

Billy asked him, "Are you alright?"

"Not really. I am feeling shooting pains in my back whenever we hit a bump."

Billy pulled over and asked Don, "Do you mind switching places with Frank? Maybe the front seat won't be as bad on his back."

He was right. Frank was still uncomfortable, but it was a lot better than sitting in the back seat.

Hulseberg, Germany

They arrived around dinner time, checked into a *gasthaus*, and agreed to meet in the restaurant downstairs. Frank ordered a ham sandwich which looked raw. Horst saw him staring at the sandwich. He said, "Ham in Germany does not have trichinosis like your American ham. It is good, try it, you'll like it."

Frank ate it but didn't care for raw looking ham. He tried to convince himself that it was fine but upchucked his meal when he got back to his room.

The next morning, Frank asked Horst about the experimental box. Horst explained, "The experimental set is designed to insert a modulation component into emitted signals from the communications detachment. The way super heterodyne receivers work is they mix the incoming detected signal with the output of an internal local oscillator in the first stage.

There would be four frequencies outputted from this stage: the received frequency, the local oscillator frequency, plus the sum and difference of the two frequencies. Filters attenuate three of the outputted frequencies from the first stage and a vacuum tube amplifies the selected frequency. The trick is that we need to be close enough to the intercepting receiver so that our unique signal is strong enough that we can detect it with the experimental set after being mixed with the local oscillator but before it gets filtered out."

Frank didn't understand how this was possible and hoping he wasn't asking a stupid question asked, "So how would that help us?"

Horst said, "It would enable us to determine the azimuth of the intercepting receiver from Detachment 5. With two, or even better three sets in different locations, we would be able to triangulate the location of the intercepting receiver, not just the azimuth. We have conducted experiments to determine the range at which we can detect the emissions from the local oscillator, but it is almost impossible to replicate the effects of interfering signals, like reflections for things like buildings and attenuation from things like trees. This will be a real-life test."

"Did you bring more experimental sets with you, so we can locate the intercepting receiver?"

"Unfortunately, no, there wasn't time to make more sets for this trip. If, however, we are successful in detecting an intercepting receiver, we will certainly make more as quick as we can. I do have several antennas, so we can experiment with them to see what works best. This, of course, all depends on whether or not there is even an intercepting receiver out there."

Frank said, "There are a lot of 'ifs' that have to come together for this to be successful. I guess that's why it's called an experiment, right?"

Horst laughed, "That about sums it up. Welcome to my world."

CHAPTER 15
Hulseberg, Germany

TSGT Billy Black saluted MAJ Best when the GEEIA team arrived at Detachment 5. MAJ Best was dressed in 1505's, the uniform more formal than the fatigues worn by the GEEIA team but less formal than the dress blue uniform. He was tall and looked more like a German than an American with blond hair and blue eyes. He was in command of Detachment 5 and although he had served in several communications sites early in his career, he had been assigned to an Air Intelligence Squadron when he made Captain and had worked in intelligence positions prior to this assignment.

MAJ Best said, "My men are ready to assist you as required, if you need them." This was said for the benefit of the Detachment 5 troops who were listening to the exchange between Billy and MAJ Best.

Billy said, "Thank you very much. I don't think we will need the support of your troops but appreciate the offer."

Don and Frank familiarized themselves with the controls on the front of the detachment's communication equipment. Gerhardt and Horst worked in the back of the equipment racks switching cables and setting up the experimental box. The troops from Detachment 5 were not too pleased to have GEEIA guys mucking around with their equipment. It became clear that they viewed it as checking up on them instead of GEEIA checking the calibration of the equipment. MAJ Best kept hovering over his guys to keep them focused on other areas of the equipment room and not what was happening in front of the equipment or behind the racks where the cabling was.

MAJ Best saw one of his airmen sneaking a peek behind the racks and challenged him, "Where are you going?"

"Just want to see what those guys are doing in the back."

"That's it! I want you guys in the break room, NOW!"

They left for the break room. MAJ Best yelled, "I don't want you guys interfering with these GEEIA guys. The sooner we get them out of here, the better."

Frank smiled as he easily overheard MAJ Best even though the break room was at the far end of the building and the white noise generated from the surrounding equipment was loud. He turned to Don and said, "I wonder how he plans to quell their curiosity after we leave for the day and they are alone on the night shift?"

Horst leaned around from the back of the equipment rack and said, "No problem. The experimental box is sealed and any attempt to open it will cause the release of a small thermite device that will melt the electronics in the box. Billy has told MAJ Best that he should impress upon his troops that the box is extremely sensitive and not to tamper with it or there would be hell to pay if they even touched it. It isn't really sensitive but only MAJ Best knows that."

Billy said, "We plan to leave it here for about a month to record any hits since we don't know when the next intercept will occur, if there are any at all."

Don said, "I hope MAJ Best told his guys not to talk about the box when they hit the local bars. You never know who might be listening to troops talk and it wouldn't take a rocket scientist to alert the bad guys to what was happening."

Horst said, "I mentioned this to MAJ Best and suggested he tell them that the box is monitoring the long-term reliability of the equipment in case any of his troops get loose lips when drinking. It is better to give them a reason for the new box and not have them speculate on their own."

Don smiled, "Good thinking but you should have told us, so we don't contradict each other."

"Sorry about that. I only thought about telling MAJ Best to suggest it when we walked in the door and should have huddled with you guys sooner."

LTC Miles Garson showed up at Detachment 5 and said, "Sorry I'm late, traffic through Bremen was a mess due to an accident. Did I miss anything?"

Billy started to answer when MAJ Best walked into the equipment room.

"Welcome to Detachment 5 Colonel Garson" using the honorific rank, "the troops were a little curious, but I explained to them that they shouldn't crowd the GEEIA guys so much. All is under control now."

"I hope so. I just came from Lindsey Air Station and Major General (MG) Jack Stone made it clear that we need to keep this close to the vest. General Stone reminded me that German General Gehlen's Organization is still active after twenty years and they have deduced that the Soviet Union has a very active intelligence network, which is no surprise. For those of you who don't him, General Gehlen was the Nazi chief of intelligence during World War II. He foresaw the collapse of the Nazi regime and prepared for post-war activities by copying his files and burying them in the Bavarian Alps for sale to the United States after the war. He surrendered to the Americans in 1945 and was interned at an American base near Oberursel, Germany. Instead of selling his files, General Gehlen offered to turn over his entire network of spies across Europe to the Americans in exchange for the Americans not turning his men and their families over to the Soviets. He feared he and his men would be tortured to expose the current Nazi network in the Soviet Union and then sent to concentration camps in Siberia or executed outright. The Army agreed, and Gehlen reported to the Army Intelligence G-2 initially and later transferred to the CIA. The CIA returned him to Germany to set up his headquarters near Oberursel, where he vigilantly maintained an anti-communist organization to spy on the activities of the Soviet Union."

Frank had never heard of General Gehlen and was impressed that the United States had the foresight to take advantage of the Gehlen Organization when the rest of the world was focused on punishing Nazis.

LTC Garson offered to buy beers for MAJ Best and the GEEIA team in the small canteen next to the building housing the Detachment 5 equipment.

LTC Garson asked Billy, "Where is your GEEIA team staying while you are here."

"The *Hofcafe* in Hulseberg."

"Yeah, me too. Let's get together for dinner. MAJ Best, please join us."

"Roger that."

Billy said, "Sounds good."

Frank said, "Sounds good to me too but no raw ham."

The GEEIA team laughed but LTC Garson and MAJ Best looked confused.

"Private joke?" asked MAJ Best. Billy explained, and they laughed too.

MAJ Best got a serious look on his face and said, "I had the canteen swept for bugs so that we can talk. We obviously can't talk about this experiment at dinner in the *Hofcafe* since there may be eyes and ears on us there. When will you be ready to 'monitor reliability'?"

Horst chuckled and said, "We have completed the installation but need to check it out tomorrow. I brought a stimulator with me to mimic the signal we are hoping to detect. I expect to be done early tomorrow and then we are a go."

"Good," said LTC Garson, "I will coordinate with MG Stone to set up a NATO artillery exercise the day after tomorrow. They exercise frequently for the NATO brass and MG Stone has made prior arrangements to have some NATO brass available."

CHAPTER 16
Bremen, Germany

Otto Kressman worked in the motor pool at Hulseberg but lived in Bremen. He wasn't the brightest light in the room, but Oleg found him useful. Oleg dated Otto's not so attractive sister Greta and told her his name was Gerhardt Knorr. Greta could not believe her luck at dating so handsome a man as Gerhardt. He took her out on picnics and boat rides but never to a restaurant or the theater. Greta did not see this as odd because Gerhardt told her that he was an artist and had little money. Greta made dinner for him and he made such a fuss about how wonderful it was that she was delighted to cook for him.

While Greta was cooking, Oleg talked with Otto about the gossip in town and how lucky he was to work at the Hulseberg motor pool.

Oleg looked into the dull eyes of Otto and said, "So how goes your work today? I envy your knowledge of so many different vehicles and how to maintain them."

Otto beamed. He didn't think his job required much knowledge but was grateful to hear that Gerhardt thought so. "I was told today to expect some NATO brass the day after tomorrow. They have such nice cars and I take great pride in caring for them while they are here."

"I bet they are impressed with the care you give their cars. How many do you expect?"

"Only two cars this time. They are probably new officers assigned to NATO and don't know which way to point an artillery piece." He laughed at his joke and so did Oleg.

"So, we can expect to hear big booms tomorrow. Hope it's not too early that I get woken up."

"I heard that it will be 1000. Are you up by then?" Otto said and smiled. He thought Gerhardt was a bum but held out hope that Greta could convince him to get a job. She told Otto that she loved Gerhardt and Otto was happy for her. She could do worse.

Greta came into the dining room, "Dinner is ready. Have you washed up?"

They both said no and one by one, slipped off to the bathroom. Oleg jotted down what Otto told him on a small piece of paper. He knew this was frowned on by his superiors, but Oleg did not want to leave anything to chance that he would forget what he heard. Besides, the paper he used was easily digestible in case he had to eat it. He saw it as a kind of dessert after Greta's dinner. He smiled at his own little joke.

The next morning Oleg checked out his gear to be sure it was functional and calibrated correctly. He had been provided a stimulator by his handler in Bremen and used it before each mission. He lived in the garage he leased and rigged it with explosives if someone broke in when he wasn't there. He thought about having the explosives set to blow when he was there but decided that he didn't want to die for the Soviets. He didn't expect to have a break-in though since he had signs in front that said the door was alarmed. Very few people felt the need for alarms since Germany was considered moderately safer than surrounding countries, except for maybe Denmark. The area where he had his garage was not the norm since most garages nearby did have alarms and the *Polizei* patrolled frequently. He felt that thieves would be discouraged since there were easier places to break into.

Oleg left the garage in Bremen at 0600 which would give him plenty of time to set up before the scheduled exercise at Hulseberg. He had four different locations that had line of sight to Hulseberg and were higher than the surrounding terrain. He stayed away from the highest terrain thinking that any surveillance would focus on the highest ground.

Oleg was right. MAJ Best had deployed two surveillance teams to the two highest ground locations. There were other locations that were almost as high but there were only two surveillance teams available to him. They reported back to MAJ Best that there was no activity at their locations. MAJ Best sent them to two other locations but didn't expect to hear back from them since the roads weren't that great and the locations were not close to each other.

Oleg was set up by 0930. He could have been there earlier but was concerned that he might stand out too much to any locals who might be hiking in the woods. Germans loved to hike, and it was a threat to Oleg. There wasn't much he could do about it so when he had been approached by hikers in the past, he talked amicably to them about protecting the environment. They did not appear to be suspicious because Germans liked a clean environment nearly as much as they liked to hike. Today was a rare hot day in northern Germany and not much to the liking of most hikers. Oleg was pleased.

CHAPTER 17
Hulseberg, Germany

"Well, here goes nothing," Horst said to no one in particular.

The Command and Control (C2) van radioed orders to the artillery battery and provided coordinates to them. The range was limited and there were only three sets of coordinates available with targets located at them. The NATO officers were taking notes in the C2 van and firing commenced.

"We got a hit at 20-200," exclaimed Horst. He wrote down the azimuth and passed it to MAJ Best. The problem with just an azimuth is that the direction could not be determined. 20-200 represented a line that meant the detected signal was along a line running from 20 degrees to 200 degrees from their location. This was based on a 360-degree circle with North being at 0-360 degrees. However, as far as their experiment was concerned, it was a success. They could detect the intercepting receiver. If they had a couple more boxes available, they could position them to possibly triangulate where the emitted signal was coming from.

"We are getting a pretty strong signal." said Horst, "The intercepting receiver must be pretty close to us."

Billy said, "How close?"

"Two or three kilometers, I would guess."

That gave Billy an idea, so he asked MAJ Best, "Do you have a 1:50,000 topographic map of the immediate area handy? Maybe I can narrow down the possible locations of high points where the emitter might be along the azimuth."

MAJ Best produced the map and Billy drew a line that depicted the azimuth along the 20-200 line. "There is only one high point along that azimuth for four kilometers in either direction." Billy said and asked Horst, "What is the margin of error?"

"At two or three kilometers, it is negligible."

Billy said, "That's what I thought too. Let's play a trick and see what happens. MAJ Best, can you ask the C2 center to send out the coordinates of the high point but not fire since it's off the range?"

MAJ Best called the C2 center, "Can you please tell the artillery battery to stand down and broadcast these coordinates? We are doing an experiment here and need some data."

After about three minutes, Horst said, "The intercepting receiver is moving."

Billy said, "Make some cuts at the new azimuths and read them out to me."

Horst provided the new azimuths and Billy plotted them on the map. "I can roughly correlate the cuts to a road leading from the high point I identified earlier."

Billy asked MAJ Best, "Can you direct your surveillance teams to this road?"

"Yes, but they are pretty far away."

You are closer. Give chase.

Frank inadvertently nodded said, "We are only two kilometers from that road. Let me go and try to catch him."

Billy said, "Our power wagon is in the motor pool for an oil change."

MAJ Best said, "Take my car and this PRC-6 walkie-talkie with you to remain in contact with us. Here are my keys. I drive the Volkswagen out front."

Billy said, "Don, you go with Frank."

Don and Frank ran out the door and got into MAJ Best's Volkswagen. "Damn, this car is older than me. Hope we are chasing a really slow driver."

Don laughed and said, "You drive, I will keep in touch with Billy and Horst on the PRC-6 radio."

Frank took off and asked Don, "Which way?"

Don got on the radio and asked Billy for an update on the intercepting receiver and the best roads to take to intercept it. Horst kept updating Billy on the new azimuths and Billy made updates on the map. He passed updates on to Don as to what roads to take and Frank drove as fast as the old Volkswagen could go.

Horst told Billy, "The suspect vehicle is driving toward Bremen and the further away he gets from us, the more intermittent the signal gets. It looks like the suspect vehicle is about to enter the road that Frank and Don are on. Ask Don if he can see a vehicle entering the road to his left."

Billy radioed to Don, "Do you see a vehicle entering your road on your left? Over."

"Yeah, a white van with lettering on the side. Looks like three words. I can see capital letters EMA but can't make out the lower-case letters. Over."

Frank overheard Don, "I think the first word is environment or something like that."

"Frank thinks the first word might be environment. Over."

"Roger that. Over," radioed Billy

The white van started accelerating down the road away from Frank and Don. "He's getting away. Can't you go faster?" Don said.

"Got the pedal to the metal."

"Suspect vehicle is getting away. Can you alert the Bremen *Polizei* to set up roadblocks or something? Over," Don asked.

"Roger. We already have. I'll keep you posted. Over," radioed Billy.

Horst told Billy, "I lost the signal. Hope they can keep an eye on him, or he will get away."

Billy radioed, "We lost the signal. Try to keep up. Over."

Don heard, "We....signal....up. Over."

Don radioed, "We must be getting out of range on the PRC-6. Over."

No response. Don turned to Frank. "It's up to us to stay with him."

The van went over a hill and seemed to accelerate even faster until Don and Frank could no longer see it. As they entered Bremen, they could see a *Polizei* check point but no white van. They slowed down, and Frank asked one of the *Polizei*, "Did a white van come through here?"

"*Bitte?*" said the cop.

"*Sprechen zie Englisch?*" Don said.

"A little... *abet... ein moment.*"

Another *Polizei* came over and said, "Can I help you?"

Don repeated his initial question.

"No, we did not see such a vehicle."

Thinking the word van might not translate right, Frank asked "How about a white truck with Environment something on the side? Big letters were EMA."

The *Polizei* smiled, "No, no van or truck."

Frank turned to Don, "He must have turned off before the check point. Let's back track and hope for the best."

Frank turned the Volkswagen around and headed back the way they just came. He figured the van's driver probably turned off when he spotted the check point so focused on a road near them. He saw some kids playing near a road that he thought might be the one the van's driver took. He asked Don, "Do you speak a little more German than you just did?"

Don said, "A bit but most German kids can speak passable English."

As Frank drove up to the kids, Don leaned out the window and asked the kids, "Did you see a white truck turn here?" One of the kids said yes and pointed down the road.

"*Danke!*" Don said.

As they drove down the road, Frank said, "One question though. What are we going to do if we catch up to him?"

Don reached behind him and pulled out a pistol. "We will detain him," he smiled.

Frank looked at the pistol, "I have not seen one like that. What is it?"

"It is a 9-millimeter Walther P-38. We need to get you one when we get back to Ramstein and a Walther PPK. We all carry German weapons since it might be advantageous if things get ugly and we don't want to use American weapons."

"I probably should have been given them before we left."

Don laughed, "You would have, after being qualified with them, if you didn't end up in the hospital. Billy was thinking of leaving you in station but that would have left the team pretty thin."

The road was wider than the streets that intersected it and they guessed the van would probably stay on it. They followed it to an intersection with an even wider road. Frank looked at Don, "What do you think, straight, right or left?"

"I think we lost him, let's go back to the detachment", Don said.

CHAPTER 18
Bremen, Germany

"What the hell happened?" Oleg asked himself out loud after he pulled into his garage. His heart was still racing.

He thought back to when he perceived that all was not well. He had only been half listening to the C2 center at Hulseberg coordinating fire when he heard new coordinates being sent and realized that he was sitting on these coordinates.

"What the hell are those idiots doing?" He panicked, thinking that artillery rounds and shrapnel were on the way, so he quickly put the van into gear and took off, dragging the antenna down the road with him from the tree where he had hoisted it earlier. He saw a dust trail behind him and after traveling down the road to what he deemed a safe distance from the blast zone, pulled over and yanked the cable and antenna back into the van. He headed out to the main road, wondering why the C2 center was calling fire onto his coordinates when it dawned on him that they knew he was there and fooled him into running. But how did they know he was there? Maybe a passerby or hiker reported a suspicious vehicle and someone in the C2 center decided to play a joke.

He continued down the road at a leisurely pace so as not to attract attention. When he got to the main road, he turned left and saw a Volkswagen bearing down on him. He accelerated and was pulling away but was concerned that he was being chased. He lost sight of the Volkswagen and almost had a heart attack when he saw a *Polizei* roadblock in front of him. He turned left, hoping the *Polizei* didn't see him and give chase. Some kids looked up when he abruptly turned. He checked his rear-view mirror and saw the kids start to play again and no *Polizei* were following him. He breathed easier and headed for his garage.

After checking the garage for any sign of tampering, he pulled in and shut down the motor. He broke into a cold sweat thinking about the close call he had. He didn't see any locals or hikers near him on that hill but wasn't really paying much attention. He chided himself for getting too complacent and almost getting caught. He started to contact his handler but thought he would be blamed for endangering the mission. He thought it best if he just pretended that he had gathered enough data and ended the mission as he usually did. He did some pros and cons thinking about this story. His superiors would probably learn from other sources that there had been some abnormal activity at Hulseberg but may not know what it was. At least, he hoped they would not find out. In any event, he would sit tight and hope for the best.

CHAPTER 19
Hulseberg, Germany

LTC Garson, MAJ Best and the GEEIA team had gathered around a table in the now closed canteen. "Well, that was exciting," said LTC Garson, "We got a bit more out of your experiment than we expected. Let me recap before I send in a report to MG Stone and General Gehlen. First, the experiment was a success. Second, we flushed out someone in a white van with the capital letters EMA on the side and the letter E may have been the word environment. And third, we tried to follow the van but lost him just outside Bremen. Billy, that was a pretty neat idea you had, tracking him with azimuths and a map."

Billy said, "It's been done before but with little success. You must have a pretty good idea on the location of the intercepting receiver and that is usually not the case. Plus, the ruse about calling in fire on him worked better than I expected. It made him move."

Frank was listening with rapt attention and reliving the chase in his mind. It was exciting and scary at the same time. He was running scenarios in his head about what he could have done differently. He thought about the P-38 that Don had and wondered what would happen if they caught up with the van. Were the people in the van also armed and with what? If they had automatic weapons, there was little chance that he and

Don would survive a gun battle.

MAJ Best said, "We have dispatched a forensics team to look over the hill he left from to see if we can find any clues to his identity."

LTC Garson turned to Frank and Don, "Did you get any more info from the kids on the corner?"

Frank started to answer when Don said, "No. We asked them if they read the lettering on the van and they looked at each other and shrugged their shoulders."

MAJ Best said, "We passed the lettering info on to the Gehlen Organization to check out. Hopefully they can track down the company, if it exists."

As if on cue, the phone rang. MAJ Best picked it up, said hello and listened. He turned to the group, "The Gehlen Organization located a company called *Environmental Monitoring and Analysis* in Bremen. They only have two of their operatives local and asked if we can help. I said, 'Of course' we would be glad to do it. I have arms and flak jackets for all if you want them."

The group opted not to wear flak jackets because they were too bulky and, except for Billy, Don and Horst who preferred to use their Walther P-38's, chose .45 caliber Colt M-1911 pistols. They chose pistols instead of rifles since they could be concealed. They didn't want to rile up the local German community in Bremen which might inadvertently give them away when approaching the *Environmental Monitoring and Analysis* office.

Bremen, Germany

They met the two operatives from the Gehlen Organization and MAJ Best asked, "What's the status and how do you want us to proceed?" The building was a two-story structure of relative modern design since a lot of the prewar buildings were turned into rubble and new buildings had sprouted up to take their place.

One of the operatives said, "There are two doors, one in the back and one in the front. It looks like there are four people inside. Two of you should cover the back door and the rest follow us in the front door, OK?"

MAJ Best said, "Sounds good. Billy and Horst - take one of the PRC-6 radios and cover the back door. Stop anyone you see leaving. Once secured, we will knock twice and then once to let you know the building is secure, then we will open the back door. Don and Frank will stay with me and keep pedestrians out of line of possible fire. Then we will follow Gehlen's men through the front door in case they need backup."

They approached the office as nonchalantly as they could to their assigned positions around the office. Billy keyed the PRC-6 radio and said, "We are in position to cover the back door."

The front door was unlocked. The two operatives walked in and pointed their weapons at the three men and one woman inside. One of the men jumped up from his seat and said in German, "Please don't kill us. You can take whatever you want." The woman started crying. Speaking in German, she said, "Please, I have two children at home." One of the operatives went through the rest of the building and found no one else present. He knocked on the back door with the pre-arranged signal and opened it for Billy and Horst.

MAJ Best asked, "Do any of you speak English?" They all nodded yes.

"Good. Where is the van?"

"What van?"

"The white one with the markings of your office painted on it."

"Oh, you must mean the data collection van?"

"Yes, where is it?"

"Our data collection technician, Hans Ludwig, has it and is out collecting data."

MAJ Best said, "Does anyone have handcuffs?" No one thought to bring handcuffs, so Frank was assigned to corral them into a corner and stand guard over them while the two operatives started going through the desks.

"So, you admit spying on Hulseberg?"

"What? No, Hans is collecting environmental data for us to forward to the main lab for analysis."

"Where is he now?" No one seemed to know.

"Where is the main lab?"

"It's in Frankfurt."

"Which Frankfurt would that be - Frankfurt am Main or Frankfurt an der Oder?" The first is in West Germany and the second is in East Germany.

The three men and one woman looked at each other confused.

One of the men said, "Frankfurt am Main, of course", then he looked at his co-workers and said, "Right?" They all still looked confused and some nodded yes.

"Let me explain," said one of the co-workers, "We call the lab when Hans delivers us the data on tape, and someone comes and picks it up. We keep logs on where Hans collected data for our records. We are also responsible for answering queries from people who are curious about the van and what it is doing across northern Germany. In addition, we pass along instructions from the lab to Hans and manage his pay and leave."

One of the operatives left the building and came back with an apparatus that he connected to the phone in the office. He turned to the man who gave the explanation and said, "Call the main lab to report that Hans has a tape to pick up."

During the phone call to the lab, the operative manipulated his apparatus. When the call was completed, he motioned to MAJ Best and Billy to follow him to the back of the building.

"The phone they called is not located in Frankfurt, but just outside Helmstedt, a border crossing to East Germany. We have a team there full time since it's a hotbed of intelligence activity. I am going to call the Gehlen Organization at Oberursel to request they raid the location and to expect resistance. Also, I think these people here don't have a clue about what they are involved in but will have it checked out thoroughly."

MAJ Best asked, "What about the van?"

"I will ask the local authorities to help us find it."

"We may have located the van," said one of the operatives about an hour later. "When I asked the *Polizei* if they could help us, one of their officers said an old lady, kind of a busy body, complained that a man was sleeping in his garage which is against city ordinance and she wanted it checked out. It was a low priority, given their other duties, so they pushed it off to check out when they had time. The officer said she told him that he drove a white van with lettering on the side. He couldn't remember if the old lady told him what it was but will check it out with her. I am going with him to meet with the old lady now and would appreciate it if you guys can come along."

MAJ Best had already returned to Detachment 5, so Billy answered, "We would be delighted to go along."

The old lady was visibly nervous with the response by so many men. She confirmed that the lettering on the van was *Environmental Monitoring and Analysis*. She went to the front window of her apartment and pointed to the garage in question. It was a small garage with two doors. One was the sliding door for the vehicle and one standard door to gain access.

The *Polizei* officer got on his radio to request assistance. The operative said, "That won't be necessary since we are all armed and should be able to handle it quietly."

"My orders are to report in and request assistance if I think there is more to this than meets the eye. My superior said that at this point in the investigation, it is a German matter and falls under the City of Bremen jurisdiction."

The operative tried to convince the officer otherwise but was unsuccessful. He turned to Billy and said, "He's right. They don't usually get involved in our business, but they do have jurisdiction. Let's split up and cover both ends of the street in case this gets ugly and they need our assistance."

Two *Polizei* vehicles pulled up at each end of the street to block traffic. Officers got out of the vehicles and approached the garage from both ends of the street. One went to the door and knocked. "*Polizei*. Open the door." He said in German. There was no response, so he motioned to one of the officers with a pry bar to break in.

MOVE BACK! GET DOWN! The voice pounded in Frank's head

Frank was visibly shocked and straightened up as if he was called to attention. He quickly moved back toward the rest of the team and began to crouch down as the officer struggled with the garage door and finally popped it open. There was a massive explosion that knocked down all the officers near the door spewing pieces of the garage like shrapnel into the buildings across the street. Frank was blown off his feet from the blast wave and skidded along the street. He was far enough away from the garage that although knocked flat on his back, he remained conscious. He felt a pressure in his lungs that left him breathless for an instant, and his ears started ringing so loud that he could hear nothing else but the ringing. Fire erupted from the garage consuming everything inside. A large cloud of acrid smoke filled the street and limited visibility to only a few yards. He saw Billy coming out of the smoke and obviously shouting something, but he could only see his lips moving. As his hearing started to return, he heard Billy yelling, "Pull those officers from the front of the garage and see what you can do for them."

Frank got up and staggered over to the fallen officers with rest of the GEEIA team. Three of them were clearly dead. They had arms and legs severed from their bodies and two were on fire. One was severely wounded with lacerations but had all his limbs attached. Within minutes, the *hee-haw hee-haw* sound of sirens could be heard. Frank and Gerhardt pulled the wounded officer back from the fire. Medics rushed to the wounded man when they ascertained that nothing could be done for the other three. Frank stared at the medics treating the wounded man and feeling nauseous, threw up on the sidewalk.

As the smoke cleared, Frank looked across the street from the garage at the apartments. Most had their windows blown out, including the one at the old lady's apartment. He made his way to the stairs leading to her apartment. He was having trouble maintaining his balance and it took him much longer to ascend than he thought it should. The door to the apartment was open, and he couldn't believe the level of the damage to the rooms he has been in only an hour before. The windows were torn from the frames and the walls and furniture looked like a madman slashed them with knives or cleavers. The old lady was sprawled out on the floor, the whole front of her body covered in glass and blood. She was not moving. He leaned down and checked her pulse. There was none. She was dead.

CHAPTER 20
Hulseberg, Germany

LTC Garson and MAJ Best were waiting for the GEEIA team's return from Bremen outside the *Hofcafe* in Hulseberg.

LTC Garson said, "Gentlemen, welcome back. That must have been a harrowing experience. We need to talk but not inside the *Hofcafe*. We have been ordered by MG Stone to report to General Gehlen in Oberursel tomorrow, provide him an update on what we know and get an update from his organization. But first, let's go to dinner and talk about more pleasant things. Be prepared to leave tomorrow at 0800, right after breakfast."

Frank went up to his room after dinner and thought about the events of the day. After hearing from Horst that he detected a signal and Billy tracking it, he heard the voice again prompting him to 'give chase'. It was as if the voice was what some people called a 'gut reaction' but it was so intense. He went on a high-speed chase with Don, or as high speed as MAJ Best's Volkswagen could go, but lost the vehicle they were chasing, then the raid on the *Environmental Monitoring and Analysis* office followed by the explosion of the garage. And that all occurred in one day. Amazing!

He got undressed and tried to go to sleep but he kept seeing the old lady dead on the floor. He wished he could unsee it.

As he was finally drifting off to sleep, he realized that his back had stopped hurting about the time he embarked on the 'high speed chase' with Don.

Sleep. Don't forget but move on. The voice comforted him.

He awoke at 0600, dressed and packed for the trip to Oberursel. He went down to the breakfast room and saw Don and Gerhardt were already there. He sat down with them and said, "Quite a day yesterday."

Don nodded and said, "We can talk later."

Frank wanted to talk it out but knew that this was not the place. He was having trouble getting the image of the old lady out of his mind. Oddly enough he wasn't having flash backs to the three dead officers and the wounded one, but the old lady kept coming back to him. He felt that he must push it to the back of his mind, or he might be consumed with it. Amazingly enough, no one on the team received any permanent physical damage but the jury was still out on any mental damage.

LTC Garson, Billy and Horst came into the breakfast room and sat at an adjoining table. They didn't talk much, focusing on their breakfast. Frank was not familiar with eating the way Germans did and kept looking around the room to see how they did things, like eating a soft-boiled egg in a special cup that had the egg stand on end. He saw people tap a knife around the top of the egg and remove the top part of the shell. They then dipped toast or bread in the exposed yoke and ate it. They then used a really, small spoon to scoop the rest of the egg out. He tried it and thought it was a unique and strange way to eat an egg.

Except for the egg, which was delivered to the table by a waitress, the breakfast was served buffet style. It was an elaborate affair and the buffet was arrayed with little silverware and tiny cups. He looked for a larger cup to have some coffee but there were none, so he poured the coffee in the little cup and added cream. The cream didn't change the color of the coffee much and when he drank it, it tasted like the strongest coffee in the world. He put it down and had a glass of juice instead. It looked like orange juice but tasted a lot different than any orange juice he ever had before.

He also saw a large bowl of white stuff that people dipped out into a bowl and mixed with fruit from small bowls near the white stuff. He thought, 'Nothing venture, nothing gained' and scooped out a small portion and mixed it with fruit. He then noticed a little placard with the word Yogurt on it. He didn't know what that was, but it tasted great. He went back for more. He also noticed displays of cold cuts and cheese on a tray. He usually ate cold cuts and cheese in a sandwich for lunch, but Germans seemed to prefer it for breakfast. He ate that too. The pastries were really, tasty, and he put several types on his plate.

Frank then noticed that the rest of the guys were looking at him and he saw that their plates were empty while he was on his third helping and he said, "What?!"

They all laughed.

CHAPTER 21
Oberursel, Germany

The ride down to Oberursel was uneventful. LTC Garson and MAJ Best drove their own cars and the GEEIA team piled into the Air Force power wagon.

Upon arrival, LTC Garson guided them to a building in Camp King and then to a conference room. General Gehlen and several aides were sitting on one side of the conference table. LTC Garson, MAJ Best and the GEEIA team sat on the other side. Frank was surprised to see how old General Gehlen looked.

LTC Garson summarized the events of the last couple days and there were few questions from General Gehlen. He had obviously read the report from LTC Garson which was very succinct.

General Gehlen said, "Good work Colonel Garson. You have kept us busy the last couple days too. My team in Bremen captured the courier from Helmstedt who came to pick up the data tapes from the *Environmental Monitoring and Analysis* office. He is being interrogated by them as we speak but I doubt he knows much except the routes and where he dropped the tapes off in Helmstedt. He and the four people captured in the office are being transferred here for more intense interrogation. Based on your report, I agree that the four people in the office didn't have any idea what they were part of."

"We also raided the house identified in Helmstedt. Our team there did not suffer any casualties but did have to kill a guard who refused to surrender. They captured two suspected East German or Soviet agents and an enormous amount of data. It will take some time to go through it and the agents refuse to talk. They will also be transported here for interrogation. It looks like they were a clearing house for Soviet and East German intelligence agents throughout Germany and, interestingly, some data from agents in France."

General Gehlen turned to TSGT Black. "I understand that you and your team will be returning to Ramstein after you leave here, correct?"

Billy said, "Yes sir."

"Your team seems to have still maintained your cover. Based on intelligence from other sources, it appears the Soviets think their illegal operation was uncovered by the Gehlen Organization instead of your GEEIA team. I made a request of MG Stone to see if he can allow your team to be available to me if there is more that you can do in future operations. Is that OK with you?"

"Yes sir."

"My men in Bremen were impressed with your team's performance there. They don't usually work well with American operatives."

He smiled at that remark and so did everyone else.

After General Gehlen and his entourage left, LTC Garson said, "I am headed back to Lindsey Air Station and MAJ Best is returning to Hulseberg. I suspect, based on what Gehlen said, that we will all be seeing each other again soon."

Billy said, "Do you think so? What if MG Stone won't honor the request?"

"He already has. I alerted him that the request was being prepared and he agreed. I told Gehlen and he thanked me for the coordination. The request is only for the files and for GEEIA to understand that you are on his and the Gehlen Organization's beck and call, if needed."

Billy said, "Sneaky," and laughed.

The GEEIA team checked into a hotel for the night and met in the restaurant for a much-deserved beer and dinner.

Frank asked Billy, "Does this mean we won't be doing any more installations?"

"No, I think it will be quite the contrary. We will be getting more jobs in the future as cover for what MG Stone and General Gehlen want us to do on the side. It will mean doing double duty. By the way, how is your back doing?"

"Oddly enough, it stopped hurting when we started chasing that white van. Adrenalin kicked in, I guess."

Don said to Billy, "When we get back you need to schedule

driver's school and weapon training for Frank. He should ace the driving and I suspect he will enjoy shooting the Walther P-38 and PPK pistols."

"Yeah, Frank and I already talked about the need for training but thanks for the reminder. This certainly has been an interesting trip."

All agreed.

CHAPTER 22
Bremen, Germany

Oleg was scared. He was lucky that he was at the grocery store shopping when the *Polizei* broke into the garage. The explosion rocked the grocery store and he, along with others, ran out into the street to see what was happening. He was totally shocked when he saw his street blocked off and his garage burning. He stood in the street with his mouth hanging open in awe until he was nudged by the *Polezie* to keep moving.

After the explosion, he wasn't sure what to do. He wandered the streets trying to calm down. Everything he owned was in that damn garage. He thought, 'I should have set up a bolt hole in case things went wrong.' He wouldn't make that mistake again.

He went to the *Environmental Monitoring and Analysis* office and saw that the *Polizei* were thick as flies around it. He thought, 'I wonder if they somehow found my garage from papers in the office. But how was that possible since the office personnel didn't know where I kept the van.' He had to think more clearly. He had to develop a story to tell his handler that would show him to be blameless for what happened today.

His alternate identity papers and his money were burnt up in the garage and he had no place to stay as well. He immediately thought of Greta and started fabricating a story on why he would need to stay with her for a couple days. He would tell her that his landlord evicted him for failing to pay his rent. She would believe that and hopefully would offer to let him stay with her; if not, he would beg her to help him for a couple days. Her brother Otto would not be so generous. He had to be sure to see Greta when Otto was at work. A couple of days should be all the time he would need to set up a meeting with his handler.

He manufactured a plausible cover up story and arranged to meet his Soviet handler. Soviets were not so forgiving of failure. Ivan Kraskov, his handler, got in touch with Oleg via a note in a dead drop to meet at a park along the Weser River in Bremen late in the afternoon. Oleg arrived at the park and saw Ivan sitting on a park bench reading a newspaper. He sat down, and Ivan smiled.

"Congratulations Comrade Oleg. My superiors are quite pleased that you managed to destroy your garage with the van in it so soon after the *Environmental Monitoring and Analysis* office was raided. You showed great initiative and I have submitted a request for you to receive a commendation or maybe even a Hero of the Soviet Union medal. It is too bad some policemen were killed but that could not have been foreseen."

Oleg thought, 'That is a better story than the one I was planning to spin.'

"Thank you, Comrade Ivan. However, my alternate identification papers and most of my money were also in the garage."

"No problem. I will provide other papers and here is some

money. Where are you staying now?"

"I have moved in with Greta and her brother Otto for a few days. I think Otto may not believe my story but deferred to his sister's generosity."

Ivan looked annoyed. "Otto works for the Germans at Hulseberg. If he notices that you, as Gerhardt Knorr, showed up the same day as the *Polizei* initiated a manhunt for Oleg Pavlov, you may be compromised. He may mention it to the security personnel at Hulseberg."

Oleg hadn't thought about that. "I will move out today but need a place to stay and a vehicle."

"Is there any time today when you are alone in Greta's house?"

"Yes. Greta and Otto visit their mother in the *altersheim* from 1700 to 1800."

"Good. Move out by 1800 today."

"I can do that. Where would you like me to go?"

Ivan looked at his watch. "Go to the dead drop in two hours. There will be a packet there for you. In the packet will be a train ticket and identifications papers in the name of Karl Ehrling. There is also a makeup kit in there for you to match your face as best you can with the photo on the identification papers while you are alone in Greta's house. It is important that you do this as well as you can. The *Polizei* will be looking for your alias, Hans Ludwig, but probably don't have a photo of you yet, and I stress the word yet."

Ivan pulled out a train schedule, studied it for a minute and said, "Go to the *Rangierbahnhof* and board the train to Karlsruhe departing at 1900. You will be met by a man in an orange jacket and a black rain hat. He will say, "Welcome Cousin Karl." Your response will be, "Where is Cousin Margo?" He will say, "At home cooking your favorite *sauerbraten* dinner." You will hand him your identification papers and he will provide you with a new set. He will take you to a *gasthaus* where you already have a reservation in the name on your new identification papers. You will stay there for at least wo days and if we do not detect any surveillance on you, he will provide you with two more sets of identification, a non-descript vehicle and an address in Strasbourg, France. You will drive to France where you will remain at the address there until I arrange another meeting. Are there any questions?"

"Will I be assigned another mission?"

"We will talk about that later. *Bon voyage!*"

CHAPTER 23
Ramstein, Germany

Frank fell into the routine of being 'in station' while at Ramstein Air Base. He left the barracks in the morning, went to breakfast, then to the warehouse and back to the barracks in the evening. He was bored and was glad to attend driving class and getting qualified on the Walther P-38 and PPK.

At night, he would join his friends at the Capri bar in the town of Ramstein. He took a taxi there with two or three other guys from the barracks. Going downtown in a car driven by a fellow airman had a downside which he only knew too well, recalling the auto wreck that landed him in Landstuhl Army Hospital.

The Capri bar had a *fussball* machine that provided the entertainment. He usually played with a partner since there were four levers to operate but also because almost all the airmen wanted to play, and partners allowed more time on the machine. He loved playing and if he and his partner were winning, they stayed on the machine. They had to get back in the queue if they lost a game.

When not playing *fussball*, he would sit at the bar and talk to Yutta, one of the bar girls, if she was not talking to someone else. Frank liked Yutta since he met her after getting out of Landstuhl Army Hospital. She was cute, rail thin and looked anemic. However, she was intelligent, and he enjoyed talking to her.

"Hi Yutta, how are you?"

"Frank, it is so good to see you. Can you buy me a cognac and coke?"

He smiled at her, "You know you like a nice sloe gin fizz, not cognac and coke."

"I think you know too much about me'" she laughed, "But you also know that Joe makes money on us when you buy us drinks and he never heard of a sloe gin fizz." Joe was the owner of the Capri bar. That was likely not his real name, but Americans can remember the name Joe. The girls asked every airman to buy them a cognac and coke. Joe made sure it was more coke than cognac. The girls called it fishing and you didn't want to be known as a fish or the girls would lose all respect for you. At least that's what they told themselves. Really, airmen were more concerned about their fellow airmen losing respect for them.

"OK. Heidi, please give Yutta a cognac and coke." Yutta smiled and said, *"Danke."*

Heidi came back to the Capri bar to bartend after her baby was born. Frank asked Yutta, "Did Heidi have a boy or a girl?"

"A boy and he looks just like that shit who got her pregnant."

Frank thought it prudent if he didn't comment on that. He did not know Jerry Sturgis, referred to as 'that shit' by Yutta, and probably shouldn't have even asked her that question. He wasn't very good at small talk.

"See that guy sitting against the wall over in the corner?" Yutta asked. "He is a German friend of Heidi's former boyfriend and sits here most nights brooding and looking at airmen. I am waiting for him to start trouble but so far, he just sits there or takes short walks outside."

Frank looked at the German and shrugged, "Does Heidi's former boyfriend still have a thing for her?"

"Thing? What does that mean?"

"Sorry, that's American slang meaning does he still have feelings for her?"

"Oh yes, but Heidi still has hopes that her American boyfriend will come back for her. Hans comes here for lunch most days and drives a taxi most nights. His customers are mostly airmen. He may have brought you here on occasion."

"Really! That must be hard on him, knowing that it is an airman who Heidi is waiting for. What's Hans's last name. I will be careful not to bring up Heidi's name if I see his name on the taxi drivers identification card."

Yutta said, "His full name is Hans Glick. His friend, the man in the corner, is Reinhart Uhler. I hope there is no trouble. I would hate to see the Capri bar put off limits to you airmen."

Frank said, "Yeah, me too."

CHAPTER 24
Ramstein, Germany

The next morning, Billy met with Frank, Gerhardt and Don, "We got another job. We are going to Lindsey Air Station to remove a ground-to-air communication system that is no longer needed. We leave on Monday which gives us three days lead time. Frank, contact the motor pool to schedule a power wagon for us. Don, check with Lindsey Air Station to see if we need to bring any special tools. The equipment is on the fourth floor and we may have to lower it from a window. Also, SMS Oliver wants to have a meeting in the SCIF at 1400 today."

Frank didn't have a car so he either walked or took the shuttle bus to get around Ramstein Air Base. The shuttle bus usually took as long to get anywhere due to its circuitous route, so he almost always walked. The motor pool was on the northern side of the base nestled in on three sides by the Woodlawn Golf Course. After scheduling the power wagon, he walked to the dining facility since they were serving steak today which was unusual. They usually served steak for dinner about once a month, not lunch. He met some guys from the GEEIA squadron along the way and they got in line to eat lunch.

After getting his helping of steak, Frank sat down at a table with about Gerhardt and some other GEEIA airmen. They noticed a full Colonel going from table to table which was very unusual since the dining facility served enlisted men. When the Colonel got to their table, he asked, "How is the food?"

Gerhardt said, "Colonel, I wish you came here every day."

The Colonel smiled and said, "Why is that?"

"Because on most days, the food served here is inedible." Airmen at the nearest table chuckled when they heard Gerhardt. Frank stared at Gerhardt and wondered what was going on.

The Colonel looked shocked and turned to one of the cooks behind him and asked, "What do you say to that?"

The cook stammered and said, "We always serve top notch meals here and this airman is obviously a troublemaker."

Gerhardt stood up and said loudly, "At breakfast, the eggs are runny and the bacon half cooked. We never have steak for lunch and only see it served at dinner about once a month, except of course, Colonel, when you are here to inspect the dining facility. We usually have processed meat and cheese for lunch, and it looks like it's been sitting around for hours before it's put out on the chow line. Dinner is the best meal but half the time it looks like dog food!"

A cheer broke out from almost all the tables in the dining facility. The Colonel stormed off with the cooks trailing behind.

Frank said, "Gerhardt, let's get out of here before they call the Air Police."

When they got outside, Frank asked, "Why did you get in the Colonel's face when you rarely eat in the dining facility?"

Gerhardt laughed, "Look on the bright side, the food in the dining facility will be great for the next month or so."

They both laughed and walked back to the GEEIA warehouse.

Billy and Don were sitting at a workbench when they arrived. Billy said, "We got about an hour before we meet with Oliver, so I will give you a little history lesson. Lindsey Air Station is in northwestern Wiesbaden. It was established in 1945 as an Air Force installation and named after Army Air Corps Captain Lindsey, who was posthumously awarded the Medal of Honor for heroism during World War II. In 1953, Lindsey Air Station was chosen as the Headquarters Command for the United States Air Forces in Europe (USAFE). Lindsey is rather small and there is no runway there. The streets are named in honor of the 31 American fatalities during Operation Vittles, also known as the Berlin Airlift. Do you guys want a ride to meet with Oliver?" They all agreed.

SMS Oliver opened the 1400 meeting in the SCIF by saying, "Your job, as Billy already told you, is to remove a ground-to-air communications system from a building operated by USAFE. The room where the equipment resides is on the fourth floor. A SCIF conference room is located adjacent to this room. You will meet with MG Stone to get an update on what the Gehlen Organization found when analyzing the data recovered from the raid on the house in Helmstedt. I, however, am not read on to the details of what was found. The code name designated for this operation is KISS. I have also been instructed to tell you to be armed, so check out your P-38's and two spare magazines."

Billy asked, "What does KISS stand for?"

SMS Oliver said rather testily, "Did you hear me say I am not read on? You will get the details at Lindsey Air Station."

Frank leaned towards Don and whispered, "Keep It Simple Stupid."

Don chuckled, and SMS Oliver looked at Don with daggers in his eyes, "Something funny Sergeant Bakersfield?"

Don reddened and said, "No, I just recalled something my daughter said on her way out the door to school."

Don mouthed the word "Thanks" sarcastically to Frank when SMS Oliver turned his back. Frank smiled.

As they were leaving the SCIF building, Frank asked Billy, "SMS Oliver seemed pissed off. Do you know what's going on?"

"Only that it has something to do with the shit storm that we ran into in Bremen. We will just have to wait until we get to Lindsey for the update. By the way Don, have you heard back from Lindsey Air Station if we will need any special tools to remove the equipment from the fourth floor?"

Don said, "Yes, they don't think we will have any problem getting the equipment down the stairs, so no special tools should be needed. They also said we could borrow some tools from their onsite workshop if we see a need for them."

"Good. What's the status on scheduling the power wagon, Frank?"

"We are good. Gerhardt and I will pick it up since I now have a driver's license and meet you guys in front of the barracks. Is that OK?" They both nodded in the affirmative.

Billy said, "Well, have a good weekend and Frank, please stay out of hospitals." They all laughed.

After breakfast on Saturday, Frank went to the arms room in the SCIF and checked out his P-38 and PPK pistols. GEEIA had its own arms room but Billy said the special team needed to keep theirs in the SCIF so that no one would know that they went armed on most TDYs. Almost all other GEEIA teams did not go armed.

He wanted to get in a little target practice on the firing range at the Ramstein Rod and Gun Club. The Club was conveniently located just behind the GEEIA barracks and next to the one of the greens of the Woodlawn Golf Course. He had joined the Rod and Gun Club a few days after arriving at Ramstein. The Club had rifles and pistols for sale as well as ammunition. German weapons were cheap compared to weapons from any other country.

After spending most of the morning on the range with other GEEIA troops, they decided to have lunch at the Club. It was the watering hole for GEEIA, and they made a decent steak for only a couple bucks. Couple that with a ceramic pop-top

Frankenthaler beer and it was hard to beat.

After he checked his pistols back into the SCIF arms room, he went back to the barracks to do some wash to be sure he would have enough clean clothes for the trip to Lindsey Air Station.

Frank and Gerhardt walked to the motor pool, checked out the power wagon and drove back to the barracks. They parked it in front of the barracks and then went to to pick up their gray B4 bags. The B4 military garment bag was issued to him when he arrived at Ramstein and held a lot of clothes as well as his shaving kit, shoes, underwear. It was the suitcase issued to all GEEIA troops for TDY trips. Frank also bought a larger than normal Samsonite brief case to carry papers, travel orders and on occasion his weapons. When he got back down from his room to the power wagon, Gerhardt, Billy and Don were waiting for him to unlock it.

"Man, you guys are punctual. I will remember that in the future."

"You better," said Billy with a smile on his face.

CHAPTER 25
Lindsey Air Station, Germany

They stopped at the SKIF to pick up their weapons and toolboxes, then drove to Lindsey Air Station. It took about two hours and could have been less if not for rush hour traffic. They entered the outer office of MG Stone and saw LTC Garson sitting at a desk that looked like it belonged to a secretary.

LTC Garson looked up and said, "Well, it seems we will be working together a lot sooner than I, and probably you, expected. Please have a seat. MG Stone was just delivered an encrypted message from Gehlen and will see us shortly."

After a few minutes, MG Stone came out of his office and asked, "Would anyone like some coffee before we start? I am having one and would be pleased if you could join me."

Billy said, "Yes sir, I could use one." Gerhardt, Don and Frank nodded their heads up and down.

MG Stone said, "I have received a message from Gehlen about operation KISS. Are you all read on to this operation?"

Billy said, "No sir. SMS Oliver said the GEEIA team would be read on when we got here."

MG Stone sighed, "OK. Here's what we know so far. The *Bundesnachrichendienst*, or BND for short, is headed by ex-General

Gehlen, as the founding president. It replaced the Gehlen Organization, but a lot of people still use that name. The BND has been analyzing the data that has been recovered in the raid at Helmstedt. In addition to verifying that the Soviets have been monitoring the command and control processes for directing artillery at Hulseberg, there is some indication that the Soviets have been in contact with the French communist party. The Soviet operation at Helmstedt appears to be a clearing house for espionage in Germany and France. The preponderance of the data is related to Germany. The French data is a surprise. The BND analysis could not conclude what the degree of cooperation is between France and the Soviet Union. That's where the GEEIA team comes in play."

"The removal of the UHF communications system from here is still on to maintain your cover. It was a stroke of genius by the CIA to have your team placed within GEEIA because GEEIA is under the command of the Air Force Logistics Command. The Soviets don't pay a lot of attention to logistics organizations. Don't get me wrong though. I am not too pleased to have Air Force personnel under the thumb of the CIA. Keep in mind that you will all eventually come back to the Air Force, so don't embarrass us."

Billy nodded, "Roger that Sir. What will be the GEEIA role in operation KISS? Also, what does KISS stand for?"

MG Stone looked at him, "It's a code word. It doesn't mean anything. In fact, most of our codes for operations are two words so it isn't inadvertently used by someone, or organization, who are not read on."

Frank smiling, "Maybe we should call it 'FRENCH KISS.'"

LTC Garson said, "That's not a bad idea but maybe it would give away the area of focus of the operation."

MG Stone chuckled, "Actually, using FRENCH KISS would seem so obvious that the Soviet paranoia would deduce that it couldn't be related to anything French. They know what Operation FRELOC is all about and if anything, would probably think it had something to do with removal of equipment from France. Let me float it by the CIA and BND to get their input. which reminds me, the BND doesn't know you are working with the CIA. I would like to keep it that way."

Billy looked confused, "General, can you clarify that statement?"

MG Stone turned to Billy, "General Gehlen asked *me*, not the CIA, to authorize your continued support to BND so I believed he thinks you are Air Force operators. That was confirmed by the CIA liaison officer to the BND complaining to his superiors that General Gehlen asked for Air Force support rather than CIA. The CIA pretended to be unhappy to keep their man thinking the same but are in fact quite delighted."

"Getting back to your role in operation FRENCH KISS. BND thinks the data they are analyzing came from Strasbourg, France. The BND doesn't know who in Strasbourg is colluding with the Soviets but surmise it is French communists. I have arranged with SMS Oliver to have your team go there as part of Operation FRELOC or something else. You will be contacted by BND personnel when you get there. Actual details will follow."

The meeting broke up and the GEEIA team headed over to the building where the UHF communications system was located. After dragging their toolboxes up to the fourth floor and checking out what needed to be done to accomplish the removal of the system, they decided to grab some lunch. When they left the building, Frank's cap was sitting way back on his head and he had just lit a cigarette. As he was putting his sunglasses on, he noticed two Air Force General officers coming in their direction. He knew he had to hurry to get squared away to salute them. He tried to quickly put his sunglasses on and take the cigarette out of my mouth, so he could salute them. Unfortunately, the sunglasses knocked the cigarette out of his mouth and up in the air. As he looked up at the cigarette, his cap started falling off his head and he ended up juggling sunglasses, cap and cigarette as the Generals walked by him. The Generals busted out laughing at his antics.

Billy laughing at Frank said, "That was quite a show you put on for the generals. I'm sure you will be a topic of humor at the officer's club this evening."

Frank was embarrassed, "Yeah but whoever was looking would surely dismiss any ideas they had on us being anything but just logistics airmen, right?"

Billy and Don looked at each other and busted out laughing. They still teased Frank about it for months afterward. Gerhardt just shook his head.

After lunch, they went back to the fourth floor of the building where the system was and started to dismantle it. The individual transmitters and receivers were heavy, and they thought about lowered them out the window.

Don said, "That might not be such a good idea because it would bring a lot of attention to us and what we don't want is attention paid to us."

They disconnected all the associated cabling between the transmitters and receivers and hefted the hardware clumsily down four flights of narrow stairs.

Billy told Don and Frank, "OK, that's enough for today. The dining facility opens in about 15 minutes so let's go get some dinner." On TDY trips, GEEIA preferred teams to stay in government furnished lodging and eat government meals. Lindsey Air Station had both available, so they would only draw a couple dollars a day for incidentals.

Gerhardt, Don and Frank went over to the Non-Commissioned Officer's club for a couple beers and to play the slot machines. Frank tired of losing at the slots but Don kept at it. He looked at Frank and smiled, "This one is going to start paying off soon." It didn't pay off though and Don asked Frank for a small loan to get him through the rest of the trip. "I'm done playing. My wife would have a fit if she heard I lost so much money, so please don't tell her." Frank looked at Don and said, "No problem."

They finished the job at Lindsey Air Station and on the ride back to Ramstein AB, they discussed planning for the trip to Strasbourg. They couldn't think of a good reason for a GEEIA team to go there since there were no American military installations located in Strasbourg.

Gerhardt asked, "Are there any military comm systems located in the American consulate and if so, they could claim that they needed to calibrate them similar to what they did in Hulseburg."

Billy smiled, "Good idea. I have never been to an embassy or consulate where they didn't have military comm systems. I will recommend it to SMS Oliver when we get back."

CHAPTER 26

Ramstein, Germany

Frank and Gerhardt were surprised on their morning walk from the barracks to the GEEIA warehouse to see Chuck Whelan and Soaring Eagle Milligan waiting for them.

"Hey guys, what are you doing here? I didn't know you were in the Air Force."

They were both in Air Force fatigues identical to Frank's except that they had a Tactical Air Command patch sewn on their right pocket where Frank had his GEEIA patch. They wore the rank of Airmen First Class so technically outranked Frank and Gerhardt.

Soaring Eagle said, "We aren't. We are dressed like this to blend in."

Chuck explained further, "We read the reports of your experience in Hulseberg and know about the interest the BND has in your team. We also know about your scheduled trip to Strasbourg and thinks things might get a little dicey."

"I wasn't aware of this. Are Billy and Don?"

"Yes, we contacted them earlier but didn't want to have to explain to your roommates in the barracks who we were, so decided to catch you on the way to the warehouse. We are here to brief you all on updates since you talked to MG Stone and to provide some additional training."

Instead of going to the warehouse, they diverted to the SCIF. Billy and Don were already there drinking coffee. SMS Oliver was not there, and Frank remembered that he was not read on to the operation. Surprisingly though, MAJ Best was there.

Frank said, "Hello Major, glad to see you again. Will you be going to Strasbourg with us?"

"No, I will be the Air Force liaison officer with the BND who share intelligence with the SDECE."

"The SDECE...What is that?"

MAJ Best turned to Chuck, "Do you want to answer Airman Logan's question?"

Chuck stood up and said, "Yes, in fact that was the first thing I was going to cover today. The SDECE is France's intelligence agency, similar to our CIA. It stands for *Service de Documentation Exterieure et de Countre-Espionnage*. The SDECE officially reports to the French Minister of Defense but in reality, it is micro-managed by French President de Gaulle himself. The German BND has entered into an agreement to share intelligence with the SDECE in exchange for allowing the SDECE to commit murder in Germany of individuals unfriendly to France, particularly those supporting Algeria where France is conducting a quasi-war. The BND makes sure any investigations by the West German *Polizei* into these murders are hindered. To make matters more complicated, de Gaulle has ordered the SDECE to break off cooperation with the CIA, thinking that the CIA is plotting to disrupt SDECE activities to get even with France for kicking out all US servicemen. That is why MAJ Best is liaising with the BND and not the SDECE."

Billy looked open mouthed at Chuck, "Complicated is an understatement. I think we are going to need a little hand holding while in Strasbourg."

"Agree," Chuck said, "That is why MAJ Best will be providing intelligence to you from BND and requested a specially trained Air Commando unit out of Sembach Air Base to provide support. They will be covertly deployed in Strasbourg and will provide support to you if you run into any trouble. In case you are discovered by Soviet operatives and need to defend yourselves, you will be armed with German weapons and Soaring Eagle will provide additional training in hand-to-hand combat to complement what you had at Keesler. Please do not engage any French authorities if you can help it.

Billy said, "We are all qualified on the Walther P-38 and the PPK."

"Good. I would like you all to spend more time on the shooting range to improve your skills on those pistols prior to departing for Strasbourg. You will also be issued and qualified with the new Heckler & Koch MP5 submachine gun. It is chambered for the same nine-millimeter Parabellum ammunition as your P-38 and PPK. The MP5 had iron sights and an effective firing range of two hundred meters. Soaring Eagle is a former USMC sniper and will coordinate with the Air Commandos to handle any trouble in excess of that range."

Frank was thinking, 'Wow. This trip sounds like it could really be interesting.' He was scared but excited to be part of this operation. He thought back to the chase from Hulseberg to Bremen and how exciting that was for him. He also thought how lucky the GEEIA team was that the German police insisted on raiding the garage in Bremen. They could have all been killed or wounded like the police and that old lady who was killed while looking out of her window at the garage when it exploded. He didn't think of her as much as he did when it happened.

Billy was pondering all that was said and asked, "Does this have anything to do with the reason de Gaulle has kicked us out of France?"

MAJ Best replied, "Maybe, but the official reason given was that France didn't agree with the NATO nuclear strategy that de Gaulle thinks was foisted on NATO by the United States."

The next day, Chuck reviewed what Billy, Don, Gerhardt and Frank had been taught at Keesler. He then taught them various new techniques that were clever and imaginative. Chuck had expanded the practical training by setting up scenarios in the towns of Ramstein and Landstuhl. He taught them various types of dead drops and then had them do them while being observed, simulating foreign surveillance, to see if he could catch them in the act. At first, he caught them all the time, but he pointed out what they were doing wrong and gave them feedback on the way they should be doing it. They got much better and even though they were doing it the way he taught them, he was hard pressed to catch them at it.

Soaring Eagle wore them out with physical training, hand-to-hand combat techniques, karate and ju-jitsu moves, knife fighting and so much range time that their fingers were raw from loading and reloading magazines for their P-38 and PPK pistols and especially the 30 round magazines for the MP5. MP5 training was harder than it looked. Keeping the muzzle trained on the targets down range and hitting them was, at first, laughable. Soaring Eagle was merciless in berating them to pay attention to his advice and eventually they learned to handle the MP5 effectively.

Soaring Eagle asked Frank after their last training session, "So what do single guys do for fun around here?"

Frank laughed, "Mostly drink bottled Frankenthaler beer in the Rod and Gun or go downtown and drink beer on tap. There is a club called the Florida Bar that opens at midnight. The bar girls usually go there after a night of fishing airmen and soldiers for watered down drinks. There is usually a band or a disc jockey providing music and a huge dance floor. It is a lot of fun, but I only go on the weekends or I would have a hard time getting up in the morning."

"Roger that. What do you say about going to the Florida Bar tonight?"

"Sounds good. I'm not sure I have any strength left after your torture sessions but I'm game."

"Great. What time do you want me to pick you up at your barracks?"

Frank thought for a minute, "We might want to take a taxi instead. They are cheap, and you won't have to worry about the *Polizei* or Air Police at the gate stopping you and administering a breathalyzer test. I am going to have a steak dinner at the Rod and Gun first. You want to meet me there?"

"OK. Steak sounds good and I would like to try one of those Frankenthaler beers too."

Frank changed into civvies in the barracks and then walked over to the Rod and Gun Club. Soaring Eagle was already there and had grabbed a table. They ordered the steaks and a couple Frankenthalers. After consuming the steaks, Frank said, "Want to shoot some darts. We can partner against the guys there now."

They shot darts for about an hour when Soaring Eagle said, "Let's go to the Capri bar for a beer or two before heading over to the Florida Bar." Frank agreed and called a taxi. When the taxi came, Frank looked down at the taxi drivers ID and was surprised to see Hans Glick's picture. He looked at the driver but was right behind him so only noticed that he had light hair. He got a better look at him when they exited the taxi at the Capri bar and kind of felt sorry for him. Losing his girlfriend to an American must have hurt.

The Capri bar was crowded. The bar seats were all taken and the *fussball* machine surrounded by loud and laughing airmen. They saw Gerhardt waving them over to his table. Yutta came over and took their order for three draft pilsner beers from Yutta.

When she brought the beers back to the table, she asked, "So who is going to buy me a cognac and coke?"

Gerhardt immediately said, "Why me of course!" Yutta motioned to Heidi to bring over a cognac and coke and she sat down next to Gerhardt. Yutta and Gerhardt put their heads together and whispered in German to each other. The bar noise was so loud that they could have talked in their normal voice and not been overheard.

Soaring Eagle nudged Frank and asked, "Do you know the guy sitting in the corner? He looks familiar to me, but I can't place him." Frank looked over and saw that it was the German who Yutta said was Hans Glick's friend.

He turned and asked Yutta, "I know you told me the name of Hans Glick's friend, but I forgot it."

She replied, "Its Reinhart Uhler. Why do you ask?"

Soaring Eagle answered, "He looks familiar, but I must be thinking of someone else since I don't know that name."

Frank told Soaring Eagle the story about Reinhart Uhler's friend Hans Glick losing his girlfriend Heidi to an American airman.

Gerhardt interjected, "Hey, the guys on the *fussball* machine are leaving. How about we play a game, Yutta and I against you two?"

They all got up. Frank and Soaring Eagle paired off on one side of the machine while Gerhardt and Yutta went to the other side.

Yutta followed and stood at the end of the machine with her empty glass, "Could I get another cognac and coke?"

Soaring Eagle said, "Sure, I'll get this one."

They played until close to midnight then caught a taxi to the Florida Bar. On the way, they noticed a Volkswagen on its roof just past a curve near where the accident that Frank was in.

Gerhardt said, "Hey that's Mike Thomas's VW."

They told the taxi driver to pull over and went to check out the VW. A2C Mike Thomas's hard hat was lying on the inside of the roof, but he was nowhere to be found. They looked in the bushes nearby but could not find Mike. They asked the taxi driver if he could call the *Poliezi* on his radio. He told them that the *Poliezi* had picked up Mike earlier. He was not injured, and a wrecker was called to remove the car from the side of the road.

They got back in the taxi and went to the Florida Bar. They were surprised to see Mike there. Frank asked, "What happened to your car?"

Mike said, "Brakes went. I was bar hopping earlier and everything was fine until I left the Capri bar. I saw you guys playing *fussball* and would have asked you if you needed a ride, but you seemed focused on the game. I guess this is your lucky night that I didn't ask. Anyway, when I left the Capri bar, I noticed the brakes were a little spongy but thought it probably only needed a little brake fluid that I would put in tomorrow. Bad move. I was probably going a little too fast around the curve when the brake pedal went to the floor. Luckily, my car did a slow roll and, although it stopped on its roof, my seatbelt held me in, and I crawled out. Not even a nick on me. How lucky can you get?"

They spent the rest of the night at the Florida Bar, dancing with the bar girls and drinking high priced beer. Mike Thomas joined them in the taxi ride back to Ramstein.

Early the next morning Soaring Eagle knocked on the door to Frank's room in the barracks. Frank and his roommates were all asleep. Frank woke up, opened the door and said, "Hey man, what's up?"

Soaring Eagle was accompanied by Chuck and said, "Get dressed, we need to talk."

Frank quietly got dressed so he wouldn't wake his roommates. He left the barracks and saw Chuck in the passenger seat and Soaring Eagle in the driver's seat of a white Opel. He got into the back seat and said, "You guys do know this is Saturday, right?"

Chuck looked at Soaring Eagle, "Yeah, so what, the SCIF is open all the time."

Frank yawned, "Not quite where I was going with my question."

"Whatever." Chuck said. "Let's go and look this guy up."

Frank said, "What guy?"

Soaring Eagle looked at Frank in the rear-view mirror, "The German guy in the Capri bar last night. What was his name?"

Frank had to think for a moment, "Uh, Reinhart something... Uhler. Reinhart Uhler. Why?"

"I was tossing and turning all night trying to think where I had seen him before, and it suddenly dawned on me that he looked like a guy in our files who is associated with the Neo-Nazis. We are going over to the SCIF and go through the files to see if I am right."

They went into the SCIF and opened the file cabinet which was really a safe. Chuck made two piles. "One for each of you since I don't know what the guy looks like that you saw last night."

After about an hour, Soaring Eagle said, "Here he is. His real name is Heinrich Lund."

Frank looked at the picture and read the text below. "It says he was born in 1941 which would make him twenty-six years old and lived in Darmstadt until five years ago when he disappeared. He was flirting with Neo-Nazis since he was fifteen."

Chuck said, "He must have moved here, changed his name and got fake papers. I wonder what he is up to now. Do you have an address for him?" He asked Frank.

"No but maybe Yutta does or that taxi driver, Hans Glick."

"Let's follow up with Yutta. Hans Glick may be involved with him in whatever Lund has going."

Soaring Eagle asked Frank, "Can you introduce me to Yutta? We kind of skipped that formality last night."

"Absolutely. You do know that I leave for Strasbourg in a couple days so how will this work?"

"I will buy her as many cognac and cokes as needed to keep her talking to me. I will somehow get her to tell me all she knows about Reinhardt Uhler, AKA Heinrich Lund."

CHAPTER 27
Ramstein, Germany

Reinhardt Uhler met Hans Glick for lunch at their usual table in a corner of the Capri bar. Reinhardt leaned close to Hans and asked, "How did you manage to sabotage that airman's car so quickly?"

Hans brightened and said, "It was easy. I put a small puncture in his brake line. I was lucky he didn't catch me because he came back out of the Capri bar a lot faster than I expected."

Reinhardt smiled, "It worked great. His VW rolled over when he tried to slow down at the curve outside the Florida Bar. Unfortunately, he managed to escape without a scratch. Bad luck but not your fault."

Hans looked apologetically at Reinhardt, "I don't plan to do this anymore. I am afraid that I am going to be arrested one of these days."

Reinhardt frowned, "Nonsense. You are too smart to get arrested."

"I almost got caught last night. No more for me. I must get back to work. *Auf Wiedersehen*, Reinhardt."

When Hans got up, Reinhardt followed him out to his taxi, "Will I see you tomorrow for lunch?"

"Sure, if I don't have a fare."

As he was driving away, Hans was thinking that he wasn't sure he wanted to meet with Reinhardt again. He felt like he was being pressured and he didn't like it.

Uhler, AKA Lund, went to the nearest public phone and relayed the information that Hans didn't seem to want to do their bidding anymore.

"*Mach Niche.* That was only icing on the cake. The information you are overhearing from the loud and boisterous airmen at the Capri bar is valuable to us. We have been successful in disrupting American plans and they have no idea how we are doing it. Keep up the good work."

Horst turned to Chuck and Soaring Eagle, "You were right. He is spying on us. This phone tap confirms it. How did you know he would use this public phone?"

Chuck said, "I didn't know but this is the closest public phone to the Capri bar. Sometimes it's better to be lucky than good."

Soaring Eagle said, "Now what? They didn't say which plans were impacted and I don't think we have enough for a German court to arrest and convict them of treason."

"I agree. We need more than just this wiretap. Horst, can you obtain the number of the phone that was called by Lund?"

"I can ask the German *Bundespost* if we can access their records. The German government is as concerned as we are about the activities of the Neo-Nazis. However, contacting the *Bundespost* is fraught with pitfalls. First, they will want to know why we want the records. We certainly can't tell them we had tapped the phone since that is illegal without authorization from the German government. Second, there are Neo-Nazi spies in all branches of the German government, including the *Bundespost* so we might want to pass this on to the BND to run it down or even take over the investigation."

Chuck pondered this suggestion, "I will bounce it off headquarters at Langley. I personally think that is a good suggestion."

SMS Oliver called Billy at the warehouse, "When can you get your team plus Horst up to the SCIF for a meeting?"

"I will have to track Horst down, but Frank and Don are here and can meet anytime."

"OK. Track Horst down and call me back. Thanks."

Billy looked at Frank and Don, "Man, Oliver was way more cordial than I have ever heard him. Do either of you know where Horst is today?"

Frank said, "He went to Ramstein with Chuck and Soaring Eagle. He said he shouldn't be long."

"OK. Let me know as soon as he shows up."

Horst walked into the warehouse about 15 minutes later. Billy called SMS Oliver and they agreed to meet at 1500.

SMS Oliver arrived at the SCIF at the same time as Billy's team. They walked into the conference room and saw LTC Garson, Chuck and Soaring Eagle sitting there drinking coffee.

SMS Oliver opened the meeting smiling, "I have been read on to FRENCH KISS. Who the hell ever thought up that name?" All glanced at Frank but didn't rat him out. "I think they decided to read me on so that if you guys screw up, I will have to explain to the brass what went wrong." He smiled and continued, "Your next assignment as a GEEIA team is to calibrate the communications equipment in the U.S. Consulate in Strasbourg. Usually the State Department would handle this but since the equipment belongs to the Air Force, I insisted that GEEIA do it. At least that is what your travel orders will read. Your real mission is to locate any receivers that are tuned to the frequency used by the Consulate to communicate with the French government. I will turn this over to LTC Garson to explain further."

LTC Garson said, "First off, I am sure that *I* will be the one who will catch hell if things go wrong." They all chuckled, "Second, the mission is more than just locating enemy receivers. That is why you have been given additional training. Once located, you will conduct surveillance on these locations and identify personnel who you suspect may be involved. You will try your best to avoid any confrontations with the French but, in-the-event that it can't be avoided, your travel orders will state that you have diplomatic immunity and are granted authorization to possess and carry arms. This will keep you out of prison if you are arrested and detained by either French civilian or military police. There is a glitch however. As you know, Horst is a contractor and a German national. If he gets caught in France, he can be tried as a spy and does not have diplomatic immunity. Billy, I need you to pick one of your team to be trained by Horst since he will not be accompanying you on this mission."

Billy looked around and said, "Gerhardt, meet with Horst after this meeting and learn as much as you can on how to operate his equipment." He turned to LTC Garson, "Can we call Horst if there are any unforeseen problems?"

LTC Garson looked at Horst who said, "That is possible."

SMS Oliver said, "Also, utilization of government quarters is not required, and civilian clothing is authorized to wear so you can move around freely in the conduct of the mission. Are there any other questions?"

Billy looked at the team who shrugged their shoulders, then said, "No more questions, seems like it's getting to be just another day at the office." They all chuckled again.

Chuck spoke next, "I would like to take this opportunity to update you all on an operation that Soaring Eagle, Horst and I were engaged in today. As some of you know, a known Neo-Nazi named Heinrich Lund, AKA Reinhardt Uhler, was identified yesterday living in Ramstein and frequenting the Capri bar. We tapped a public phone in Ramstein that Lund used after talking to a taxi driver named Hans Glick in the Capri bar.

It is not clear how Glick is involved with Lund but from the phone conversation it appears Glick wants out. We thought about following up with the German *Bundespost* to get the phone number of the person Lund was talking to, but Horst pointed out that we would probably get mired in the legal aspects of tapping a phone in Germany without authorization. He suggested turning the investigation over to the BND who wants to stop the Neo-Nazis and can override any resistance from the German bureaucracy. I informed the CIA at Langley that I support this suggestion and am awaiting their decision. Are there any questions?"

Frank asked, "What do you think the CIA will say to illegally tapping the phone?"

Chuck smiled, "I have done worse, so they will probably let it go but I also suggested to Langley that we not mention to the BND about tapping the phone but just say we observed Lund on the phone at a certain time and day. Tapping the phone was really for our benefit to confirm that Lund is up to something bad for us and to not go on a wild goose chase to find the number of someone who may not be involved. He could have been making an innocuous call."

LTC Garson nodded, "Thanks for the update. Can you keep us posted on how it turns out, so we can reply intelligently to General Gehlen if he brings it up in a future conversation?"

"Roger that."

CHAPTER 28
Strasbourg, France

Oleg Pavlov made the journey to Strasbourg, via Karlsruhe, precisely as planned by Ivan Kraskov. The contact he met in Karlsruhe relieved him of the identification papers in the name of Karl Ehrling and provided him with three new, but artificially aged sets of identification papers and passports. He decided to pick the one in the name of Herbert Mueller. He had been at the house in Strasbourg for weeks now. The house was of German design and although small, had ample room for him. The kitchen was well stocked with food and beverages. They even stocked the pantry with vodka and beer. He was taught how to cook by his mother and took the time to make use of the recipe book that was on a shelf in the kitchen. The living room had a bookshelf with classics in French and German. He found a book on the history of Strasbourg. He was not particularly interested in it but read it to pass away the time. He knew that Strasbourg had a history of passing back and forth between Germany and France for centuries but didn't know the details. King Philip of Swabia declared Strasbourg an Imperial Free City about 1262. It wasn't until after the Thirty Years War, that King Louis XIV of France surrounded the Free City with his army and annexed Strasbourg for France in 1681. At the end of the Franco-Prussian War in 1871, the city was transferred from France to the German Empire. Following the defeat of the German Empire in World

War I, Strasbourg was again annexed by France in 1919. With the German defeat of France in 1940, Strasbourg was again annexed by Germany. In 1944, Strasbourg was liberated from the Germans and returned to France.

Oleg was sitting in the living room and looking out at passersby on the street. He was trying to figure out if they were German or French. He thought enough time may have passed since the end of the war twenty years ago that most of the animosity towards Germans had probably dissipated but knew that the French had long memories.

He had not heard from Ivan Kraskov since he occupied the house. He wondered if the Russian was being extra careful that he was not under surveillance before setting up a meeting. While Oleg was recounting the history of Strasbourg, he saw Ivan Kraskov walking down the street to the safe house. He was surprised to see him arrive unexpected and jumped up to greet Ivan at the front door.

Almost out of breath Oleg greeted Ivan, "Comrade, it is so good to see you again. I wasn't expecting you."

Ivan looked around the room, "Nice accommodations. I trust that this house has been acceptable to you and you did not see the need to wander around the streets of Strasbourg."

Oleg thought Ivan probably already knew he had not left the house but replied, "Of course not. I have been waiting for further instructions from you and used the time here to catch up on some reading."

"Oh, and what have you been reading? Nothing on capitalist nonsense, I hope."

"No comrade, mainly newspapers that the housekeepers here have discarded and books that were here." Oleg did not mention that he learned from the newspapers of the 'accidental' deaths of Greta and Otto Kressmann in Bremen. The newspaper report said that there was a gas leak in their home and a subsequent explosion. He wanted Ivan to think he did not know of their fate for he was almost sure that Ivan had them killed.

"I have a mission for you. I would have been here sooner, but our experts were trying to determine if you were somehow detected listening in on Hulseberg. They concluded that you were probably observed when you were dropping off data to the *Environmental Monitoring and Analysis* office in Bremen. We think the BND must have had the office under surveillance for some time."

Oleg nodded sagely, thinking that he believed that *he* was detected, maybe by a hiker or camper nearby that he had not noticed, and reported his van as suspicious. He did not know why that old VW chased him but thought they might have been the local *Polizei* in a private car. They may have noted the *Environmental Monitoring and Analysis* logo on the side of his van which led them to the office. He did not share that belief to Ivan since there was a better than even chance that he would be blamed for the blown operation and Soviet punishment for such a mistake was brutal at best.

Ivan looked at Oleg for any reaction and not detecting any nervousness continued, "Another van has been constructed for your use. It is an improved version of the one that was destroyed in Bremen. You can find it in a garage at the address in this note and here is the key to the lock. The target is the U.S. Consulate. The frequencies we want you to monitor and record are also on the note. Memorize everything written and burn the note."

Ivan picked up an ashtray from the table and held out a pack of matches. "Please do that now."

Oleg had received training on memorization techniques so read the note a couple times and burned the note in the ashtray. Ivan smiled, "Very good *comrade*."

CHAPTER 29

Ramstein, Germany

Frank entered the GEEIA warehouse on Ramstein AB on the day before they were planning to depart for Strasbourg and saw Billy, Don and Gerhardt looking over new toolboxes. Other GEEIA troops were milling around them complaining that they didn't get new toolboxes.

Billy turned to the complainers, "I guess someone didn't want us showing up in a State Department Consulate with the ratty toolboxes that we currently have so sent us new ones."

Billy turned to his team and smiled, "OK, let's go get our old toolboxes and do a switch." The four of them picked up their new empty toolboxes, followed Billy to his car and he drove us to the SCIF.

Their team kept their toolboxes in the SCIF. Billy said, "You will notice that the new toolbox is deeper than your current one. It has a false bottom that we will use to store all our weapons and ammo. It has places for the MP-5, P-38 and PPK so it will be a lot heavier than you are used to lugging around. After you transfer the weapons, ammo and of course, your tools, we will transfer them to the power wagon tomorrow."

The next day, Frank lugged the heavy toolboxes from the SCIF into the power wagon. He drove to the GEEIA warehouse to pick up Billy, Don and Gerhardt. He was surprised to see LTC Garson, Chuck and Soaring Eagle sitting in two cars by the warehouse loading dock. They were all wearing civilian clothes.

Billy asked, "Sir, are you guys going with us?"

LTC Garson answered, "Yes, we are going to follow you. We wanted to leave about the same time as you so we will arrive at the U.S. Consulate in Strasbourg at about the same time."

Billy, Don and Gerhardt came out of the warehouse and the three vehicles left Ramstein for Strasbourg.

Billy looked at his map, "Head for the *autobahn* number 6, then head south on number 5. I want to stay in Germany as-long-as we can before crossing the border into France. We can fuel up just before crossing the Rhine."

Frank responded, "Roger that."

Strasbourg, France

About two hours later, they crossed the Rhine River into Strasbourg, France. They had to stop at the customs booth.

Billy asked, "Do any of you speak French. I learned a little in Indochina but am not fluent."

Frank said, "I had two years of French in high school."

"Good, take our orders and passports in and find out if they need anything else."

Frank walked up to a French border guard who asked, "*Parlez-vous Francaise?*"

Frank said, "*Oui.*"

The border guard spoke French so fast that Frank just stared at him. The border guard smiled and said, "Would you rather speak English?"

Frank nodded yes.

When he got back in the power wagon Billy asked, "How did it go?"

"Fine." He wasn't about to tell them what really happened. They would hound him for months. He started the truck and they continued to the U.S. Consulate.

Frank pulled up in front of the consulate, "Hey, where are LTC Garson, Chuck and Soaring Eagle?" A minute later, LTC Garson walked up to them. Frank wondered why he had not driven up to them in his car but didn't get a chance to ask him before Billy turned to the team and said, "Wait here. LTC Garson and I will find our contact in the consulate and let him know we are here. After that, we will come back and we all will go grab some lunch somewhere."

After about an hour, Billy and LTC Garson came out of the consulate, "Okay, slight change in plans. We are going to drop off our toolboxes in the consulate SCIF which is near where they keep the communications systems. Our contact is named Mary Wright and she said we could have lunch at the consulate cafeteria. We can park our power wagon in the consulate parking lot." LTC Garson opted to park their civilian cars outside the consulate in case the consulate is under surveillance. That is why they parked so far away."

After parking the power wagon and unloading their toolboxes, the team met Mary. She was a beautiful girl with blonde hair, soft blue eyes and a physique that was perfectly proportioned. Frank thought, 'She must send a lot of time in the gym.'

Mary smiled at them, "I am to be your point of contact while you are here, so let me know if there is anything you need. Have you obtained lodging yet in Strasbourg?"

Billy said, "Not yet. We were going to look for a place nearby after lunch."

"The consulate gets a discount rate at the *Hotel Fountainebleu* around the corner from here. Would you like me to call in reservations? I know the hotel manager and he can provide some nice rooms."

"Yeah, that would be great. We will need four rooms."

"They have a large suite on the top floor that has a parlor with four bedrooms. Would that work?"

Billy looked at the group and they all nodded yes. "Sounds good. Is there an elevator in the hotel?"

Mary said, "*Mais oui.*"

Don asked, "May we what?"

She laughed, "*Mais oui* means 'but yes'. I should have said *bien sur* which means 'of course' but *mais oui* is kind of a slang term for 'of course' that is used here."

They checked into the *Hotel Fountainebleu* and took the elevator up to the top floor. The parlor was huge. It had two sofas separated by a coffee table with a fireplace at one end of the sofas, multiple other chairs scattered throughout the parlor and a conference table with six chairs. Three of the bedrooms had two single beds each and the other had a large canopy bed. Billy and Don took one of the rooms, while Frank and Gerhardt took another, and Chuck and Soaring Eagle took the last one. They all agreed that LTC Garson should take the room with the large bed.

LTC Garson sat down at the conference table and placed a small box with an extension cord in the middle of the table and plugged it into an outlet. He smiled and said, "This is a wideband jammer so we can talk in private. Let's go over how we are going to approach this mission in a little more detail. As you know, GEEIA Research made two more boxes for us to use since the one in Hulseberg worked well to find the azimuth of the intercepting receiver. Now we can triangulate with what they are calling the 'outlier' boxes. I coordinated with the consulate to request using two buildings on American installations near here that are in the approximate location to enable triangulation and are high enough to cover most of the area around the consulate. The consulate made arrangements with these installations to provide power and a place to mount the antenna of the outlier boxes. Gerhardt and Frank will set up what I am calling the main box in the consulate. Billy and Soaring Eagle will set up one of the outlier boxes and Don and Chuck will set up the other outlier box. We will run some tests with the stimulator that Horst provided to Gerhardt to see how well we can triangulate in an urban environment. Gerhardt, can you explain further?"

"The main problem with operating in urban environments is a phenomenon called multipath. The signal we are looking for is weak to begin with. Depending on the structures in an urban environment, the amplitude of the signal may be diminished, or sometimes even enhanced, due to reflections. I have incorporated a filter in the time domain versus the frequency domain that should mitigate some of the multipath. Also, the time of arrival of the signal we are looking for will probably be delayed at the boxes due to the distance from the target receiver. We will have to take all this into account to get even a general location of the target."

Chuck looked confused, "Could you put that into English for us common folks?" Everyone laughed except Gerhardt.

Looking a little annoyed, Gerhardt said, "I guess. The bottom line is that we may have a difficult time locating the intercepting receiver. We will know more about how well the filter works when we employ the stimulator in various parts of the city."

Chuck shook his head, "Okay, I can understand that, I think."

LTC Garson smiled at Gerhardt, "Horst taught you well. Let's get some dinner downstairs then get a good night sleep so we can start early in the morning."

CHAPTER 30
Strasbourg, France

They had breakfast at the *Hotel Fountainebleu* then walked to the consulate. The team split up to go to their assigned locations and to get the equipment set up in the consulate and the outlier sites. Gerhardt was now directing Frank over their walkie-talkies to move the stimulator around Strasbourg. Frank was glad because it gave him a chance to see the neighborhood around the consulate. Strasbourg was a pretty city with a lot of new buildings sprinkled among a lot of older buildings. There were many tourists strolling through the streets and the restaurants were getting ready for the lunch crowd. Frank was getting hungry. He thought about going into a restaurant but rejected it immediately. The radio and headset would certainly draw curious stares and if he was called, he would have to jump up and leave. LTC Garson let Frank use his car to drive around the town to the various sites that he and Gerhardt had agreed on before he left the consulate. The small antenna for the stimulator was attached to the roof with a suction cup and did not attract any attention.

The PRC-6 squawked into Frank's headset, "Bulldog to Rover, Over." Bulldog was Gerhardt's call sign in the consulate and Frank was Rover. Frank chuckled at 'Rover Over'. Apparently, LTC Garson did not think this assignment of call signs all the way through. The call signs for the outlier's boxes were Spaniel and Collie.

"Rover to Bulldog, got you five by five, Over."

"Rover, move out to next site, Over."

"Roger, Rover out."

They kept this up all morning and Frank was looking forward to finishing and having lunch.

"Bulldog to Rover, Spaniel and Collie. That's it for the day. Return to base for lunch, Over."

Frank drove back to the consulate and after dropping off the walkie-talkie and stimulator, headed to the cafeteria. LTC Garson and Gerhardt were sitting at a large table with Mary Wright. She smiled at him and asked, "So how did you like Strasbourg?"

"It was great. It sure beats sitting in the consulate all day."

"If you guys are still here over the weekend, I would be glad to show you some of the more interesting attractions in the city."

Frank smiled, "That would be great." He would love to spend more time with Mary, even if it was with the whole group.

They waited for Billy. Don, Chuck and Soaring Eagle, then got into the cafeteria line.

Frank asked Mary, "So what is good to eat here?"

She smiled and said, "The State Department allows the consulate to bring in French cooks and they all think they are master Chefs, so everything is good. I don't care for things like snails that the French really like but I'm sure you will find the food wonderful."

After lunch, LTC Garson convened a meeting with them in the consulates SCIF to lay out their assignments during the collection phase of the operation.

LTC Garson said, "We have two vehicles and I don't think the power wagon is appropriate, so we will have to rent a couple more vehicles."

Mary replied, "I suggest we could use my car. We could even borrow a couple cars from other consulate personnel. They don't have embassy markings on them and the one you have, Colonel, has USA plates so that may be a non-starter." Privately owned cars belonging to U.S. Forces in Germany had USA embossed at the top of their license plates to distinguish them from cars owned by Germans.

Frank was surprised to see Mary sitting at the back of the room. It seems she was more than just an admin type with a pretty face.

LTC Garson smiled, "Good catch Mary. Can you inquire on the availability of the cars?"

"Yes sir."

"Okay, thanks. I will stay here at the consulate with Gerhardt to coordinate the operation. One of you will not be partnered up since there are only five of us in three cars."

Mary suggested, "I can be the sixth person and drive since I know the city well."

LTC Garson thought about it for a few seconds. "Well, you are certainly qualified. Who do we need to check with to see if it's okay?"

"I have already been cleared to work with you guys to include providing assistance and support to you in the field."

"Good. Who would you like to ride with you?"

She looked at us all, "If it's okay with you I would like Frank to ride with me."

LTC Garson said, "Done. Let's roll as soon as you can get the other cars."

CHAPTER 31
Strasbourg, France

Oleg Pavlov thought the new van was not as advanced as Ivan Kraskov led him to believe. In fact, the van wasn't even new. It also did not have any marking on the side. He was told to act like a tourist and was provided with plastic chairs and a small table to set outside of the van when he parked it. Inside the van were the same type receivers in it that he used in Hulseberg but they were hidden behind panels in case he was stopped by authorities who wanted to look inside. He wondered if the consulate even used VHF/UHF communications equipment. He thought they would prefer to use microwave as the primary communication.

His first day out with the van, he drove near the U.S. Consulate but parked his van out of sight of it in case they had cameras. He strolled around the whole complex, looking at the antennas on the roof. He did not see any microwave antennas so thought they probably did use VHF/UHF communications. He saw some HF antennas, but he didn't have the equipment to intercept signals from HF communication systems. He also did not see any cameras which surprised him. He wondered why the Soviets wanted to monitor signals from here. It seemed like the Americans did not hold this consulate in high regard, but he chuckled to himself, "You are not being paid to think."

He checked the topographic map that he was provided and decided to go to one of the sites that he had chosen earlier to collect data. The Soviet engineers had placed a luggage rack on the top of the van which was really a radome for the antenna. He hoped they had chosen a material for the radome that was nearly transparent at VHF/UHF frequencies to minimize attenuation of the signal. The site he had chosen was on a small knoll in a park about three kilometers from the consulate. He set the plastic chairs and table outside the van and then went back inside to turn on the receivers. He set them to monitor the frequencies Ivan had provided him. He then turned on the tape recorder and went back outside with a little snack and a drink.

Gerhardt exclaimed, "We got a hit! Spaniel got it too. I am still waiting for Collie. Between us and Spaniel, it looks like it's coming from an area called *Hautepierre*. Collie just came up on their radio. He confirmed they have the signal also and we have triangulated the signal to a park there."

LTC Garson picked up the PRC-6 radio. It was equipped with a scrambler in case *they* were being monitored by the same people who were intercepting signals from the consulate. The PRC-6 was on the VHF frequency band and if intercepted, all that would be heard is static.

He keyed the radio, "Bulldog to Rover, Over."

Mary laughed, "Did I just hear Rover over?"

Frank stifled a laugh and replied, "Rover to Bulldog, Over."

"Rover, head to the park on Hautepierre. Over."

Mary said to Frank, "I know where that park is. We can be there in about ten minutes."

"Bulldog, ETA is about ten minutes, over."

Mary navigated through the small streets until she got to the entrance of an *autoroute* or highway leading out of downtown Strasbourg and hit the gas. They got to the park in *Hautepierre* in under ten minutes and slowed to a crawl.

"Do you know what we are looking for?" Mary asked.

"They used a van the last time so let's look for a van. I'll ask the Colonel or Gerhardt."

"Rover to Bulldog. We are at the park but not sure what we are looking for. Can you give us any help? Over."

"Rover. No clue but they used a van last time. Over."

"Bulldog. Roger that. We're snaking through the park looking for anything suspicious. Over."

"Spaniel to Rover. We are on site at the north end of the park. Where are you?"

Frank looked at Mary, "Do you know where we are?"

"The east end of the park heading west."

"Spaniel, we are at the east end heading west. Over."

"Roger that. We will head to the south end. Over."

Frank keyed the radio, "Bulldog. I see a van with a guy sitting outside. He seems to be catching some sun. Over."

LTC Garson came back, "Rover, park your car and take a leisurely walk but not directly toward the van. Spaniel, you keep looking for any other vans in the park. Over."

Mary smiled, "It would look more natural if we held hands while strolling through the park."

Frank was delighted, "Agree. You can pretend you are showing me the sights."

Mary laughed, "I was hoping he might think we were lovers."

Frank blushed a little bit because he was thinking the same thing. Mary pulled a blanket out of the back seat and hoped it would look like a random walk they were taking but kept the van in sight. Mary stopped and spread the blanket out on the grass. "Let's sit and enjoy the view for a while."

They didn't have long to wait. The guy picked up his chair and table, put them into the van, and started to leave.

Frank and Mary strolled back to the car and Frank picked up his radio, "Rover to Bulldog, the van is leaving, and we are preparing to follow. Please advise. Over."

"Rover, do you think you can follow him without being detected? Over."

"Spaniel to Bulldog, we can assist Rover. We have both vehicles in sight. Over."

"Good. Stay on the radios and take turns following him so he doesn't spot you. Over."

"Collie to Bulldog. I have joined the fun and have all vehicles in sight. Over."

They maintained a tag team approach until the suspect van pulled up to a garage about two kilometers from the park. The driver exited the van and rolled up the door. He pulled the van inside and rolled the door back down.

"Spaniel to Bulldog, the van pulled into a garage. I parked a distance away but have eyes on the garage. Do you want me to take the first watch? Over."

"Roger that. Rover and Collie return to base. Over."

CHAPTER 32

Strasbourg, France

Soaring Eagle and Billy were the Spaniel team. Soaring Eagle turned to Billy, "I am going to take a walk around the back of the garage to see if there is another door that we need to watch." He came back about ten minutes later, "Nope, no other door. I wonder if he lives in there like the guy in Hulseberg."

Billy said, "He might *be* the guy from Hulseberg, or he might be an innocent guy who just likes sitting in the park."

Soaring Eagle thought for a minute, "Yeah, but he was in the only van we saw in the park and Gerhardt seemed pretty confident that the intercepting receiver was in the park."

Billy shrugged and picked up the radio, "Spaniel to Bulldog. Did the signal stop when the van left the park? Over."

"Roger that. I think you are sitting on our guy. Over."

The three teams took turns watching the garage. In the meantime, LTC Garson updated MAJ Best and asked him, as the liaison with the BND, to inform them that they were monitoring the activities of a suspicious individual, who they now referred to as 'Sunny', and to request the BND provide support. Obviously, BND operatives would blend in a lot easier with the locals than the GEEIA team, even in their civilian clothes.

The next morning Frank and Mary were taking their turn sitting in her car outside the garage. The two BND operatives who were going to take over the surveillance were sitting in the back seat of her car when they saw Sunny exit the garage on foot with a newspaper under his arm. Sunny took a roundabout route to another park nearby. Frank and one of the BND operatives followed him and saw him sit at a park bench reading his newspaper. He then got up and walked to the other side of the park and put a chalk mark on a light pole and returned to the garage.

Frank told the BND operative, "He must have put a package near the park bench he was sitting on, but I didn't actually see it. He was pretty smooth."

The operative said, "I will hide in those bushes overlooking the bench to see if someone comes by to pick it up, assuming there is a package there. You go back to the car and report in and ask BND to send more agents to seal off the park."

Frank reported to LTC Garson, "Rover to Bulldog. BND support arrived and has been briefed. We observed Sunny leaving the garage and making a chalk mark on a pole in a nearby park. We think he left a package near a bench he was sitting on, just prior to making the chalk mark. The BND operative is still there, hiding in some bushes, waiting to see if anyone suspicious comes by the pole. He asked for more BND agents to seal off the park. Over."

"Roger. Let the BND handle the surveillance and return to base. Over."

Frank turned to Mary, "Looks like we get to relax a little."

Mary made a face, "Just when it was getting to be fun."

CHAPTER 33
Strasbourg, France

LTC Garson convened another meeting in the consulate to summarize recent events and to discuss his plan going forward, "The BND is staking out the garage but no further activity there or in the park since the chalk mark was made. I called MAJ Best and told him to coordinate with the BND to have the Air Commando snipers from Sembach provide support to their surveillance team as needed. I would hate for them and the BND to get in each other's way or shoot at each other. The frequency channel that was intercepted was the one from the consulate to the French government. We don't know what they are hoping to discover in these communications, but we are analyzing the recorded tapes here during the time the consulate folks were on the air and who they were communicating with at the French end."

Gerhardt said, "A quick run through of the tape does not indicate anything significant. Chuck and some of the consulate staff are looking at it in detail."

Look at it from another angle.

Frank heard the voice and had an idea, "Maybe they are monitoring the chatter between the consulate and the French to see if there is any increase lately. You know, like to detect that there is something abnormal going on."

LTC Garson looked thoughtful, "It is interesting that you would say that since there has been no increase. I presume you are thinking that there would be a lot more chatter if we or the French had detected something that would concern us."

"Exactly. I doubt if Sunny could tell us anything so maybe we just keep tracking him but not arrest him. The guy we want is whoever retrieves the package Sunny left in the park."

LTC Garson called MAJ Best, "Jim, can you ask BND to follow whoever picks up the package instead of whatever action they were planning? We think that the Soviets are looking for abnormally heavy chatter instead of something that was actually said between us and the French."

MAJ Best said, "Can do. General Gehlen is here so I will bounce this idea off him to get his reaction. He has a meeting scheduled with the SDECE today. I can't attend since de Gaulle has put out the word that the SDECE doesn't cooperate with the CIA. General Gehlen said he would back brief me if it concerned us."

They all went down to the consulate cafeteria for lunch. Frank saw an egg burger on the menu sign board, 'never saw that before' he thought and ordered it and a cup of coffee. He liked coffee with little cream and sugar but could take it black if that was all that was available. He saw Mary waving at him from a table across the room. Don and Gerhardt were pulling another table towards the one she was at so that they could all sit down together. He sat down and soon Billy and LTC Garson joined them. Chuck was still working with the consulate staff to see if there was anything interesting on the recorded tapes.

After lunch, Billy said, "Until something breaks, we should get back to hooking up the remote from the Air Force communications system to maintain our cover."

Don said, "I already ran the cable from the receivers to the consulate command center. All we need to do is hook it up and test it."

Frank smiled, "Well, in that case, I am going to see what they have for dessert."

Mary nodded, "Me too."

LTC Garson said, "I am going to write my report to MG Stone. We can get together in an hour to review it before I send it out. Frank, you and Mary enjoy dessert."

When everyone else left, Mary said, "If we have the time, I could still show you around Strasbourg."

"I would like that. Would you like to go to dinner tonight? Just you and me."

"Yes, I would like that very much."

They found the rest of the group, minus LTC Garson, in the SCIF comparing notes.

Billy asked Frank, "So you didn't actually see Sunny hide a package near the bench he sat on?"

"No, neither did the BND guy. Hopefully, Sunny did though or we may be spinning our wheels waiting for someone to pick it up."

LTC Garson walking into the SCIF, "I just got word that Sunny's van is on the move again. He is being followed by the BND guys to see where he goes this time. This might be an opportunity to check out his garage, but we need to be very careful that it's not rigged to blow like the one in Hulseberg."

Mary said, "I can ask the consulate explosive ordnance disposal, or EOD, guys on staff for help after I clear it with the consulate chief of staff."

"Great. The Air Commando snipers have been surveilling the surrounding area and they have not detected anyone else watching the garage."

Billy asked Mary, "Is there any chance you can rustle up some kind of maintenance uniforms or something similar in case the garage is being watched?"

Mary brightened, "Yes, as a matter of fact, some French electrical workers have been upgrading the service to the consulate and keep spare uniforms here in case they need them. I think I can sneak them out of the closet where they are kept but I will need them back by the end of the day, so they are not missed."

The uniforms were small and only Frank and Soaring Eagle could fit into them. Mary showed up with an EOD guy who was small enough to fit in one also. The three of them changed into the uniforms and headed for the garage.

When they got to the garage, the EOD guy checked for trip wires and pressure plates but finding none, turned to Frank and Soaring Eagle, "You might want to cover your ears because if I missed something, the sound will be really loud."

Frank and Soaring Eagle looked at each other, then back at the smiling EOD guy who burst out laughing. "Gallows humor" said the EOD guy.

Soaring Eagle didn't think it was funny as he picked the lock on the garage. It took him about thirty seconds. They entered the garage. There was a faint smell of oil and diesel fuel. A bed and a small refrigerator were tucked into a corner. A bucket with a cover on it was across the other side of the garage and when they lifted the cover, the smell of feces filled their noses, so they put it back down quickly. "Hell of a way to live," croaked Frank. They searched the garage but found nothing suspicious. They took pictures, put everything back the way they found it and left the garage.

They changed out of the uniforms in the car, folded them and placed them in the paper bag that Mary used to sneak them out of the closet. They drove back to the consulate, thanked the EOD guy and reported to the rest of the group in the SCIF, again minus LTC Garson. "We didn't find anything there to help us to identify Sunny. He must keep everything in the van."

Gerhardt said, "Speaking of which, Sunny is monitoring the consulate from a knoll in another park. BND says he looks like he is sunning himself, so we gave him the right name. I wonder what he will do on a rainy day."

All chuckled but stopped when LTC Garson came into the SCIF, "MAJ Best just called. The BND observed a guy taking something from the bottom of the park bench and putting it in his pocket. He wasn't as smooth as Sunny. It looked like he had difficulty retrieving it. They followed him to a house on Avenue de Colmar. They informed the SDECE who immediately raided the house and took into custody a Frenchman named Francois Langevin. General Gehlen is not particularly pleased with this and told the SDECE that he had hoped to continue observing the individual they arrested to see where he would lead them. The SDECE was not apologetic and demanded that General Gehlen tell them how he suspected Langevin. General Gehlen did not mention Sunny but instead concocted a story that one of his BND operatives was strolling through the park on his day off and observed someone attaching something to the bottom of the bench. The SDECE was not pleased and suspected that the BND was conducting an operation in Strasbourg without informing the French government."

Frank said, "This might not be all that bad. Sunny may not know that Langevin has been arrested so will continue monitoring the consulate and passing tapes until his handler contacts him to let him know that Langevin has been arrested. His handler will either pull him out of Strasbourg or direct him to a new contact or maybe even kill him. My money is on Sunny being pulled out because once the French figure out that the tape has scrambled data on it and it is from a scrambler that is used between the consulate and them, they will be on the lookout for Sunny. We on the other hand, already know about Sunny and can continue observing him until his handler contacts him and we can arrest them both."

Good call, the voice in his head said.

LTC Garson looked surprised, "That is a very good idea. Let's all discuss it to see if we can find any holes in it before I make a recommendation to MG Stone and, if he approves, share it with General Gehlen. I will also ask General Gehlen *not* to share it with the SDECE."

CHAPTER 34
Strasbourg, France

Frank and Mary were given some time off while LTC Garson was coordinating details of the proposed plan with MG Stone and General Gehlen.

Frank asked Mary, "Is now a good time for taking that promised tour of Strasbourg and having that dinner I promised?"

Mary smiled and took his arm, "I think it is and we better grab it before something else comes up. You better take the PRC-6 radio just in case though."

"Good idea, it's bulky as hell though to carry around town. It would be nice if there was something a little more compact that could fit in your pocket."

Mary smiled, "Dream on. I'll bring a big handbag and we can put it in there."

They drove into *Petite France*, the historic quarter of Strasbourg and parked the car. They strolled along the canals where there were beautiful medieval structures that were home to the tanners, millers and fishermen and was now a tourist attraction. From there, they went to the *Barrage Vauban,* a bridge and defensive work on the Ill river that was constructed in the 17th century. They crossed over the Ill river to the *Grand Ile* and continued to the *Place Kleber*. This was Strasbourg's main square and was populated with several shops and cafes. They read the dinner menus displayed in front of the cafes in the square and selected one that looked good and was in their price range.

Frank said, "This has really been an eye opener. I am so glad you made the offer to show me around. I had no idea that there were so many buildings that were constructed well before America was even discovered and they are still standing. It's amazing!"

Mary smiled, "I'm glad you like it here. After dinner, we can stop at the *St. Thomas Eglise.* It is the only hall church in the Alsace region and was originally built in the ninth century although earlier versions of the church burnt down. The current fortress like building was started in 1196 and was not completed until 1521."

Frank looked awed, "How do you know so much about this church?"

"My brother's name is Thomas and I wanted to learn as much about it as I could about the church with his name on it. I could go into a lot more detail if you would like."

"That sounds great. Let's order dinner first, okay?"

Mary nodded, "I would recommend you try the *Choucroute Garnie.* It is *the* most famous Alsatian meal in Strasbourg. It is pickled cabbage, similar to sauerkraut, but made with wine. It is served with smoked ham hocks, sausages and potatoes."

"It does sound good to me. I like sauerkraut, sausages and potatoes but what are ham hocks?"

Mary laughed, "Its pig's ankle. I know it sounds gross but it's tasty the way the French cook it."

"Okay. What are you having?"

"The *Matelote* which consists of local fish filets in a creamy Riesling sauce and served with noodles."

"Wow. Have you gone native?"

She laughed again, "Two words I love, Food and Free. French food is delicious, and you are paying for dinner."

Frank laughed with her, "How about some wine with dinner? Do you have a recommendation?"

"As a matter of fact, I do. *Gewurztraminer* is a white wine that is aromatic. I prefer *Hugel and Fils Gewurztraminer*. It has a peppery, spicy scent. Does that sound okay?"

"Sure does. Here comes the waiter."

Mary ordered in French which took Frank by surprise but when he thought about it, was not really surprised. Mary was always surprising him. The wine had an unusual taste and the *Choucroute Garnie* was delicious. They didn't say much while eating which Frank guessed that it must be because the food was so good.

After dinner, they walked hand in hand to the *St. Thomas*

Eglise. The church was originally Catholic but converted to Protestant in the 1500's. It possessed an organ that was once played by Wolfgang Amadeus Mozart and had several tombs, one of which was created by Jean-Baptiste Pigalle. His name is most commonly known since the Pigalle red-light district in Paris is located around the square named in his honor. They left the church and re-crossed the Ill River at the *Pont St. Thomas* Bridge on the way back to her car.

Mary said, "Would you like to see where I live?"

"Do you have more of that wine that we had for dinner?"

"No, but I'm sure I can find something you will like."

Her apartment was not far from the consulate which meant it was not far from his hotel. They climbed to the third floor which the French call the second floor. The French consider the ground floor as zero and the floor above it the first floor and so on. Frank smiled and thought, 'That would really confuse an American mailman.'

They entered the apartment and Mary said, "Have a seat on the couch and I will see what I have to drink. I think I have some beer and maybe a bottle of wine."

"Either works for me as long as it's cold or just cool."

She came back with a corkscrew and a bottle of Chardonnay. She smiled, "Will this do, I must have drunk the beer after one of our more exciting days."

Frank was not familiar with the type of corkscrew that she

brought and looked confused. She offered to show him how it worked. She leaned in close with her breast pushed up against his arm. He felt himself getting excited and tried to hide it but then her arm slipped, and her elbow came down on his leg and she felt something hard.

Mary smiled, "Do you really want some wine?" and then kissed him. He put the bottle down and put his arms around her. She got up, took his hand and headed to the bedroom. He followed while unbuttoning his shirt.

Frank woke up alone in the bed. He listened for Mary but didn't hear anything. He got up, found his underwear and pants, put them on and went into the living room. Mary wasn't in the apartment. He was about to finish getting dressed when he heard the lock in the door being opened.

Mary came in and saw him standing in the living room. "I went shopping at the market and got us some breakfast. We don't need to be at the consulate until 0900. Are you hungry?"

Frank was famished, "Yes, what did you buy?"

"I just got some croissants and pastries. I don't think we have time for *jambon* and eggs." She laughed.

He smiled, "sounds great. By the way, what is *jambon?*"

"Ham" and she grabbed a handful of her shapely buttocks. "This will help you remember what *jambon* is." She said laughing.

"I will never forget and will smile whenever I have ham for breakfast."

CHAPTER 35
Strasbourg, France

Oleg was enjoying the sun when a beautiful girl in hiking clothes startled him, "It sure is a beautiful day for getting some sun," she said in French. He didn't speak much French and asked her. "*Sprichst du Deutsch?*" He used the familiar '*du*' instead of '*zie*' because she was so pretty.

She answered in French accented German, "Yes I do," and continued in German, "I said this sure is a beautiful day for getting some sun."

"Yes, but it's getting hot. Would you like something to drink? I have water and cola."

"Water would be good. Do you have an extra chair inside that I can use to rest a little?"

Oleg looked around to see if anyone was paying attention to them. It looked clear, so he pointed to his chair, "Take that one and I will bring another one out with the drink."

When Oleg went into the van, she nodded to a man hiding in the bushes on the other side of the van.

Oleg emerged with the chair and a glass of water, "Here you go. Do you hike here often?"

"No, this is the first time. I am visiting my brother who lives nearby with his family. I was born in Strasbourg but now live in Stuttgart where I work."

"Stuttgart is a beautiful city. What do you do at work?"

"I am a secretary at the American base called Kelley Barracks."

Oleg was stunned for a minute. He was envisioning that he could ask Ivan if he could try to recruit this girl to their side. He fantasized becoming her lover and moving to Stuttgart. He was pulled back to the present when she asked, "What is your name?"

Oleg couldn't remember his cover name for a second, "Mueller, eh…Herbert Mueller."

Just then she saw the man moving away from the van. She smiled, "My name is Monica Schiller. I must go now. My brother worries when I am gone too long. It was very nice to meet you and thank you for the water."

Oleg saw his dream vanishing, "Would it be possible to see you again and maybe go to a movie or have dinner?"

She acted like she was thinking about it then said, "I would like that. Do you have some paper and a pencil? I will write my phone number down."

After she hiked back to her car and got in, she turned to Soaring Eagle, "Did you put the transponder in a place where it is secure, and he won't see it?"

He looked at her, "*Mais Oui Mademoiselle.* How was my French?"

Mary laughed, "It's getting better."

Mary and Soaring Eagle went to the consulate to update LTC Garson who was in the SCIF with Billy, Don, Frank and Chuck.

Mary addressed the group, "The transponder is in place, so the BND can track his van. Sunny is going by the name of Herbert Mueller. We may even have a date later if he calls me."

Frank felt a tinge of jealousy when she mentioned a date with Sunny but pushed it out of his mind. He had feelings for Mary that he never had for Barb and it made him think of how he was going to break it to her that he met someone else. He saw everyone in the room looking at him and realized someone must have asked him a question, "I'm sorry, can you repeat that?"

Don't get distracted. You have his confidence. Don't blow it.

Frank felt like he was slapped. His face suddenly flushed.

LTC Garson looked at Frank, wondering if he was feeling ill, and said, "Based on your plan, do you think it would be better to arrest Mueller as soon as he meets with his handler or have Mary go out on a date with him to see what she can learn?"

Frank's immediate thought was to stick to the original plan, but what if Mueller's handler opted to just replace the contact who was arrested and continue monitoring the consulate. "Why not do both? His handler may opt to just replace the contact and having Mary meet with him may give us another alternative. If, however, he meets with his handler, I suggest we arrest both and interrogate them or have BND do it. They seem to get better results."

LTC Garson frowned, "I don't know about BND getting better results, but I like your idea of pursuing both options. I will recommend it to MG Stone. If he approves, I want you and Soaring Eagle to shadow Mary and make sure nothing happens to her."

Mary said, "I think we should also ask BND to provide an agent to act as my brother and to provide a safe house. I gave Mueller my apartment phone number, so we should transfer it to the safe house. I suggest we do this pretty quick since we don't know when Mueller will call, if he does."

LTC Garson nodded, "Good point. I will include that in my recommendation to MG Stone." He picked up the secure phone and called MG Stone who approved the operation.

Billy asked, "What do you want the rest of us to do?"

"Good question. Gerhardt should stay here in the consulate and keep track on the data that is intercepted in case our plan goes haywire. The rest of you should be armed and ready to assist Frank and Soaring Eagle as the need arises."

The BND Watchers at the garage, reported some unusual activity. They tracked Oleg Pavlov, who they knew as Herbert

Mueller, as he left the garage and headed toward the Rhine River. The transponder tracked him through U-turns, sudden stops, and circling blocks. He was obviously trying to lose anyone following him. Then he turned before crossing over the Rhine River, returned to the garage and drove the van into it. They surmised that he may have learned that his contact had been arrested and his handler had him go through these gyrations to see if he was blown.

Mueller left the garage on foot and headed to the park where he made the drop previously. The BND Watchers were good and there was little chance that they would be detected by Mueller. What they were concerned about was being detected by someone who was watching for the Watchers. They used extra men, women, couples and faux mothers with baby carriages to track Mueller. They had various tricks to avoid detection, including reversible jackets, wigs, and hats that were changed constantly as they handed off Mueller to another Watcher. It was tedious work and the longer Mueller walked around the park the higher the chances were that they would be detected by whoever might be watching for them.

Mueller finally sat down on a bench and was joined shortly by a man that one of the Watchers recognized. He was an attaché at the Soviet embassy in Frankfurt named Ivan Kraskov. The Watcher, when they weren't watching, spent their time memorizing the faces of embassy officials from various embassies. If Americans arrested Kraskov, they knew he would claim diplomatic immunity and must be released to the Soviet Embassy who would recall him to the Soviet Union. The BND however, had a different set of rules. They would quietly arrest an obvious spy with diplomatic immunity and that said spy would simply disappear. They would try to turn the spy and if unsuccessful, would dispose of him or her.

The Watchers observed Mueller visibly react to something Kraskov said. They surmised that Kraskov told him that Langevin was arrested. After Kraskov calmed Mueller down, they parted company and headed for different exits from the park. The BND Watcher alerted their operator teams who stationed themselves at all the exits from the park. They pulled up their vans and were provided updates from the Watchers about where Kraskov and Mueller were at all times.

Two of the operators split off from the others and pretended to get into loud fierce argument that escalated into a fist fight. The diversion was staged to focus the attention of any passersby so that snatching Mueller at one exit and Kraskov at another would be hardly noticed. The snatch operation did not go as planned however. Mueller, who was more than a little paranoid from his experience at Hulseberg, pulled a pistol from his jacket and shot the closest BND operator. The bullet hit the operator squarely in the chest but was stopped by the armored vest worn by the operator. It had enough force to knock the operator down though. Mueller just stared at the fallen BND operator and did not see another operator approach him from behind. The other operator hit Mueller on the back of his head. Mueller was surprised to see the ground as he fell and blacked out when he hit the pavement with his forehead.

Kraskov heard the shot and ran toward his car. A BND operator tripped him and then pretending to help him up, he inserted a syringe into Kraskov's neck. Kraskov started to say something then passed out. The BND operator was assisted by another operator and they lifted him into a van that drove up to them.

The two vans containing Mueller and Kraskov drove to a warehouse in Strasbourg where they were bound, gagged and hooked up to an intravenous drip to keep them unconscious. They were then loaded into a truck behind several crates of fruit and driven across the border into Germany.

Karlsruhe, Germany

The truck drove to a remote safe house on a well maintained farm operated by the BND. Upon arrival, Mueller and Kraskov were moved to separate soundproof rooms. They were stripped of all clothing and secured to a chair that was bolted to the floor. Next to them on a table were various surgical instruments that were mainly to scare them but would be used if necessary.

Oleg Pavlov, AKA Herbert Mueller, slowly regained consciousness and jerked when he saw that he was naked and secured to a chair. He initially thought he was snatched by Soviet operators and almost panicked when he saw the surgical instruments. The BND interrogators saw his reaction and smiled. He would be easy to break, they thought.

Oleg said, "Who are you and what are you doing?"

A BND interrogator in a white smock with dried blood stains on it came into the room and asked, "What is your name?"

Oleg gulped, "Herbert Mueller."

He was immediately smacked on the back of his head by another man in the room that he couldn't see, who said, "Your real name, you lousy spy."

"I am not a spy," he screamed.

"We have your van with the radio intercept equipment. I will only ask one more time and then I will ask my friend in the smock to help you remember."

Oleg looked at the man in the smock walk over to the table with the surgical instruments and select one. He then turned to Oleg with a crazy look on his face and was breathing rapidly like he was excited. Just then, Oleg's head was pulled back and he felt a strap tighten across his forehead. The man with the smock pushed a metal contraption into his mouth and turned screws that forced his mouth open.

"We are going to pull your teeth out one by one. Blink your eyes rapidly if you are ready to tell me your name."

Oleg thought, 'So what if they know my name,' then blinked his eyes. The metal contraption was removed from this mouth. "My name is Oleg Pavlov."

"Your accent indicates that you are from northern Germany.

Where specifically are you from?"

Oleg rationalized that it would be of no consequence to answer, "Bremen."

Both men then left Oleg in the room alone. He could not help but stare at the tray holding the surgical instruments. He felt something trickling down his face and thought he was cut somehow, then realized they were tears, and he started crying.

The GEEIA team along with Mary, Chuck and Soaring Eagle were sitting in the consulate SCIF when LTC Garson entered.

"The man we know as Mueller is really Oleg Pavlov from Bremen, Germany. General Gehlen confirmed with the *Polizei* in Bremen that an Oleg Pavlov lived there until 1955 and then disappeared. They thought he moved somewhere else in Germany without the proper authorization but that was happening a lot, so they didn't pursue it. General Gehlen thinks he was recruited by the Soviets, trained in East Germany or the Soviet Union and then returned to West Germany. The BND is still interrogating him to learn why he was monitoring radio traffic from the consulate to the French government. General Gehlen also said the SDECE is upset about the commotion in the park where we snatched Pavlov but are not aware that the BND was involved. They think it might have been a Soviet operation and are filing a protest with the embassy."

Mary said, "What about the other guy who was snatched?"

"Gehlen said they are interrogating him. They think he is Pavlov's handler but don't know for sure what his role is yet. He obviously is not as cooperative as Pavlov."

Billy asked, "So where do we go from here?"

"Your work here is done, so pack up your stuff, check out of the hotel and return to Ramstein."

Frank looked at Mary, but she was heading for the door. He caught up to her and said, "I want to keep seeing you. I get weekends off when we are in station and could catch a train down here."

"I would like that. I thought you would forget about me when you left."

"I don't think so. I never met any girl like you and want to keep seeing you."

She smiled, "Me too."

CHAPTER 36
Karlsruhe, Germany

Meanwhile, in the safe house, Oleg awoke. He couldn't believe he fell asleep tied to a chair with his head strapped back. His whole body ached. His fingers looked white and he guessed that was from the tight bindings reducing the blood flow to his hands. He looked at the surgical instruments and started crying again. Try as he might, he couldn't stop the tears running down his face.

He regained his composure a few minutes later. He wondered if they kidnapped Ivan also. They had not been back since he told them his name and where he was from. He looked around the room for the first time but could not see what was behind him. It looked like the walls were made of metal and he could see no windows. The only furniture in the room was the chair he was sitting in, at least as far as he could see with his head immobilized.

The door opened and a man in a hood walked in and went behind him, "Oleg, we have verified that is your name and you are from Bremen. You seem to have aged a lot since the photo on your old identification papers. That may have been due to the coarse image faxed from Bremen or because you were only about eighteen years old then. Where have you been for the last ten years? Don't lie to me or you will be relieved of some of your most precious body parts, one by one."

"I went to East Germany. They arrested me there and forced me to work for them."

"Exactly who did you work for?"

"Do you mean his name?"

"Yes, and his organization."

He thought that if they had Ivan and he lied, he would be tortured, "Ivan Kraskov, at least that's what he told me his name was, but I don't know who he works for."

"Where were you trained?"

"Somewhere in East Germany."

"Did you ever go to the Soviet Union?"

"After they arrested me in East Germany, I was tortured and interrogated, then sent to the Soviet Union for more interrogation."

"Were you trained at the Dzerzhinsky School?"

Oleg panicked, "I don't know where I was interrogated."

"Not interrogated, trained."

"I was trained in East Germany to operate the equipment in the van."

The man with the hood left the room and Oleg relaxed a little.

That changed when the man in the bloodied smock entered the room. He swung the contraption around one of his fingers that he had inserted in Oleg's mouth previously and said, "Thank you for lying." He roughly reinserted the contraption into Oleg's mouth.

Oleg screamed and struggled as two of his back teeth were slowly pulled and shoved back and forth into their sockets to grate against the nerve. He felt like he was going to drown in his own blood and gagged while trying to swallow the blood and not let it go into his lungs. When the teeth were finally yanked free, the man in the smock was sweating and said, "This is hard work. I think I will take a little rest and then we will work on the front teeth. They should be easier."

Oleg groaned and with his mouth held open by the contraption, he had a hard time swallowing the blood and breathing so that some of the blood leaked into his lungs causing coughing fits. The door opened, and Oleg started crying again but it was the man in the hood. He walked behind Oleg again and putting his mouth close to Oleg's ear whispered, "Blink fast if you are ready to truthfully answer my question. Were you trained at the Dzerzhinsky School?"

Oleg blinked so fast he forgot about the blood going into his lungs and broke out into another coughing fit. The contraption was removed from his mouth and Oleg had a hard time talking. His jaw ached so much he could not form words.

"I'm waiting," the man in the hood smiled.

"Yessh, Yessh, I was trained there."

"Very good, now you will tell me what your training consisted of and how long you were there."

The strap was removed from his head and Oleg bent down to redirect the flow of blood to the front of his mouth and onto his naked chest. The man in the hood went to the door and returned with a nurse who cleaned out his mouth and packed the sockets where his teeth once were. Oleg felt his penis getting hard when the nurse moved against him. She looked down and laughed and pointed it out to the man in the hood who laughed with her. Oleg was embarrassed and then got scared that it would give them the idea that this could be the first body part they 'relieved him of'. Oleg told the hooded man everything that had happened to him from 1955 to the present. He also told them about his father being abused by Germans during the war, the pastry shop being destroyed by Allied bombers and the death of his father by the British soldiers as a way of justifying his spying for the Soviets.

CHAPTER 37
Ramstein, Germany

Frank got back to Ramstein AB from Strasbourg late on a Friday night. He was sound asleep when his roommates came into their barracks room hooting and hollering. They had been downtown and were really, drunk. Frank pulled his pillow over his head to block out the noise but that only encouraged gthem to make more noise. A1C Tony D'Angelo, the barracks chief had a room across the hall and came bursting in and yelling for quiet. His roommates shut up and went to their lockers.

"I am putting the whole room on report to the First Sergeant first thing tomorrow! You will be on detail for at least a week." He turned and slammed the door on the way out. His roommates starting giggling like little girls. Frank was pissed. "Thanks Assholes!" They giggled louder, then both plopped into their bunks fully clothed and passed out. They left the light on and in no time, they were snoring so loud that Frank couldn't get back to sleep. "I'm going to have to move into another room soon but where?"

The next morning, Frank looked over at his roommates snoring away and stinking to high heaven. He wondered what they had to drink last night. He thought about making a huge racket to wake them up but remembered the threat that Tony

D'Angelo, the barracks chief, made last night. Tony didn't make threats often and if you stopped doing whatever it was you were doing; he usually didn't follow through. He was really a nice guy and very quiet. He worked for the First Sergeant and carried the implied authority that went with his job. It was sort of like the Commanding General's wife who thought she carried the same rank as her husband and could be quite vindictive to other officer's wives. Tony didn't abuse the implied authority though and Frank got along with him well. They were both from Philadelphia and Tony usually gave him the benefit of the doubt. Frank didn't know if Tony knew about his other 'mission' and obviously couldn't ask him.

Frank sat down at the desk in their room and tried to draft a letter to Barb expressing doubts about their relationship since meeting Mary. Fifteen minutes later, he was still looking at a blank piece of paper. He decided to get dressed, go have breakfast and think about the letter later.

He saw Tony at breakfast in the cafeteria across the street from his barracks and after getting his food, he sat down with him. "Sorry about the noise last night."

Tony looked at Frank and said, "No problem. You guys quieted down right away so I will give you a onetime pass,"

Frank decided to ask Tony for advice. "I am having a relationship problem. I met this girl on my last TDY and we hit it off really well. The issue is that I have a girlfriend back in the States and I feel like a dog for cheating on her."

Tony looked at Frank with a smile. "Do you know how many guys get 'Dear John' letters from their girlfriends back home? That's because their girlfriends meet somebody and that somebody is there, not across the Big Pond. Do you think your girlfriend is any different or for that matter, are you any different?"

Frank reeled back. He had not looked at his predicament that way. He poked at his breakfast but had lost his appetite.

Tony said, "So, what I'm saying is that crap about absence making the heart grow fonder is for romance novels, not real life. Do what you think is best for you."

Frank said, "Yeah, I guess."

Frank left the cafeteria and walked to the GEEIA warehouse. He saw Billy, Don and Gerhardt pouring over some Technical Manuals. "What's up? Are we going to try to resurrect some old communications equipment again?"

Billy smiled, "Nope, we are going TDY to Sembach AB to check out the status of their equipment. We are looking at the TMs to get more familiar with the systems there. We also have a meeting scheduled with SMS Oliver after lunch."

They had lunch at the Rod and Gun, and then went to the SCIF. SMS Oliver was there already, as was MAJ Best. They shook hands all around and took their seats.

SMS Oliver opened the meeting, "We are going to get an update from MAJ Best before we talk about your TDY trip to

Sembach AB.

MAJ Best thanked SMS Oliver, "After further interrogation, the BND broke Oleg Pavlov. It turns out that he was a German citizen of Russian ethnicity who was born in Bremen. During World War II, his father's business was destroyed by allied bombers and was later killed in a crossfire between the German army defending Bremen and British forces attacking it. Oleg witnessed his father's death. He crossed the lax border between West and East Germany in 1955 and offered to help the Soviet Union do whatever they wanted him to do against the west. He eventually came to the attention of the Soviet KGB who trained him in intelligence gathering and sent him back to West Germany. He not only spied in Strasbourg but was the intelligence collector you guys chased from Hulseberg to Bremen."

Billy interrupted, "Really! What are the odds of that happening?"

MAJ Best continued, "The odds were actually pretty good since he lost his van in Bremen and had to be redeployed somewhere. The next bit of information from Gehlen is where things get a bit dicey. The BND also captured Oleg's handler, who was identified as Ivan Kraskov, a Soviet embassy official with diplomatic immunity. It turns out that after 'extreme interrogation', in Gehlen's words, Kraskov shed some light on the data the BND captured in Helmstedt regarding the French. It appears the Soviets are looking for a way to exploit the division between the French and NATO. As you know, de Gaulle is not happy with NATO adopting the U.S. policy regarding nuclear weapons as the NATO policy, so he told all NATO forces to pack up and leave France. We still don't know why the Soviets were monitoring the radio traffic out of the consulate to the French so Chuck and Soaring Eagle, along with Mary Wright, are quietly investigating the recipients on the French side of the conversations. Charles de Gaulle told the SDECE not to cooperate with the U.S. a couple years ago and the BND has pissed the French off by conducting the operation that identified Oleg's contact, Francois Langevin, so we don't expect any help from them."

Billy asked, "Are the Soviets screaming to get their diplomat back?"

MAJ Best fell silent for a second, "Yes, their embassy has demanded his return, but the German and American governments are denying having anything to do with his disappearance."

Billy looked confused, "I don't understand. When it comes out in Kraskov's trial that they both arranged to have Kraskov snatched, it will all get out anyway."

"It won't be coming out. Kraskov didn't survive the interrogation."

Everyone got really quiet, then SMS Oliver said, "You're right. This is really getting dicey."

MAJ Best nodded, "Changing the subject, Gehlen updated me on the neo-Nazi agent named Heinrich Lund who we knew as Reinhardt Uhler from the Capri bar in Ramstein. The BND obtained the record of calls from the public phone that Chuck asked them to investigate. They also pulled the records of the calls from Lund's home phone. There were numerous calls to a *gasthaus* in Kaiserslautern from both phones. The BND have dispatched surveillance teams, called Watchers, and are taking pictures of people coming and going to see if anything pops."

Frank said, "We are familiar with BND Watchers. They are really good at staying invisible."

Don asked, "So why are we going to Sembach?"

MAJ Best tapped his forehead, "Sorry, I got distracted. The BND exploitation of the data from Helmstedt contained a request for more information on Sembach from their French contact but whoever they asked had not responded before the BND raided the house. You are going there to meet with WO4 Jim Woodrow to see if you can come up with some possible reasons. I know this is a long shot, but we just don't have any good intelligence to work with. Good luck."

CHAPTER 38
Sembach, Germany

Billy decided that it would be easier to drive them in his own car to Sembach since it was only about twenty kilometers from Ramstein. Horst was the only one who needed to bring a toolbox since they were only checking calibration and not doing an installation.

When they got to Sembach AB, they met with MAJ Ted Burns, 1LT Kerry Alexander and WO4 Jim Woodrow, who were assigned to the Tactical Missile Wing (TMW). The Wing was responsible for the operation and maintenance of the TM-76 MACE, a tactical cruise missile armed with either a conventional or a nuclear warhead. MAJ Burns was the missile squadron commander for six launchers and 1LT Alexander was one of the launch officers of a mobile variant. WO4 Woodrow was the chief technical officer for the Wing.

Introductions were made, and Billy said, "We are here to check the calibration of your communications systems and should be completed in a couple days. Are there any questions?"

MAJ Burns responded, "Not really but you know that our people will be sensitive to your presence here as they feel you are checking up on their competence."

Billy nodded, "We get that all the time. Unfortunately, one of the responsibilities of the GEEIA squadron is to periodically check on communications systems and file a report that probably no one will read."

MAJ Burns smiled knowingly. "Okay, 1LT Alexander and I have other duties but WO4 Woodrow will be available to you for any support required."

After they departed, WO4 Woodrow said, "I apologize for them being here, but MAJ Burns insisted on greeting you. Neither of them is read on to FRENCH KISS. This conference room was swept this morning, so we can talk here; plus, a guard will be at the door until you are finished with the 'calibration'. So, what can I do for you?"

WO4 Woodrow was a crusty old man of forty-three but was a towering six foot three and solidly build and was one of the last warrant officers to still be in the Air Force. He had entered the Army Air Corps in 1942 and served as an armaments specialist for bombers stationed in England during World War II. He had demonstrated a remarkable knack for learning new things and was cross trained to be one of the first maintenance warrant officers for the MACE missile. After he had been assigned to the TMW, he was recruited by the CIA to keep on top of any abnormal interest in the nuclear warheads mounted in the MACE missiles. He had been read on to FRENCH KISS when the CIA learned that Sembach was mentioned in the data from the Helmstedt raid.

Billy said, "In addition to checking on your communications systems, our other mission is to try to determine why the

Soviets are interested in learning something about Sembach other than the obvious – that it was an American air base."

WO4 Woodrow added, "Of course there are the nukes. They are well guarded however, and we patrol at irregular times to keep from establishing a pattern. Attack dogs accompany each patrol and are trained to detect odors and noises that are unusual. Would you like to take a tour to see what there is to see?"

Billy said, "That would be great. Thanks."

They all piled into WO4 Woodrow's four door Mercedes-Benz. He drove them past a lot of MACE missiles in various stages of being packed up.

Frank asked, "Are they being sent somewhere?"

WO4 Woodrow answered, "Yes, the TMW is in the last phase of inactivation at Sembach. Most of the MACE missiles and the nukes warheads are being sent to Bitburg AB and some are going back to the states. I have orders assigning me to Bitburg, which will be my last assignment before I retire."

Don chuckled, "Did you notice that they are all pointed toward France?"

They all laughed and continued the tour. They drove by a Tactical Control Group who provided, operated and maintained Tactical Air Control Systems for offensive forces, a Tactical Control Squadron whose mission was to provide Aircraft Control and Warning, a Mobile Communications Group (MOB) whose mission was to install, operate and maintain all communications systems within USAFE and subordinate units and the Air Commando Squadron who operated C-47, C-23 and U-10 aircraft and were trained for special operations.

Frank commented, "The Air Commando snipers supported us on our last mission."

WO4 Woodrow looked in his rear-view mirror at Frank, "I didn't know they had snipers."

Don said, "We requested sniper support from the Air Commandos, so they may have arranged for some Army snipers to provide the support. They work with them from time to time."

"That makes sense."

They drove back to the conference room to recap their observations.

Billy suggested, "How about we put the potential targets in priority order and focus our efforts on them. If you guys have a better suggestion, I am open to hear them."

WO4 Woodrow nodded, "It sounds like a good plan to me. We really don't have enough information at this time."

Frank noted, "Based on what we have encountered with the Soviets so far, I think they may try to intercept the communications set up by the MOB."

Don't be obsessed about communications. Think a bit out of the box.

Don pondered Frank's suggestion, "That's logical but I guess I thought they were asking for more info on the layout of Sembach. Why would they be interested in that?"

Billy said, "Good point. In that case, I would put the MACE missiles or the nuke warheads as my priority."

WO4 Woodrow agreed, "The warheads would be more valuable since the Air Force is downsizing the MACE inventory and most likely will retire them in a couple years."

Billy said, "Good. Now let's focus on how they would get to them. Chief, could you arrange for us to look at the storage site for the nukes?"

WO4 Woodrow looked a little skeptical, "If you want to go in, MAJ Burns would have to approve it and he would want to know why a GEEIA team is interested in seeing the storage site."

Billy said, "No problem. I just want to see the outside of the site as a criminal would do while casing the joint."

Billy made a scrambled call to SMS Oliver, "We spent most of the day looking at potential targets at Sembach. The most obvious one is the nuke warheads, but they are well guarded and are surrounded by two chain link fences set about ten feet apart and topped with concertina wire. The second priority is the communications operated by the MOB in support of USAFE. I had Gerhardt install the three boxes we used at the consulate to determine if they are being monitored but no hits so far."

SMS Oliver said, "Okay, why don't you guys finish the calibration of their comm systems, pack up and head back to Ramstein. Chuck and Soaring Eagle will return tomorrow, and we can update the whole team. MAJ Best and LTC Garson will be here also. Tell your team that we will meet in the SCIF at 0900."

Billy told the team, "Oliver wants us to finish with the comm systems. pack up and return to Ramstein. I want to thank you WO4 Woodrow for your hospitality and assistance. Here are contact numbers for me and SSGT Don Bakersfield in case you think of something that we missed."

"Thanks. I will alert the guards to be extra vigilant until we get the nukes packed up and shipped off to Bitburg."

Frank was pondering what the voice said and had a thought, "What is the mode of transportation of the nukes from here to Bitburg?"

WO4 Woodrow said, "Not sure. Someone else is handling that but I will check it out and get back to Billy and Don at the numbers Billy provided."

Gerhardt retrieved the experimental boxes and put them in Billy's car trunk for the trip back to Ramstein. When they got on the road, Billy looked in his rear-view mirror at Frank, "That was a good catch about the mode of transportation. That may be the best opportunity for the Soviets to snatch the nukes."

"Thanks. There is something else bothering me, but I can't put my finger on it yet. I guess I will let my subconscious work on it a bit and let you know."

You need to do some research.

CHAPTER 39
Ramstein, Germany

They all convened at the SCIF and Billy updated them on the trip to Sembach AB.

LTC Garson asked, "When do you expect to hear from WO4 Woodrow? I agree that we need to look closer at the transporting of the nukes."

Billy answered saying, "I expect to hear within the next couple days. If not, I will call him."

Chuck followed, "Soaring Eagle, Mary Wright and I have been observing the French officer who was on the other end of the conversations from the consulate. He is COL Pierre LaCroix, an intelligence officer in the French army attached to a foreign office detachment in Strasbourg. The foreign office in Paris set up the detachment to interact with several consulates face-to-face in lieu of telephonically. COL LaCroix served as a Lieutenant on General Leclerc's staff in the liberation of Strasbourg during World War II. General Leclerc was the *nom de guerre* of Philippe Leclerc de Hauteclocque who commanded the French 2nd Armored Division and died in a plane crash in 1947. After Leclerc's death, Charles de Gaulle took LaCroix under his wing and mentored him throughout his career. Mary Wright met LaCroix at several social functions in Strasbourg in the past and plans to get to know him better."

Frank thought, 'Mary is way more than meets the eye. She really knows her way around the diplomatic landmines but has yet to tell him she is with the CIA and not the State Department. But then again, he was not with the CIA, but it would be hard to tell the difference, so maybe she is with State in a joint effort. What a tangled web the CIA weaves.'

MAJ Best broke Frank out of his musings with an update, "So far, what I have learned as liaison to the BND is that they have mended fences with the SDECE who have been interrogating Francois Langevin. They were shocked to find out that he is the brother-in-law to COL LaCroix. They have not yet questioned COL LaCroix since he is a confidant of de Gaulle and they wanted to be sure he is involved before incurring the wrath of de Gaulle. The SDECE upper management subsequently decided that they didn't want anything to do with Langevin and proposed to the BND that they take credit for capturing Langevin and take him off their hands. Gehlen met with the SDECE and when he was told that Langevin is an avowed communist, he saw another potential link to the intelligence that was discovered from the raid at Helmstedt. He pretended to reluctantly agree to take Langevin from the SDECE for an undisclosed favor."

Billy said, "Holy shit. This is getting really complicated."

SMS Oliver asked, "Does Director Helms know about this?"

LTC Garson, "Yes, MG Stone ran it up the flagpole to him and he has already passed it on to the President in this morning's brief. The President told the Director to tread carefully with this as he does not want to involve the United States in another confrontation with de Gaulle after the Sapphire Affair."

Frank looked around in confusion so asked, "What was the Sapphire Affair?"

"That was the catalyst to the SDECE breaking off cooperation with the CIA. Then President Kennedy alerted de Gaulle of a Soviet spy ring called Sapphire within the SDECE after a KGB defector told the CIA of its existence. Charles de Gaulle didn't believe Kennedy and saw it as a CIA plot to cause discord within the SDECE. Several years later, it was found to be true but the SDECE still does not work with the CIA. Stubborn bastards!"

MAJ Best continued, "I have been invited to observe the interrogation of Langevin, so I believe that the BND is being up front with us on this. Langevin may only be the tip of the iceberg but he may have knowledge of Soviet planning or the name of his handler in France who I suspect is Ivan Kraskov who we already know about, so that is probably a dead end, no pun intended. The BND is going to press Langevin about the interest in Sembach in particular."

LTC Garson stood up, "Okay, here is what I want us to do in the meantime. Chuck and Soaring Eagle will continue to support Mary Wright in Strasbourg. MAJ Best will continue to liaise with BND and update us on the results of the interrogation of Langevin. The GEEIA team will install an updated communication system at Bitburg in the alert facility. The alert facility houses the F-102 Delta Dagger that includes in its armament a nuclear missile called the Falcon or GAR-11. Frank, since you are the youngest member of the team, I want you to act curious about the aircraft and pose some innocent sounding questions about the nukes. Also, it will probably take at least a week to do the installation, so I would like the rest of the team to monitor the nuke storage facility there for any unusual activity. I will coordinate with MG Stone to relay any direction from the CIA. Are there any questions?"

CHAPTER 40
Ramstein, Germany

Billy dropped Frank off at the barracks to prepare for the TDY to Bitburg AB.

"SMS Oliver is going to cut orders for us to leave for Bitburg on Monday so that gives us three days. Please reserve a power wagon and we will all meet you then at the SCIF to pick up our tools and weapons. Have a nice weekend and stay out of trouble."

Frank smiled, "You know me Billy."

Billy laughed and took off for his home in the housing area.

On the way into the barracks, he was surprised to see Chuck and Soaring Eagle.

"Hey guys, I thought you would be on your way to Strasbourg."

Chuck said, "It's rush hour so we decided to leave tomorrow. Soaring Eagle told me about the Rod and Gun, and we thought you might like to go for a beer or two and get something to eat."

"Okay, I will meet you there after I change into my civvies."

Frank went back to his room, made a quick change and walked to the Rod and Gun Club. Chuck and Soaring Eagle were drinking Frankenthaler beers and had one sitting there for him. Chuck stood up and waved him over.

"Soaring Eagle was telling me about the Capri bar. I would like to see it and maybe get a glimpse at this Heinrich Lund aka Reinhardt Uhler. Would you like to join us?"

"That sounds good to me. We could play the *fussball* machine which would give you an opportunity to scan the bar without seeming to be looking at anything in particular. That's assuming Uhler is there and if not, at least we get to play some *fussball*."

They called a taxi and by chance, the driver was Hans Glick. Frank pointed to Glick's license to drive a taxi which displayed his picture. They made small talk while studying the data on the license for anything that stood out, but it was generic stuff. Hans Glick pulled up to the Capri bar and instead of dropping them off, he went inside with them and headed for a table in the back room of the bar where Uhler was sitting.

"Interesting...I sure wish we knew what they were saying" said Soaring Eagle.

Since it was early evening, there weren't many airmen in the Capri bar and the *fussball* machine was available to them. Chuck went to the side of the machine where he had a good view of Reinhart Uhler and Hans Glick. Soaring Eagle went to the other side and Frank took a seat at the bar and asked Heidi for three beers. Yutta may have had the night off or would be coming in later when more airmen arrived.

"So how are you this fine evening?" he asked Heidi.

"Okay. Business is slow, and Joe is always complaining. He makes good money from you guys and when it slacks off, he gets upset that his customers have found a new place to drink beer."

"Business being slow probably has more to do with when we get paid and that won't be until week." They both laughed.

"Is your son getting big?"

Heidi beamed, "Yes he will be a big boy, like his father." then she looked sad and he knew she had not heard from Jerry Sturgis. "My mother takes care of him while I work". She turned away and started busying herself behind the bar, but Frank noticed her eyes getting moist.

He thought, 'Good move, you idiot, now you probably ruined her night.'

Frank turned back to Chuck and Soaring Eagle. They were just about finished with their game and it would be his turn to take on the winner. They played a few more games and watched Glick leave. Uhler left a few minutes later.

They left by taxi about an hour later and the driver dropped them off at the Rod and Gun. As Chuck was heading to his car, he told them, "I'll tell Gehlen, he might want to keep close tabs on that Glick fellow in addition to Lund. There may be something more to their friendship than meets the eye."

The next morning, Frank picked up the power wagon from the

motor pool and drove to the SCIF to meet Billy, Don and Gerhardt. They loaded their toolboxes and weapons and left for Bitburg AB. The trip was about an hour and a half from Ramstein AB and the way they went took them through the beautiful city of Trier and across the Moselle River.

Bitburg, Germany

The French Army, under contract to the Air Force, did the initial construction of the Bitburg AB since it resides in France's zone of occupation. It had an elaborate camouflage scheme. Huge nets which resembled volleyball nets were randomly scattered around the base. Supposedly, these nets looked like forests when viewed from aircraft. Fake runways with old derelict planes parked on fake tarmacs crisscrossed the real runway that was painted green to blend in with the surrounding grass. Frank wondered if it would really confuse an attacking aircraft. They checked in at a building that was painted with a camouflage pattern like most of the buildings on the base. He heard that some called Bitburg AB the 'paint by numbers base'. They were issued flight line badges and given directions to the alert facility.

Billy said, "Head for the flight line and look for a four-bay concrete hanger."

They were stopped at two gates. One was the entrance to the flight line and the other was at the entrance to the alert facility. At both, heavily armed sentries demanded to see their flight line badges. Don asked Frank, "Have you heard the story about GEN Curtis Lemay lighting up a cigar on the flight line? It seems that an Air Policeman told him that smoking was not allowed on the flight line as it could cause a fire and possibly cause one of the aircraft to blow up. Lemay looked at the aircraft and said, 'It wouldn't dare'".

Frank looked at Don, "You're making that up."

Don said, "No, it's the truth. He also once drove a jeep past the checkpoint and the guard shot up the jeep. Lemay stepped out of the jeep and chastised the guard for missing him with all the shots fired."

Billy laughed, "Stop feeding Frank those war stories. He may actually believe you."

Don looked at Frank, "You believe me, right?"

Frank snickered, "Yeah, sure."

The drove up to the hangar which had four sturdy looking doors for aircraft and a regular door in the middle of the hangar for humans to enter. Above this door was a narrow slot with a window set back into the concrete which looked to be about a couple feet thick. Billy said, "That's the control tower for this fortified hangar."

They entered the hangar and passed a fireman's pole next to some steps. They went up the stairs to the control room manned by two NCOs sitting before a panel which was bracketed with two revolvers on each end.

Frank was thinking, 'This is really cool but bizarre at the same time.'

Billy approached one of the NCOs, "Good afternoon. We are the GEEIA team that will install the communications system. Where would you like us to set it up?"

The NCO looked at Billy and without smiling said, "Follow me." He took them through a large room with beds on each side and proceeded to the far wall. He pointed and said, "Right here will be fine."

Don looked at the beds, "Are you sure? The system fans are pretty noisy and if pilots normally sleep here, they will be sure to complain."

The NCO scowled, "Damn, I knew this wouldn't be as easy as I was told. Wait here while I call the boss." He stalked away leaving them in the room.

Frank said, "We could ask the base engineers to have a wall installed between the system and the beds."

Billy agreed, "That would work. Let's get the equipment installed first so we know how much room we will need."

The other NCO walked into the room, "I heard 'Old Grouchy' on the phone with MAJ Olsen complaining about you guys. Don't pay too much attention to him. He has been like that since I got here. MAJ Olsen is pretty levelheaded though and I'm sure he will be open to suggestions."

"Good, we thought of a solution to ask the base engineers to put up a wall."

"That should work. Would you like a tour of our alert hangar while we are waiting for MAJ Olsen?"

"That would be great."

They headed to the stairs, and Frank asked, "Do you mind if I use the pole to go down?"

"Knock yourself out. The pilots use it all the time when we get an alert."

Don and Frank slid down the pole. The NCO smiled, "You are supposed to wrap your arms around the pole rather than using your hands. It's safer."

The NCO opened the door to one of the hangars, "Gentlemen, feast your eyes on the F-102 Delta Dagger. It is the world's first super-sonic jet interceptor. The primary mission of the F-102 is to intercept and destroy enemy aircraft. It is usually armed with six guided missiles and 24 unguided 2.75-inch rockets."

Frank stared in awe at this magnificent looking airplane. He almost forgot that Billy wanted him to ask about nuclear armament, "Sarge, is the Delta Dagger capable of carrying a nuclear weapon?"

The NCO looked surprised, "Yes, the F-102 can be armed with a Falcon nuclear missile but we only fly with a non-nuclear version of the missile for training purposes. The Germans would really get upset if we accidently fired off a nuke over their country."

An officer walked in the hangar, "Gentlemen, my name is MAJ

Olsen and I am the acting squadron commander. I will be your point of contact for this installation. TSGT Smith said there may be a problem."

"Major, I am Tech Sergeant Billy Black, team leader of the GEEIA team. Glad to make your acquaintance. I think we have a possible solution but need your approval and assistance. We are thinking that a wall with an access door could be built between the beds upstairs and the communication system. If you approve, could you make a request of the base engineers to construct it?"

"Sounds like a good plan. I will make the request today."

"We would like to install the equipment first to be sure there is enough room so there is no rush on our end."

"Great. I don't know how long it would take to have them respond. How long will it take to install the equipment?"

"We should have it done and checked out in about a week."

A couple F-102 pilots joined them, "Hi Sir, what's going on?"

MAJ Olsen said, "These are GEEIA guys from Ramstein who will be installing some equipment. They suggested putting a wall up so the noise of the system won't bother you guys."

"Great. We just wanted to offer up our ready room to them for coffee and snacks when they take breaks."

Billy smiled, "Thanks. I thought we would have to go all the way back to the base coffee shop."

After MAJ Olsen and the pilots left, Billy said, "Okay, let's go check out the nuke storage site so I can report back to LTC Garson."

They drove past the nuke storage site and it was about like the one they saw at Sembach. It was virtually impregnable.

Billy located a phone with a scrambler device and called LTC Garson, "Sir, we drove by the nuke storage site at Bitburg and it looks like a carbon copy of the one at Sembach, formidable and is well guarded."

"No surprise there but I was hoping for something that didn't look right. What about the alert facility?"

"We checked in and after being told where they wanted it installed, we highlighted a potential issue. The location is in the area where the pilots sleep. Frank suggested erecting a wall to separate the sleeping area from the comm system. MAJ Olsen, the acting squadron commander, approved the suggestion and agreed to coordinate with the base engineers to have it done. We were provided a tour of the facility and determined that although the F-102 can carry nuclear missiles, they train on a non-nuclear variant. It wasn't mentioned where they store the nukes in the event of an incursion by the Warsaw Pact. The pilots offered us the use of their ready room for breaks, so Frank and Don will make small talk with the pilots to learn more. I had the impression that they are bored stiff when not training in their aircraft."

LTC Garson chuckled, "I hear you. Pilots are only happy when they are flying. Speaking of flying, WO4 Woodson got back to me on how they plan to transport the MACE missiles and their nuke payloads. Initially they planned to go overland but with the potential threat, they decided to fly them from Sembach to Bitburg in C-141's."

"That's good to hear. Have you received any news from the rest of the guys?"

"Chuck and Soaring Eagle are working with Mary on surveilling COL LaCroix but so far, he hasn't done anything unusual. MAJ Best passed on Chuck's suggestion to the BND to monitor the taxi driver, Hans Glick in addition to Lund. He reported that they have not yet identified who Lund reports to but are eliminating folks one by one who reside in the *gasthaus*."

Billy smiled, "By *eliminating*, I take it you mean no longer suspected, right?"

Laughing LTC Garson said, "Yeah, I guess I could have used a better choice of words."

Since they finished the installation and did not discover anything suspicious at Bitburg, they returned to Ramstein to await further orders from LTC Garson.

CHAPTER 41
Ramstein, Germany

The next morning Frank thought back to what the voice in his head said about doing some research and had an idea. He boarded the base shuttle bus for Kaiserslautern which had a large concentration of U.S. Army soldiers and dependents. They had a decent library and since he had off for the weekend, he planned to visit the library and some bookstores. He was going to see if he could learn more about Sembach AB. He couldn't figure out what the Soviets and French had planned and though he might learn something from reading about the history of Sembach AB.

He went to the library first and with the help of the librarian, found the section that dealt with the history of Sembach. There was only one book that dealt with the history of the area that contained Kaiserslautern, Sembach and several other towns. He read that after World War I, French occupation troops had built an airfield at Sembach whose facilities included 10 sheet-iron barracks and over 20 canvas topped wooden hangars. They abandoned the airfield in 1930 as part of a general withdrawal of French occupation troops from the left bank of the Rhine River. In 1939, the German *Luftwaffe* used the airfield as a fighter base. The original French facilities were gone, so the Germans constructed temporary buildings connected by tunnels but abandoned it in 1940 after France had surrendered at the start of World War II. In 1950, the French constructed a modern airfield despite resistance from German farmers who wanted it kept for farming. An 8,500 concrete runway and taxiways were completed in 1951. Although in the French zone of occupation, it was intended to be used by NATO forces and in particular, to be an American airbase. In 1952, surveys were conducted to build barracks buildings. German farmers protested even more vehemently than before, saying the site being considered was ideal farmland. A compromise was agreed on to build the barracks on a different site that was somewhat sandy and not desirable as farmland.

Frank thought, "Tunnels?" He wondered where they were and if they were still there. He asked the librarian if there were copies available of the surveys done over the years. She did not know and suggested he may find them in the German state survey office. Sembach AB is located in the *Rhineland-Pfaltz* state so she gave him the address and phone number but said since its Saturday, she did not think it was open. He called and got a recording that confirmed that the office was not open on the weekend.

He took the shuttle bus back to Ramstein, walked to the SCIF and called Mary Wright in Strasbourg. He could have used the phone in the orderly room of the GEEIA squadron but didn't want to chance someone overhearing him.

She answered, "Hello."

"Hi Mary. Do you have a scrambler devise for your phone?"

"Yes, wait a second. Okay, all set."

"I would like to discuss some info with you that I found on Sembach before I alert the rest of the team."

"How are you too," she laughed.

"Sorry, I guess I could have been more civil. How are you?"

"Lonely and wanting to see you again. I would ask you to come down to Strasbourg, but Chuck and Soaring Eagle have been keeping me so busy I only get back to my room to sleep."

"Uh-oh, did I wake you?"

"I needed to get up anyway. I have wash to do before they call me again. Anyway, how can I help?"

He told her about his morning in the library and asked what she thought of his findings.

"Have you thought about asking Chuck? He could check with Langley to see if they have info on any tunnels."

"Good idea. I was going to check it out by myself to see if the tunnels even exist before getting the rest of the team involved but your idea could save time. Can you get in touch with him today?"

"Yes, he and Soaring Eagle are staying at the *Hotel Fountainebleu*. I will ask them to meet me at the consulate in an hour. Can we get in touch with you at this number?"

"Yes. I will grab some lunch and will be back here in an hour."

Frank gave her the number and headed for the cafeteria to get an egg burger.

The phone in the SCIF rang about an hour and a half later.

"Hello"

"Hi Frank." It was Chuck, "What is this about there being tunnels at Sembach?"

Frank explained, "According to what I read in the library, the Germans planned to use Sembach as a reserve airfield at the start of World War II. They hastily built flimsy buildings and flight faculties connected by tunnels to serve as protection in the event of an air attack. However, they abandoned Sembach shortly after the French surrendered in 1940. When French occupation troops rebuilt the airfield in 1951, I couldn't find any reference to tunnels in any of the documentation associated with that construction or any since. I was hoping there were survey notes that referenced the tunnels if they still exist."

"So, you think this may have something to do with the Soviet interest in Sembach?"

"It may but since we didn't see anything suspicious when we were there a couple weeks ago, I was looking for something that was not so obvious."

"Okay, there has been some tunnels found in other places that the Germans built during the war, but this is the first I heard of any at Sembach. I will ask Langley to research it, but the BND might be a better source. LTC Garson is coming down to Strasbourg this afternoon so I will ask him if I can request the BND to look into it."

Mary asked, "How was your trip to Bitburg?"

"Interesting. We installed a communication system in an Alert Facility for F-102 Delta Daggers. The facility is a concrete hanger for four aircraft. I don't know what kind of concrete they used to build it, but our Ramset stud driver couldn't penetrate it. We had to set the studs the old-fashioned way using a hammer and a star drill."

Mary laughed, "Ramset? I don't know what that is but don't think it would be of interest. What about the storage site?"

Frank could hear Chuck and Soaring Eagle laughing in the background. He said, "Oh, yeah, our surveillance of the storage sites revealed nothing unusual. Have you guys learned anything new?"

"Well, we have been surveilling COL LaCroix. Chuck has set up a tap on his phone after seeing Horst do it in Ramstein. So far, we haven't heard anything of interest. LaCroix's wife called and is upset about her brother Francois being arrested and has asked him to find out what he can. LaCroix is smart enough not to push SDECE or he may find himself being looked at harder by them. He doesn't seem to know that the BND has Francois now, not the SDECE, but we have no doubt that he soon will."

Chuck came back on the phone, "Okay, regarding the tunnels

at Sembach, I put in a call to Langley and they said they will get back to me in about four hours. Will you be at this phone later?"

Frank looked at his watch, "I suggest we plan to talk at 1800. That will give Langley five hours but don't tell them."

Chuck laughed, "That works for us."

The phone rang at 1800 on the dot. Chuck said, "Hi Frank. I have good news and bad news. The good news is that Langley found some documentation that confirms that tunnels were built at Sembach by the Germans between buildings at the beginning of World War II. The bad news is that they can't find any drawings that show where they are, and the buildings no longer exist. They have contacted the BND and requested assistance."

"I was thinking that maybe we could ask WO4 Woodson if he heard any rumors of tunnels at Sembach. He might have heard about some locals talking about them."

"That's a good idea. Hang on the line and I'll call him right now."

Frank hung on for about an hour and started thinking about hanging up when Chuck came back on the line. "Sorry for the delay. WO4 Woodson had to round up the base engineer since he was off this weekend. They rummaged through some old drawings, but they only dated back to the French construction in 1951. The base engineer suggested asking the Germans or the French to look in their archives. I told him we have put in a request to the BND. We will see what we can find in Strasbourg."

"Darn. I didn't think this would get so involved."

"No problem. As Mary said, we are just monitoring COL LaCroix and we only have heard idle chit chat so far."

CHAPTER 42
Karlsruhe, Germany

Oleg was being treated as well as could be expected given that he was a virtual prisoner of war. The BND held daily interviews with him on details of his life from boyhood in Bremen to spying for the Soviet Union. He could not call the interviews interrogations since he could not detect them trying to trap him into lying. His mouth had healed from the teeth extractions and he was finally able to move his jaw without wincing. He was not held in a cell but had two rooms to himself, a bedroom and a living room. He did not have a kitchen but was provided three meals a day and two beers after dinner. He was also provided books to read and occasionally a newspaper with some pages missing, presumably these pages contained something he was not permitted to see.

Oleg heard the lock on his door being disengaged and in walked the man Oleg now knew as Fritz. He thought that it was Fritz who wore the hood when he was first interrogated and tortured. Fritz Brenner was a BND interrogator who was born in 1939. His father was a German officer who was involved in the plot to kill Hitler and was arrested by the Gestapo. He was awaiting sentencing in a prison near Stuttgart when the Nazi guards were replaced by American soldiers and he was eventually released.

"Good morning Oleg. How are you this morning?" said Fritz in

German.

"I am doing fine. What shall we talk about today?"

"Well, we are going to talk about when your father was killed. There seems to be a discrepancy in what you told us before and you know that causes us some concern."

"I don't understand. What kind of discrepancy?"

"Before we get to that, please tell me in excruciating detail what happened that day."

Oleg was nervous that Fritz was trying to catch him in a lie and focused his mind on that dreadful day, "My father and I were going to a food distribution warehouse to beg for food and water. We saw a German patrol turning a corner and my father pushed me into a bombed out building and told me to hide. I saw the Germans stop my father and ask for his papers. As I was looking past the Germans, I saw some British soldiers approaching and I heard a shot ring out. I ducked my head when bullets started hitting the building I was hiding in and the Germans retreated. I waited until the British soldiers passed by me to chase the Germans and then I saw my father lying on the ground. I ran to him, but he had been hit in the head and was dead."

"Did you actually see your father being shot?"

"Yes, well not really, but it had to be the British who started shooting at the Germans talking to my father."

"That's the discrepancy. When you first told us your father

was killed by the British, you said you witnessed it. We now know that was not true. Did you know that the Germans were SS troops and they filmed executions as proof to their superiors?"

"Executions? I don't understand."

"Your father was executed by the SS. German *Gestapo* records indicate that they captured a Soviet spy a week before your father was executed and under torture the spy provided them a list of names of Soviet agents in Bremen. His name was Alek Popov."

"What! He was my father's friend. He would never tell them my father was a traitor."

"I'm sorry but under torture, people will do almost anything to make it stop."

"I don't believe it!"

"I have the film of the execution. Would you like to see it?"

"Yes! There has to be a mistake."

Oleg watched the film. He saw a German officer looking at his father's papers, then draw his 9mm Luger and shoot his father in the head. Almost simultaneously, he saw the Germans ducking and looking around in confusion as the British opened fire. The film was suddenly jerky and continued as the cameraman appeared to be running, then the film ended. Oleg's eyes began tearing up and he felt like he was eight years old again. He felt the same hopelessness that he felt that day so many years ago. He started crying and dropped his head toward his lap. He heard Fritz stop the projector and leave the room.

The next morning, Fritz entered Oleg's room and asked, "Are you okay?"

Oleg nodded, "Yes, I can't believe that I thought the British had killed my father and all along, it was the Germans."

"Well, that was because the Soviets told them he was a spy. I hate to ask, but do you think your father may have been a spy?"

Oleg looked shocked, "My father was a baker, what could he have spied on? He didn't know any secrets or have access to them."

Fritz said, "He may have been duped by Popov. Your father may have provided information of troop movements without knowing he was doing it."

"My father knew nothing about troop movements. How would he possibly know?"

"When German troops are alerted to being deployed, one of the last things they do is to stock up on *brot*. Your father would be happy to sell so much bread and likely tell his friends, including Popov."

Oleg thought back to when he had used a similar ploy with Greta and Otto in Bremen to get information on activities in Hulseberg. He also knew the Soviets had killed them to keep his identity secret. Now he learned they also had a hand in killing his father and he felt sick about spying for them.

He looked at Fritz, "I am sorry I agreed to work for them. I even joined the communist party to show my loyalty."

"You were played, and you are not the first."

"I am lost. I am a German citizen who was born to a Russian family. Now I don't feel like I belong to either. I am almost looking forward to being shot as a traitor."

Fritz smiled since he felt this could be the first step in turning a Soviet agent to work for the BND.

CHAPTER 43
Ramstein, Germany

Frank heard a knock on his door as he was getting dressed in the morning. He opened the door and saw an airman standing there who said, "You have a call in the orderly room from TSGT Black."

Frank quickly finished dressing and sprinted down the stairs to the orderly room. He picked up the receiver, "Airman Logan speaking."

Billy said, "Hi Frank. Can you rustle up Gerhardt and meet Don and I in front of your barracks in about an hour. Get some breakfast and dress in civvies. We are going on a quick trip but will be back this evening so there is no need to pack. Is there any reason why you can't be there?"

"Nope. See you in an hour."

"Out here" Billy said, and the line went dead.

Frank went to Gerhardt's room and they both went to the cafeteria for breakfast.

Gerhardt said, "So what's up?"

"We will have to wait for Billy to pick us up to find out."

They were standing in front of the barracks an hour later when

Don drove up and parked his car. He came over to Frank and asked, "Do you know what's going on?"

Frank was surprised, "No, I thought you might know."

A few minutes later, Billy drove up and Don got in the in the passenger seat. Frank and Gerhardt got in the back seat and Billy headed for the front gate of Ramstein AB. He looked in the rear-view mirror, "Sorry for the late notice. LTC Garson called me this morning and told me that MG Stone and General, excuse me, *Herr* Gehlen want to meet with us in Wiesbaden after lunch. I don't know what it's about, so we will all find out together."

Wiesbaden, Germany

They parked in front of the Headquarters GEEIA European Region at Wiesbaden Air Force Base. Parking was difficult here but LTC Garson arranged for a reserved spot for them. They called him from the lobby, and he met them there.

"Welcome to HQ. It's now 1130, so let's get some lunch in the cafeteria before we meet with MG Stone at 1300."

Frank checked the menu for an egg burger, but it seemed like the only place he found it so far was at Ramstein AB and the consulate at Strasbourg. He ordered a tuna salad sandwich and coffee. He saw Chuck, Soaring Eagle and Mary come into the cafeteria. "Over here," he called to them.

Billy said, "It looks like old home week seeing you guys again."

Mary slid into the seat next to Frank. She smiled, "Hi, great to see you again." He resisted the impulse to hold hands with her as the whole table was looking at them. He thought, 'They know.'

LTC Garson looked at his watch, "Okay, finish your meal and let's go. We don't want to keep the General waiting." When they got upstairs, the executive officer, or XO as they were called, told them that MG Stone was running a little late. No surprise there, generals are always running late because whoever was in there, like everyone else, wanted as much face time with the General as possible. They waited about twenty minutes when the XO called them, "The General will see you now."

MG Stone was sitting at the conference table with General Gehlen and MAJ Best. The conference table only seated seven, so as the junior guys in the room, he and Gerhardt were relegated to a seat against the wall behind Billy and Don. The XO brought in coffee and enough mugs for everyone and then departed, closing the door behind him.

MG Stone addressed the group, "*Herr* Gehlen asked that I host this meeting to bring everyone up to speed on his interrogation of Francois Langevin and the information he has learned. LTC Garson suggested we meet at GEEIA HQ instead of my office at Lindsey Air Station since it would be less noticeable for TSGT Black's GEEIA team to have a meeting here."

He turned to General Gehlen who said, "Langevin, as you probably know, is COL LaCroix's brother-in-law which led us to suspect COL LaCroix might be involved in whatever is going on. Langevin however, told us he collects the intercepted scrambled data from Oleg Pavlov and provides it to Jean Monsate, a civilian who works for COL LaCroix. Monsate has access to the device in COL LaCroix's office to unscramble it. He then provides the unscrambled data to Ivan Kraskov. We asked him what Kraskov was interested in learning and he told us he was not cleared to know but he thought it was to confirm that COL LaCroix did not suspect whatever was going on. We coordinated with Mary, Chuck and Soaring Eagle and they confirmed that they did not observe COL LaCroix doing anything unusual."

Chuck interrupted, "We are now quietly investigating Jean Monsate."

Gehlen frowned, "I was getting to that." Chuck muttered an apology.

"As I was saying, we also learned from Langevin that he and Monsate were both sympathetic to the aims of the French communist party (FCP). The FCP emerged around 1920 and in a few years, had members elected to the French parliament. The party leader, Maurice Thorez, encouraged a Stalinist alignment of the party which grew in popular support after the great depression and won the parliamentary elections in 1936. However, the invasion of Poland by the Germans and Soviets in 1939, and the French communist party support for the Soviets, caused the party to be outlawed by France and many of its members jailed. Thorez was drafted into the army when France declared war against Germany but instead fled to Moscow. He was sentenced to death, *in abstentia*, for desertion and lost his citizenship. When the Germans invaded the Soviet Union, the FCP were predominant in the *Maqui*, the French resistance group, and violently engaged the occupying Germans in a guerilla war until liberation in 1945. As a result, the FCP became the largest political party in France because of its anti-Nazi resistance movement in the war. Thorez was pardoned by France and shortly after his return from Moscow, his citizenship was restored. He was subsequently elected to a leadership role in French politics. France soon became wary of Soviet influence in their country and the FCP lost popular support. Thorez stayed as the leader of the FCP and an elected official in France until his death in 1964. He was idolized by the followers and many of them sought vindication by supporting candidate Francois Mitterand to be President of France in 1965 instead of Charles de Gaulle. However, Charles de Gaulle won the election. The FCP, and in particular, Thorez followers, had been marginalized and in retaliation, fomented widespread protests by students."

LTC Garson said, "If I understand this, you are establishing a motive for the cooperation of the Soviets and the French communists to escalate the resistance to a higher level, correct?"

General Gehlen replied, "Precisely. I don't think Francois Langevin knows what is being planned and probably Jean Monsate doesn't either. They seem to be little more than middlemen in this operation. We need to know who the mastermind is in the FCP and monitoring Monsate is our only link at this point. I can provide surveillance with our Watchers but would rather not provide any technical support that may be tracked back to the BND and endanger our relationship with France. Can you provide that Colonel?"

LTC Garson looked at Billy, "Looks like your GEEIA team is up at bat but this must be handled off the books, so to speak, and not as part of a GEEIA project."

Billy looked at his team, "I am up for it, but I would rather you guys volunteer than be ordered to do it." Almost in unison, Gerhardt, Frank and Don nodded assent. "Good. We will start by establishing taps on Monsate's home and office phones. The next logical step will be to tap the local FCP office phone and the phones of all the commies in that office. I don't expect them to use VHF or UHF radios, but we need to take the intercepting devices if they do."

Chuck added, "Soaring Eagle and I can break into the FCP office and plant bugs. We will look around to see if they are dumb enough to leave any incriminating evidence. We can also check to see if they have any radios there."

Mary said, "I can arrange for consulate support as needed."

MG Stone looked pleased, "With that, I will provide my sage advice. Don't get caught!"

The GEEIA team returned to Ramstein AB that evening with Chuck and Soaring Eagle. The next morning, Horst provided refresher training to the team on the various techniques of planting bugs and tapping French phones. It was similar to techniques Frank learned from Soaring Eagle at Keesler AFB, but the French junction boxes were unfamiliar to him. Planting bugs in electric outlets was straight forward since the bugs were adapted by Horst to be compatible with the power provided by the French electric company.

CHAPTER 44
Strasbourg, France

Chuck arranged to get two non-descript cars with French license plates for their trip. They departed Ramstein and drove straight to Strasbourg. Mary had the same suite reserved for them at the *Hotel Fountainebleu* that they used on the previous visit. They split up into teams to set up the taps on the phones. Billy, Frank and Soaring Eagle took the task to tap Jean Monsate's home phone and plant bugs. Gerhardt, Chuck and Don were going to do the same at Monsates's office.

Mary Wright scheduled a social at the consulate and invited COL LaCroix and Jean Monsate. When they showed up, it was well after sundown. Billy contacted the BND Watcher and ascertained that Monsate's neighborhood was not being surveilled by anyone else. Billy, Frank and Soaring Eagle drove over to Monsate's house and waited for the signal from the Watchers that all was quiet. Monsate was not married nor did he have a dog which might have been a problem. They did not know if Monsate had an alarm system, so they disconnected the power to his house and Soaring Eagle picked the lock on his back door. Billy sat outside the house in one of the non-descript cars and stayed in contact with Frank over handheld radios to warn them if Monsate made an unscheduled return to the house, or worse, a security team showed up. Soaring Eagle inserted the bugs into the outlets and Frank searched the house for any radios but found none. Frank searched Monsate's desk for his address book and took pictures of each page. He looked at documents that were in the desk, but they were of no apparent use to them. He photographed them anyway and carefully placed them back in the same place he got them. On their way out, they reset the electric clocks throughout the house and turned the power back on. They then located the telephone junction box outside and tapped Monsates's phone. The Watchers would monitor the bugs and the phone tap.

Frank turned to Billy and Soaring Eagle, "Man that was easier than I thought, and it only took fifteen minutes."

Billy laughed, "You guys did well. Let's check to see how Chuck, Gerhardt and Don made out."

They drove back to the hotel and went up to the suite. Chuck, Gerhardt and Don were sitting at the table in the common area looking at the drawing of the office layout they put together.

Billy asked, "So how does it look?"

Chuck said, "Well, getting to the junction box was easy enough but planting bugs may be harder. They posted a guard inside that we were not expecting. We might have barged in on him if we had not seen him escort the cleaning crew out."

Don looked up from the drawing, "We were looking at the layout to see if we could somehow distract him."

Mary.

Frank started at the voice, composed himself and said, "We could ask Mary if she could knock on the door after the office closes tomorrow night. The guard would have to disengage any alarm system to open the door and give us time to plant the bugs. It only took us fifteen minutes at Monsate's home."

Chuck said, "That might work. Don and Gerhardt checked the lock on the back door, and we could get in pretty quick."

Chuck called Mary and she agreed to try to distract the guard. She said, "The social will probably run past midnight as diplomats like free booze and *hors d'oeuvres*. I will call you when the consulate general lets me wrap this up."

Quickly changing clothes upon arrival at her apartment, Mary then drove to Jean Monsate's office and knocked hard on the door. She wore a low-cut blouse and a very short skirt and completed her outfit with a wig and smoked glasses popular in France at the time. She hoped the guard would focus on her body rather than her face which most Frenchmen were prone to do. That way he would have a difficult time describing her if asked.

The guard came to the door and waved her away mouthing, "the office is closed". Mary feigned fear and frantically looked behind her, imploring the guard, "Please open the door". The guard looked in the direction that Mary was looking and, very reluctantly, finally disengaged the alarm and opened the door a crack.

"We are closed. Come back tomorrow." The guard said in French.

Mary pleaded with him in French, "*S'il vous plait*, a man is following me, and I am scared. Can you call me a taxi?"

He looked at her breasts and slid his eyes down her body, then opened the door and motioned her to enter. He never took his eyes off her body while he dialed for a taxi.

Chuck answered, "*Taxi Parsien*", in a faux Middle Eastern accent. He was sitting next to one of the BND Watchers who was close to laughing out loud at his accent. The guard made a disgusting sound and asked. "Please send a taxi to 24 *Rue St. Germain* as soon as possible."

Chuck told the guard he would be there in ten minutes.

The guard turned to Mary and said, "Damn foreigners."

Mary kept talking to the guard in a near hysterical voice describing the man who she claimed was following her. The guard stared at her breasts swaying back and forth as she waved her arms up and down in exaggerated motions. When she sat down, he stared at her legs. Meanwhile, Gerhardt aligned the last of the tumblers in the locks and it clicked opened. He gently pushed on the door and it did not make any squeaking noises. He heard Mary talking loudly and was grateful for the noise she was making. The door slid open all the way. He and Don tiptoed inside to Monsate's office. Don stayed near the office door and Gerhardt inserted a bug in each of two outlets in the room. Six minutes later, they made their way to the back door and re-engaged the locks.

Chuck saw them exit so started up the taxi he had 'borrowed' and drove to the front of the office. The guard opened the door for Mary and after giving him a peck on the cheek, she climbed into the back seat of the taxi, lifting her skirt a little higher for the guard to get a view.

Chuck said, "Nice outfit and with that wig and glasses, I wasn't sure it was you."

She smiled, "That was the plan."

Chuck provided the Watchers a list of words that he hoped to hear from the phone taps and bugs. He was rewarded two days later when one of the Watchers called and said he heard the word 'Sembach' on one of the bugs in Monsate's office. Chuck collected the tape and met the rest of the team in the consulate SCIF.

The tape captured a conversation between Monsate and someone in his office. The building where Monsate had his office was not in the same building as COL LaCroix. COL LaCroix was in a French government building while Monsate had his office in a public building with other tenants. Chuck loaded the tape in a player, and they listened to the conversation. A paper with a translation was provided to all who did not speak French.

"Jean, may I come in? I have the information that you asked for last week about Sembach."

"Please close the door and lower your voice."

"Sorry. Anyway, I found the tunnel plans in a French Army warehouse. Apparently, the French Army collected every document at Sembach when they occupied the base after World War II. It doesn't seem like anyone has looked at the documents since then or maybe even at all. The plans were in a huge trunk with other documents and the dust on top was thick."

"When can you go and check to see if the tunnels are accessible?"

"I plan to leave in the morning. It looks like one of the tunnels extends beyond the current fence around the base. I will be in touch later tomorrow."

"Good Henri. Keep me posted."

Chuck turned off the tape player. "There was no more on Sembach. I alerted WO4 Woodson who will start looking but reminded me that the base covers a large area and if the alleged tunnel is far beyond the fence, it might be a long time before he discovers it. He asked if we had the tunnel plans, which of course, we don't."

Frank said, "Maybe we don't need them. If Henri resides in the building, we might be able to identify him and find out if he owns a car. A French license plate will stick out a bit in Germany."

Chuck smiled, "I checked to see if there is anyone in the building with the first name of Henri but no luck."

Don suggested, "Maybe we can locate the French Army warehouse that stores old documents and maybe there is a sign in sheet that identifies whoever entered in the last week."

Mary said, "I might be able to help with that. I will make a couple calls."

Chuck turned to Billy, "I suggest we leave Gerhardt here to coordinate with the BND Watcher and work with Mary on locating the warehouse. The rest of us will check out of the hotel and hotfoot it over to Sembach."

Billy looked at Gerhardt who nodded okay, "Agreed."

CHAPTER 45
Karlsruhe, Germany

Henri Deveraux hated going to Germany, even if it was to contribute to the success of the mission of saving France from the excesses of de Gaulle and his goddamn Fifth Republic. If it wasn't for men like his father who really drove the Germans out of France, France would still be occupied. His father was a leader in the *Maqui*, the French resistance movement, during the war and a devout communist. He believed France should have adopted a communist philosophy after the war, but de Gaulle banned the FCP from holding government positions in 1947 due to the concern over Soviet influence in French affairs. Henri's father became deeply depressed over what he perceived as a misled France. He committed suicide when Henri was five years old and his mother, herself a devout communist, reverted to her maiden name. Henri's mother focused all her attention on him and pushed him to achieve excellent grades in school. That enabled him to be accepted and graduate from Saint Cyr, the French military academy. Henri thought about formally joining the FCP and mentioned it to his friend, Jean Monsate, who cautioned him to not make it public that he was a communist. Monsate told him that they should work together within the French government to eventually bring the FCP to power in France.

Monsate told Henri that de Gaulle was the reason the FCP was banned and something had to be done to get rid of him. Monsate became close friends with now COL LaCroix and after resigning from the French Army, worked as a confidant of COL LaCroix. Henri was assigned to an engineering battalion and left the army after being passed over three times for promotion to Captain. He formed his own company which focused on building facilities which his friend Monsate helped make successful by issuing contracts to him from the army.

Henri drove his own car to Karlsruhe where he met a man that Monsate told him he could trust. He saw the man standing in front of the *Bahnhof* wearing a black leather coat and a Bavarian style hat with a poppy in the brim, just as Monsate said he would look. He parked his car in the *Bahnhof* parking garage and strolled up to the man.

"*Excusez moi, parlez vous francais?*"

The man sneered, "*Nein*".

Continuing in French, Henri said, "Where can I rent a car?"

The man handed Henri a driver's license in the name of Hans Lieppman and said in German, "How good do you speak German?"

"*Zehr gut.*"

The man sneered again, "You have the accent of someone from Strasbourg."

Henri shrugged his shoulders. They entered the *Bahnhof* and proceeded to a car rental agency. "This is as far as I go. Use the license I gave you and be sure you get a car with German license plates. Insist on paying cash and when you return the car, destroy the driver's license. Good luck."

CHAPTER 46
Sembach, Germany

The GEEIA/CIA team arrived at Sembach AB and checked in with WO4 Woodson at the conference room they met in the last time they were there.

"Any luck with finding the tunnel?" Billy said.

WO4 Woodson shook his head, "No, but the Air Commandos have agreed to help. I was thinking of asking the local *Burgomeister* if he knew of any tunnels but wanted to check with you guys to see if it was too sensitive."

Chuck shook his head, "Let's hold off on that for now. We don't want to stir up the locals if we don't have to."

"Okay," Woodson said as he laid out a map on the table in the conference room, "This is the layout of the air base and the proximity of the town of Sembach. As you can see, the base perimeter is right up against the town on the north side and by farmland on the other three sides. We drove along the perimeter on all four sides several times but didn't see anything that looks like an entrance to a tunnel. We really didn't expect to see anything but wanted to rule out the obvious. You say the tunnels were built about 25 years ago, right?"

Chuck said, "Yes, maybe even over 25 years ago. We really don't know if they were well constructed or not. They may not even exist but the data the BND confiscated at Helmstedt indicates an interest in finding them. We don't know why, precisely, but may have something to do with a plan to infiltrate Sembach and we want to put an end to it."

Billy asked, "Did you see anything out of the ordinary around the perimeter like a vehicle with French tags?"

Woodson smiled, "No. I think we would have spotted that. The base has a fair amount of traffic with airmen and especially their families going on and off the base. I checked visitor logs for the past few days and found nothing unusual there. There are several contractors here helping us to pack up the MACE missiles for transport to Bitburg, but they were expected."

Chuck looked at Billy, "We have two cars with French tags that I can outfit with German tags in about an hour. I suggest we conduct a grid search for the next few days of the area outside the base to see if anything pops. What do you think?"

"Sounds good. Don, take Frank and Soaring Eagle and scout out the three sides with the farmland. Chuck, you and I will search the town. Be on the lookout for any vehicle that looks suspicious."

When Chuck showed up with the tags from Kaiserslautern, Frank remarked, "Is there any significance to the first letters being KA?"

Chuck smiled, "Sembach is in the Kaiserslautern, Rhineland Palatinate, and has the prefix code KA as the first two letters of the license plate. Other regions and cities have up to three letters depending on their size generally. Bigger cities, like Berlin for example, only have one letter, B."

"That's cool. Maybe we should recommend that the USA plates here begin with the first two letters of the state the Serviceman is from. It might help boost morale."

Billy laughed, "That would really confuse the admin weenies who have to keep track of such things."

Frank got the job of switching plates and they started their search. Don drove, and they stopped often to check out likely spots. The farmland around the base was lightly populated but they noticed curtains being drawn aside on many of the houses they passed.

A car approached them, and Frank noticed the license plate had the prefix KL. He asked Soaring Eagle, "Where is that car from with a KL on the plate?"

"Karlsruhe."

Just then, the car turned into a driveway of a house. "He must be visiting someone."

They continued their search until it got dark and went back to the base. Chuck and Billy were waiting in the conference room.

"Any luck?" said Chuck.

Soaring Eagle answered, "Nope and we covered about half the

farmland out to about a kilometer. Maybe we'll get lucky tomorrow."

"We didn't see anything unusual in the town of Sembach either but who knows what might be in any of the houses. I sure wish we had the layout of the tunnel locations that were in that French Army warehouse."

They completed the grid search the next day and met with WO4 Woodson in the conference room. Chuck looked frustrated, "Okay Chief, I agree to ask the Sembach *Burgomeister* if he has knowledge of any tunnels built by the Germans."

WO4 Woodson called the *Burgomeister* but he said he heard of that rumor but no one in town knew of any tunnels.

Billy said, "Let's wrap up here and head back to Strasbourg."

Chuck suggested, "Maybe we should leave Soaring Eagle and Frank here to continue looking for Henri."

Billy looked to WO4 Woodson. "Is that okay?"

"I think they should lodge in a *gasthaus* in town because MAJ Burns is going to wonder why they are still here. I will relay any of your instructions and intel to them. Also, they can use the phones to stay in touch with you."

CHAPTER 47
Sembach, Germany

Henri Deveraux pulled into the driveway of the farmhouse and looked back at the car with the two men in it but decided they were no threat when he saw them continue down the road.

He checked the plat he had from the French warehouse to confirm that he was at the tunnel entrance but was surprised to see that a house was built on the location. He looked closer and could see that the house rested on a concrete slab that looked much older than the house. The door of the house opened, and a man stared at him. The man was in his late forties, had a bit of a paunch and had a rose-colored tint to his face from many days in the sun.

"Can I help you?" the man said in German.

"*Guten Abend*, my name is Herr Lieppman and I am from the State Archives. Can I ask you a few questions about your house?"

The man looked a bit apprehensive but invited him in, "You have a strange accent."

"Yes, I was born in Strasbourg."

The man nodded and invited Henri into the house. They both

sat down in the living room. Henri couldn't see the whole house but since it was small, surmised it only had two bedrooms. A moment later, a woman entered the living room. "This is my wife. Now, what was it about our house?"

"Do you live here alone?"

"Yes, our only son is not interested in farming and lives in Berlin with this wife."

Henri was surprised that the man was so forthcoming and then realized that the man was disappointed in his son not wanting to be a farmer.

"Is your house built on an old concrete slab from the war?"

The man became very defensive, "We have done nothing wrong. This slab was supposedly built by the French when they occupied the old German airbase. I bought the property after the war ended and built this house on it."

"Do you know what the slab was originally used for?"

"No, the French tore down the buildings that used to be here before they sold the land to me. I presume the slab was what one of the buildings sat on."

"Good, that answers all my questions. Do you have a phone I can use to report in? I will reverse the charges."

The man looked relieved, "Yes, it is in the kitchen."

Henri waited until the man joined his wife in the living room and in as low a voice as he could talk, called Monsate to report. He got his secretary instead. "Is Jean available, this is Henri."

"Not here, he is in his other office." Henri knew that Jean had a small apartment located near his regular office that he used for sensitive work for the FCP. Jean told his secretary it was 'his other office'.

"Okay. I will call him there."

"Jean, this is Henri. The object we are looking for is under a slab of concrete that has a house sitting on it. What are your instructions?"

"Are you confident the tunnel is under the concrete?"

"It is on the coordinates that appears on the plat from the French Army warehouse. There is no way of really knowing if the tunnel still exists under the slab, but it looks like it hasn't been disturbed since the Germans abandoned the airfield."

"Okay. Can you stay near the phone you are calling from? I will get right back to you."

Henri hung up after giving Monsate the number. He went back to the man and woman in the living room and asked if he could stay for about ten minutes, so his boss could call back with instructions. The man looked concerned. "Is there a problem?"

"No, my boss had to go to another room to get your file, so we can close it out."

His wife said, "Would you like some tea and pastries while we wait?"

"Yes, thank you."

About a half hour later, the phone rang. The man picked it up and said, "There is no Henri here." He then turned to 'Herr Lieppman' and said, "Is your first name Henri?"

Henri jumped up, "Yes, thank you. It must be my boss."

The man handed Henri the phone.

"A team is on the way to break through the concrete. Take care of the occupants so that they cannot identify you."

Henri was glad that the operation was going to proceed. He liked the man and woman, but they were after all, Germans. When he went back to the living room, he took out a Walther 7.65mm PPK and shot both the man and woman in the head. He looked down at them and sarcastically said, "You should feel honored. You were shot with the same type pistol that your *Fuhrer*, Adolph Hitler, used to commit suicide."

CHAPTER 48
Sembach, Germany

Frank and Soaring Eagle checked into the *gasthaus* that WO4 Woodson recommended. The *gasthaus* had a large restaurant at the street level and they decided to have dinner. The restaurant was crowded, and they sat at the only empty table. The din of the customers ebbed, and they felt eyes looking at them.

Frank whispered, "Did we do something wrong?"

Soaring Eagle looked around, "If we did, I don't know what it was. Maybe they don't see many Americans in this *gasthaus* or we dress funny or both."

Frank laughed. The waitress ignored them. A man entered and walked over to their table and said something in German.

Frank said, "*Mien Deutch sprechen ist bisschen.*"

The man smiled and responded in accented English, "That explains it. Did you know that you are sitting at the *Stammtisch*? This is the regular table for the *burgomeister, forestmeister* and other officials of the town."

Frank and Soaring Eagle started to rise, and the man waved them down. "You are my guests tonight." He gestured to the waitress and held up three fingers. "*Drie Pils, Bitte.*"

He then turned to them, "I hope you like beer."

They both nodded. "You must be newly posted to Germany not to know of the *Stammtisch*. Where are you from in the states?"

Frank said "Pennsylvania" and Soaring Eagle said "Oklahoma."

Frank asked, "Which town official are you?"

"I am the *Jagermeister*. My name is Nils Haupmann."

Frank was confused, "I thought *Jagermeister* was a drink."

The man smiled, "Yes that is true. However, the name means Hunt Master. It is the title of the official in charge of hunting and game keeping. The term has been in use for many centuries in Germany. The inventor of the drink was an avid hunter and honored the profession by naming his new drink *Jagermeister*."

"Very interesting, I did not know that."

Soaring Eagle asked, "That sounds like what we call a game warden in the states."

"Not quite. The laws for hunting in Germany are very strict. Hunters must go through a rigorous training course that may take several months and pass a test of their knowledge of the law, identification of species and German hunting traditions. Hunters have to get permission and be assigned hunting locations by the local *Jagermeister*."

Frank asked, "So as the local *Jagermeister* how large is the area you are responsible for?"

"The primary hunting areas are the forests east and west of Sembach. Farms occupy most of the area north and south. Animals roam from the forests to the farms for food and water in the early evening through the early morning then return to bed down during the day. I am responsible for controlling over-hunting a particular area and as such, assign hunters an area or a blind from which to hunt."

"I imagine you are quite familiar with the area surrounding Sembach."

"Yes, would you like a tour of the hunting areas? I check with farmers on the edge of the forests to get an estimate of the numbers of animals they see regularly. I usually do this on monthly cycle, and you are invited to accompany me."

"I would be honored," said Frank and looked at Soaring Eagle who said, "Count me in too."

CHAPTER 49
Sembach, Germany

Henri opened the barn doors when the trucks arrived with the equipment to break through the concrete slab. He was surprised to see that they were Germans instead of the French that he expected Monsate to send. They left the barn and the German in charge walked around the house to look at the slab.

He turned to Henri, "We are going to set up in the center of the house where I think the entrance to the tunnel should be. I estimate about an hour to break through the concrete cap."

Henri nodded and said, "I will keep an eye out for any visitors or police."

The man nodded and told his men to start moving the drilling equipment into the house. No one came by the farmhouse and the cap was breached in ninety minutes. They found stairs leading down about thirty feet deep. The odor coming from the hole was putrid. The German provided Henri with what look like a fireman's mask and oxygen tank to strap on his back. They descended and found smooth concrete walls heading towards the air base. The tunnel was in much better shape than Henri expected. They used flashlights to see and dropped off battery powered night lights about every ten feet. The Germans had a wheeled device that measured distance and marked the tunnel 100-meter intervals as they proceeded.

Henri told them to stop at 951 meters.

"We should be under the ammo bunkers where the nuke warheads are stored."

The German nodded and assembled a portable drill to get through the tunnel ceiling. In about an hour, he broke through and the drill passed easily through dirt until it contacted the concrete at the bottom of the bunker.

"Are you sure nobody is in the bunker?"

Henri told the German, "The bunker is not occupied. I checked with our contact and he assured me that nobody will be in it."

The German turned to his men, "Go get the heavy drill so we can cut a hole big enough to climb through. Also, bring the big fans down so we can circulate the air in here."

Henri returned to the house to keep watch while the Germans cut a hole into the bunker. He thought again what Monsate had told him about the construction of the ammo bunker. The top and sides of the bunker were more sturdily built than the floor since the threat was to protect the ammo from aircraft and missiles striking the top of the bunker. No one apparently thought of an attack from below. He laughed while making another cup of tea and eating more of the pastries.

CHAPTER 50
Sembach, Germany

Jagermeister Nils Haupmann picked up Frank and Soaring Eagle at the *gasthaus* and they drove east toward the forest. Nils stopped at several farmhouses and chatted with the farmers. At one of the houses, as Nils was talking to the farmer, a young girl approached the car where Frank and Soaring Eagle were waiting.

She looked at them and said, "Nils said Americans you are. I study English in school and would like you, uh, say something to me to see if I understand. Thank you."

Frank said, "You speak English well. The grammar may need a little work, but I understand you. How old are you?"

The girl smiled, "Thank you. I am thirteen years. How old are you?"

"I am twenty-one years old."

She looked at Soaring Eagle. "I am thirty-one years old."

"Do you always say 'old' after you say your age?"

"Yes, that is standard in America. England may be different though."

Nils came out of the house. "Monica - are you practicing your

English?"

She smiled, "Yes. Will they be coming with you next month?"

"No, this is the only time."

The next stop they made, a young boy came running out of the house, "The Americans are here!" he yelled back to his father who was coming through the door of the house.

Nils laughed, "You are famous. I bet Monica called everyone she knows to tell them she met you."

At almost every stop they made that day, they were peppered with questions. Frank and Soaring Eagle were taking in the lay of the land as they went from house to house but saw nothing that would help them locate a tunnel.

Nils dropped them off at the *gasthaus*.

Frank said, "Thanks for the tour. Let us buy you dinner tonight to show our gratitude."

Nils smiled, "I can't accept. My wife is making dinner for you two and asked me to pick you up at seven o'clock tonight."

"Well, thank you very much. We will bring the wine."

"*Danke*. Heidi prefers a *qualitateswien* which is a nice *reisling* that will go well with dinner. Don't be talked into something more expensive because they are usually too sweet for our taste."

Frank turned to Soaring Eagle, "Okay, let's find a wine shop."

As they were walking to a wine shop Soaring Eagle said, "The tour was nice, but each farm was too far away from the base."

"Agree. I wonder how we might ask Nils if he heard about a tunnel in a way that would not make him suspicious of our motive."

"Maybe we tell him we heard a rumor about a tunnel from one of the airmen on the base."

Nils showed up promptly at seven o'clock to pick them up. Frank showed Nils the two bottles of wine that they bought. He nodded his approval. Nils lived on a farm just outside of the town of Sembach.

"Heidi is all excited and nervous about having Americans for dinner. She is excited because we never had any Americans over to the house and nervous because she hopes you will like what she prepared."

"I am sure we will like it."

Nils's house was not large. It had what looked like white stucco walls and a terra cotta roof. There was a barn in the rear of the house and a fenced in area with several cows. On the side of the house was a vegetable garden. All the fences were made of rough wood and the pattern was cross hatched. The windows were like those in the barracks. They opened sideways or tilted back with a handle on the side. In other words, it was a typical German house.

They were shown into a small dining room which overlooked the field with the cows and a small hill in the background. Heidi entered the dining room. She was an attractive woman with blond curly locks and a bright smile, "Welcome to our house. Would you like something to drink?"

Frank said, "We brought wine."

"I will chill it before dinner. Could I offer you some cognac or a beer?"

"Beer would be fine," Frank looked at Soaring Eagle who said, "Sounds good."

Nils said, "Let me show you the rest of the house."

After the tour, they returned to the dining room and the beers were set out on the table. "Heidi is finishing the dinner, so we will sit and talk, *ya*?"

"*Ya*. You have a very nice house. Have you lived here long?"

"It was built by my father. He was the previous *Jagermeister* and supplemented his income by farming. Both of my parents passed away in an automobile accident over two years ago. Heidi and I moved here from an apartment in Sembach."

Soaring Eagle asked, "One of the guys on the base mentioned a rumor that there was a tunnel built nearby. Have you heard this rumor?"

Nils said, "My father mentioned it, but nobody here knows of it. There is a farmhouse near the base that is built on a concrete slab that is different from all the other houses in the area, but they think it was a left-over foundation from another building. We passed it on our way here. I will point it out later when I take you back to the *gasthaus*."

Heidi served beef *Rouladen* with fried potatoes, green beans and a salad with a creamy dressing that Frank had not tasted before. The *Rouladen* she served was made from a thin slice of steak rolled with a filling of onions, bacon and pickles. She topped it off with a cheesecake that melted in your mouth like custard and was not real sweet. The dinner was delicious.

After they had eaten, Heidi cleared off the table and Nils brought out small glasses and filled them with cognac. He put a small plate of nuts and chocolate on the table. "This is good for digestion."

They sat around after dinner and talked about the differences between German and American life. Frank, who was raised in the city, asked Nils about life on a farm. Heidi joined them and asked about what women in America wore and what they usually cooked. Soaring Eagle had their rapt attention, including Frank's, when he started talking about life on an Indian reservation in Oklahoma. Frank started feeling sleepy from the food and alcohol.

Nils drove them back to the *gasthaus* and pointed out the house on the concrete foundation on the way. Frank had to really look hard to pick up the edges of the foundation. After Nils dropped them off, Frank told Soaring Eagle, "We should take a ride out to that farmhouse and talk to the owner."

Soaring Eagle nodded, "Tomorrow. I need to sleep off the dinner."

In the morning, Soaring Eagle was already sitting at a table in the *gasthaus* drinking a cup of coffee when Frank walked in for breakfast.

"I couldn't eat a bite after that dinner."

Frank laughed, "I hear you, but I think I can choke down one of those delicious pastries with my coffee."

On the drive out to the farmhouse with the concrete foundation, Frank said, "I'm sure glad you speak some German. I doubt that a farmer would have much need to learn English."

They pulled up to the house and knocked on the door. No one answered so Soaring Eagle said, "Maybe they are in the barn."

They walked around to the barn and opened one of the large doors. The barn was empty, and the farmer's tractor was jammed into one of the stalls which looked a bit odd.

Frank held his nose. "What is that stink?"

"It smells like burnt oil. Look at the truck tracks and the number of footprints in the dirt. Seems like there was a lot of work done here recently but on what?"

They left the barn and walked completely around it; then did the same to the house.

"It's kind of late in the year to be working in the garden but look at that pile of dirt. Kind of looks like a grave." They quickly looked at each other and nodded. They both pulled their weapons at the same time and cautiously approached the house.

Frank picked the lock on the back door as Soaring Eagle provided cover for him. They entered the kitchen and fanned out to the other rooms. Frank saw blood sprayed on the wall in the living room. Soaring Eagle walked in and said, "The rest of the house is empty but there is a big hole in the dining room floor." He looked at the blood spray on the wall and said, "Time to call Chuck and see how he wants to handle this."

Soaring Eagle took out his handkerchief and picked up the phone to call Chuck.

Chuck answered, and Soaring Eagle told him what they found. "Try not to leave any fingerprints but check out that hole. I will call the BND and request assistance. We will pack up here in Strasbourg and head back to Sembach. Can you give me directions to the farmhouse?"

"Yes, and you might want to ask the BND to bring some breathing devices. The odor from that hole is strong. I don't think we can go too far down it."

The BND showed up first. Frank saw that they brought masks and oxygen tanks. The BND operator in charge gave his men instructions to fan out around the house and barn to be sure the area was secured. He then told one of his men to dig up the suspected grave in the garden.

"Have you been in the house?" the BND operator asked.

Frank said, "Yes, there is a lot of blood sprayed on the living room wall and a large hole in the dining room that emits a foul odor. We tried not to touch anything, but we probably left some prints while searching the house."

The man assigned to the garden reported that he found two bodies – a man and a woman. They had both been shot in the head.

The BND operator motioned to his men to don the breathing devices and enter the house. He turned to Frank and Soaring Eagle, "Follow me and point out what you found."

They showed the operator the blood spray and the hole. He started down the ladder in the hole and they followed with weapons drawn. Someone had strung lights along the tunnel. They proceeded cautiously. They came to another ladder which led up into a hole in the ceiling of the tunnel. The BND operator sent one of his men further along the tunnel and another up the ladder into the hole.

The man who was sent further along the tunnel returned first, and said, "the tunnel ended in an open area that contained some heavy equipment that must have been left behind by whoever broke into the tunnel."

The man who was sent up the hole called down and said, "all

clear". They climbed up and found themselves in a large concrete bunker. Frank noticed a steel I-beam mounted on rails that ran the length of the ceiling of the bunker and a heavy-duty chain block and tackle mounted on the I-beam. There were several different types of munitions sitting in cradles on the floor. A lot of the cradles were empty, and he wondered how many and what type of munitions were stolen. He turned to Soaring Eagle, "We have to get in touch with WO4 Woodrow and tell him what we found and if he has access to the inventory of the munitions that were stored here."

WO4 Woodrow arrived about 45 minutes later carrying an envelope and had a scowl on his face.

"I have the inventory list but what the hell are all these armed civilians doing here. This bunker is classified and there will be hell to pay when MAJ Burns finds out."

Frank said, "I think this goes way beyond MAJ Burns. Can you look over the munitions and compare them to the inventory list?"

"Yes, but we need to clear the bunker of these civilians. You also need to get all the names of the BND team, so we can vet them."

The BND leader was not happy but understood. He contacted General Gehlen and obtained permission before releasing the names of his team. Frank wondered if the names given were really their real names…probably not.

WO4 Woodrow conducted the inventory and told Frank and Soaring Eagle, "Two MACE nuclear warheads are missing. They are the lightweight versions of the bomb but are still heavy. The saving grace is that an arming device is needed before they can be detonated."

"Where are the arming devices stored?"

"MAJ Burns has them in his safe and would only dispense them to the Launch Officers just before the warheads are inserted into the MACE missiles. When we train with the warheads, they are never armed so no accidents happen."

They went down into the tunnel and could see tracks in the tunnel floor made by the trolley found at the other end of the tunnel. They must have used the block and tackle mounted on the I-beam in the bunker to lower the warheads down into the tunnel and moved them along the tunnel on the trolley to the hole in the dining room. Other equipment found in the tunnel was probably used to raise the warheads out of the tunnel and then onto their trucks.

Frank wondered why they buried the German couple and had the thought that maybe they planned to return. He found the BND leader and told him that they should make the area look like they had not found the tunnel. The BND leader looked at him and said, "I think it's a little late for that, but I'll see what I can do."

LTC Garson arrived from Wiesbaden and Chuck Whelan arrived from Strasbourg. LTC Garson convened a meeting in the base conference room to update the group on what he heard from headquarters and to discuss options on their next move.

"I talked to MG Stone and told him that two nukes have been stolen and we need to inform MAJ Burns who has the arming devices. He agreed and told me he would call him. He also said he would request satellite imagery but don't hold your breath. It takes a while to process the data and that's if the satellite was looking at the area at the time when we suspect the trucks were here. I have contacted the folks who are charged with investigating nuclear events to help locate the trucks. They are fanning out throughout the area with devices that can pick up minute amounts of radiation. Again, don't hold your breath. They have limited resources and must cover an ever-enlarging area since we don't know which way the trucks went and how far away they might be. They are covering the *autobahns* primarily. Thanks to Frank's quick thinking that they might return, we have evacuated the area around the farmhouse and will leave a joint CIA/BND assault team in the barn. The BND has agreed to set up covert observation points in every direction from the farm. Comments?"

WO4 Woodrow said, "We should schedule a meeting with MAJ Burns to give him the details. Someone may need to access the bunker at any time and we need to control access."

"Good point. Can you set it up? Also, is there a sign in sheet when the bunker is accessed and who has the authority to approve access?"

"Yes, I will set it up and get the sign in sheet. MAJ Burns approves access to the bunker. All personnel who are approved have to be escorted by MAJ Burns, which would be rare, or one of the six launch officers or myself."

WO4 Woodrow called MAJ Burns and he showed up in the conference room about ten minutes later. He looked very upset and shouted at WO4 Woodrow, "This is all your fault. You have killed both of our careers and I am going to meet with the Judge Advocate to start the process to court martial you."

LTC Garson stared at MAJ Burns in disgust, "Calm down Major, this is not WO4 Woodrow's fault and it certainly is not about you and your career. I asked you here to provide details on what we know so far and to ensure that the arming devices are secure."

MAJ Burns looked nervous, "Sorry Colonel but I think Woodrow should be put under guard until this mess is sorted out."

"That's not going to happen. Please answer my question, are the arming devices accounted for and secure?"

"I will check when I get back to my office, sir."

"Go now and then return here."

MAJ Burns returned about 15 minutes later, "All devices are secure in my safe except for the one I provided to 1LT Alexander to conduct refresher training. All launch officers are required to conduct periodic training on the device and it's his turn."

"Please escort us to where 1LT Alexander is training."

They went to the Bachelor Officers Quarters where 1LT Alexander roomed.

MAJ Burns knocked on the door, "Kerry, it's MAJ Burns, can I come in?"

There was no answer so LTC Garson tried turning the knob and the door opened. The room was small with a government issued steel gray bed, table, chair and locker. 1LT Alexander was sprawled in the middle of the floor with his throat cut and was quite dead.

CHAPTER 51
Kaiserslautern, Germany

Henri followed the two trucks driven by the Germans in his rental car. They pulled into an abandoned warehouse in Kaiserslautern and parked in a high bay area. Henri Deveraux did not like the Germans he was working with to steal the nukes. He had to admit that they were very efficient, but they were rude to him. Being a Frenchman, he was well versed in being rude, but the Germans lost two wars to France and they should have been more respectful. He was also angry that one of the Germans dug a hole in the garden and buried the farmer and his wife. Dumb Germans! Too sentimental! Then he laughed to himself as he thought, 'Germans are anything but sentimental!' He was planning to just leave the farmer and his wife in the house, so no one would notice anything different. It would be just like a nosy neighbor to see the fresh turned dirt in the garden and knock on the door to chuckle at the folly of planting this late in the season. Then to top it off, the Germans complained to him about leaving their tools in the tunnel. He finally convinced them that they needed to move the nukes while they had the chance. Who knows who might come visiting? Besides, they could always come back and pick them up later if nobody discovered what they did at the farmhouse. His contact at Sembach assured him that no one would access the bunker, so it was unlikely that anyone would know the nukes were missing. Henri didn't really care if they got their tools or not since he had no intention of returning to the German couples' farmhouse. At least the tools couldn't be traced back to him or the FCP.

Jean Monsate was waiting in the warehouse and congratulated Henri with a hug and a kiss on each cheek, "Did you have difficulties?"

"No, everything worked out as we planned. How was the train ride?"

"My *faux* papers passed inspection and with the disguise I applied, no one would be able to identify me. I told my secretary that I would be working from home and was not to be disturbed."

Henri walked to where the trucks were parked and said to the German neo-Nazi leader, "This is where we part ways. I will provide the arming device when my comrades deliver it to me."

"I don't like it. Why do you not have the device here?"

"I told you before. If we stole the arming device before we accessed the warheads, it would alert the Americans. Besides, you don't need it until the American air show at Ramstein which is two days away."

The German leader grunted as Henri climbed into one of the trucks. Jean drove Henri's rental car and they left the warehouse. They drove in a circuitous route taking back roads where there was little or no traffic to be sure they were not followed. Henri turned off the back road to a dirt road that led to a barn located on a dead-end road outside of Kaiserslautern. As he approached it, the door to the barn opened and he drove in followed by Jean. The barn was in much better condition than the abandoned warehouse. There were six men in the barn who were all Frenchmen and belonged to the French Communist Party. "*Comrades*, we were totally successful and soon we will bring France under communist rule as it should have been done twenty years ago." The men in the barn cheered.

They moved the warhead from the German truck to another truck with U.S. Air Force markings. Henri and Jean left the barn and drove to Karlsruhe to turn in the rental car and retrieve Henri's car from the *Bahnhof* parking garage. Jean caught a train to Strasbourg from the *Bahnhof* and Henri returned to the barn to pick up the U.S. Air Force truck with the warhead in it. His comrades were in the process of disguising the warhead to look like a large hot water tank. When he was satisfied that the disguise would pass a cursory inspection, he changed clothes and now wore the fatigue uniform of an Airman Second Class. He climbed into the cab of the Air Force truck and pulled out of the barn.

CHAPTER 52
Sembach, Germany

The phone rang in the conference room where LTC Garson and the rest of the group were perusing a map to try to identify likely routes that the trucks may have taken. Frank picked up the phone, "Hello. Airman Logan at your service, can I help you?"

"Frank, this is MAJ Jim Best, is LTC Garson available?"

"Yes, hold on. LTC Garson, MAJ Best would like to talk to you."

LTC Garson said, "Put him on the speaker. Hi Jim, What's up?"

"I have just been briefed by the BND. The Watchers have reported an increase in activity at the *gasthaus* in Kaiserslautern. Two men in workman's clothes got into a heated discussion with the owner and he hustled them back to the rear of the building. They then left together and drove to an abandoned warehouse. One of the Watchers got a peek inside the warehouse and saw a truck parked in there. The men were arguing while looking in the back of the truck. Gehlen heard from his BND team near Sembach that there has been a breach in an ammo bunker, and you are looking for two trucks. It seems like too much of a coincidence and he wants to know how you would like to proceed."

"I am going to send Frank and Soaring Eagle over to Kaiserslautern to take a look. They have a casting of the tire tracks of the trucks from the farmhouse at Sembach and can compare them to the truck there. Can you ask the BND to provide an assault team at the warehouse to meet up with them?"

MAJ Best laughed, "Great minds travel in the same channels. Gehlen already alerted an assault team and they are standing by for your direction. How soon can Frank and Soaring Eagle get to Kaiserslautern?"

"They are leaving now and will be there in about 20 minutes. They will be armed with their P-38's and HK MP5's and have vests with them. Where should they meet the assault team?"

"They will meet with a man in a black leather coat carrying a violin case at the entrance of the Kaiserslautern *Hauptfriedhof* or cemetery. He will take them to the assault team staging area."

LTC Garson turned to Frank, "Did you get that?"

"Roger, on my way."

Kaiserslautern, Germany

Frank drove to Kaiserslautern as fast as he could and saw a man standing in front of the cemetery… a very large man carrying a violin case. His first thought was of a movie he remembered about gangsters in the 20's. He laughed and Soaring Eagle looked at him, "What's so funny?"

Frank said, "Who does he remind you of?"

Soaring Eagle looked at the man and smiled, "a gangster?"

"Yeah!"

They picked up the man who saw their smiling faces, . "Such happy Americans", he said as he opened the violin case and brought out an HK MP5 and four magazines in a pouch. "Just like an American gangster, *ya*?" All three broke out laughing.

The man directed them to a small garage where they met the rest of the BND assault team. They were all in civilian clothes and armed. Frank noticed they wore wide belts with spare magazines and one with a red cross on it. Fritz Brenner, the team leader followed Frank's gaze and said, "Just in case we need quick medical attention. Come and look at the layout of the warehouse." They went to a table and perused the layout. The entrances were marked, and the location of the truck was also indicated.

"My men will lead the assault with you two following. We will go in all the entrances at the same time. Once we have secured the warehouse, I was ordered to leave the disposition of the contents of the truck up to you."

Frank acknowledged, and the team left the garage in ones and twos until they had surrounded the warehouse. The BND leader spoke into a small radio and on command, the assault force crashed through the doors of the warehouse. There was a continuous burst of gunfire and two of the BND men were down. Frank and Soaring Eagle entered and saw one other man sprawled on the floor in a pool of blood and three BND operators pinned down behind boxes. Frank went right and Soaring Eagle left to protect the flanks for the pinned down BND men. One of the BND men pointed to loft in the garage. Frank moved further into the garage when a man popped up and pointed a weapon at Frank. Frank froze for a second.

MOVE TO YOUR LEFT! The voice shouted as Frank ducked to his left.

The man fired where Frank was standing but missed since he was no longer there. Soaring Eagle fired a three round burst that hit the man in the stomach, chest and head. The man fell from the loft and made a thump when he hit the cement floor.

Frank was breathing hard and stayed behind the box that he rolled to for cover. He was scared but remembered what Soaring Eagle had drilled into him in training. *You will be scared but must conquer your fear or it will haunt you forever.* Frank nodded a thanks to Soaring Eagle and they proceeded forward along a parallel path on each side of the warehouse. The BND guys moved forward box by box down the center of the warehouse. Two men ran into an office and fired their weapons on fully automatic from behind file cabinets in the office at the BND men. Frank had a direct view of the two men and fired his weapon, hitting both and heard their weapons clattering to the floor. He rushed into the office and saw them on the floor, one with a hole in the center of his forehead and the other clutching his shoulder. Frank had had some cable wraps in this pocket from the last installation they were on and used them to secure the wounded man's hands behind his back. The wounded man screamed as his arm was pulled back, but Frank was more interested in who else was in the warehouse. Soaring Eagle walked into the office behind two men with their hands raised. Frank reached into his pocket and pulled out more cable wraps. He noticed his hands were shaking and he tried to hold him MP5 tighter to hide his shaking hands.

Soaring Eagle looked at him and smiled, "First time is a bitch, but it gets easier the next time."

Frank was surprised that he felt no remorse. The shaking in his hands abated and he looked around the warehouse and his eyes settled on the truck.

Frank went over to the truck and saw the warhead inside and breathed a sigh of relief. He compared the truck tires to the plaster cast he had and although he thought it was obviously one of the trucks they were looking for, confirmed that this was indeed one of the trucks at the site of the farmhouse.

Fritz Brenner came over to Frank and said, "They were not professional soldiers. They did not even post sentries. We believe they are Neo-Nazis."

Frank saw a telephone in the warehouse office and called LTC Garson, "Sir, the warehouse is secured, and we found one of the trucks with a warhead inside. Three of the bad guys resisted and were killed but three others were captured with one wounded. Soaring Eagle speaks German and is interrogating them now."

"Good work. Give my congratulations to the BND for me. It looks like there were more than six men at the farmhouse. Ask the three that were captured where the others went and what happened to the other warhead. I am sending WO4 Woodson out with his team to inspect and pick up the warhead."

"Roger that."

Frank passed on the questions to Soaring Eagle who said, "The youngest one speaks English and is being cooperative. He is scared and said he didn't realize what his neo-Nazi friends were up to until he got here. He wasn't one of the crew at the farmhouse or, so he said. Do you want to interrogate him? Don't be too gentle."

Frank took the young English speaking German into the office, sat him down in a chair and tied his arms and legs to it. The German was on the verge of panicking and pleaded, "I will cooperate. Please don't hurt me."

"Where is the other truck?"

"The Frenchmen took it."

"Men? - describe them."

"One was old and a bit fat. He came here before the trucks arrived. The other was young and followed the trucks in his car. The young one seemed to be in control of the operation but deferred to the older man. He got into an argument with our leader about an arming device."

Frank was sure the young Frenchman was Henri but wondered who the other man was, "Give me a better description of the older man."

"He spoke German with a Strasbourg accent. Most people from Strasbourg speak both German and French. He had a small mustache and a moon shaped head."

That description fit Jean Monsate, but Frank thought he was under surveillance by the BND Watchers. He wondered if they lost him and would check with LTC Garson after interrogating the young German.

"Did they both leave in the truck?"

"No, the young Frenchman drove the truck and the older man drove the car the younger man came here in."

"Tell me more about this arming device."

"Our leader wanted to know why the young Frenchman didn't provide it and was told he would have it in plenty of time before the Ramstein air show."

Frank tried to hide his surprise, "What was the plan regarding the air show?"

Frank could see a noticeable change in the attitude of the German. He thought that the German had not meant to mention the air show and was thinking about how to plead ignorance.

"Uh...that was only a reference to when the device would be available."

"You are lying. Tell me about the plan involving the air show."

The German didn't respond so Frank reached into his pocket

and retrieved his switchblade knife. The knife was not part of his official weapons but was available for purchase in stores in Kaiserslautern. They were not illegal in Germany. Most GEEIA troops had one as they came in handy when performing installations. He pressed the button on the handle and the blade snapped open.

"I don't want to use this, but I will. Tell me about the air show!"

The German squirmed in the chair but did not say anything. Frank grabbed the German's left hand and positioned the blade under his fingernail. "This is your last chance to tell the truth." The German gritted his teeth and Frank could see that his threat was apparently something the German could live with, so Frank changed tactics. He moved the razor-sharp blade from the fingernail to the pants leg and slit the pants up to the crouch and exposed the man's penis. The man looked shocked and tried in vain to break the bonds holding him in the chair. As Frank repositioned himself to get a better angle to make the cut that would sever the man's penis, the German screamed, "We were going to smuggle the warhead onto a German F-104 that would be displayed at the air show!"

Frank thought about his friends there and the people in the town of Ramstein and got angry, but he refolded the knife and said, "I want all the names of those involved. If you hold back, I will make you a woman and then blind you."

The German shuttered and rattled off names so fast that Frank had to stop him to get some paper and a pen. He named the weapons technician at the German airbase who would load the warhead into the F-104, the leader of the team that broke into the Sembach ammo bunker, the owner of the *gasthaus* in Kaiserslautern and a name that Frank was familiar with, Heinrich Lund aka Reinhardt Uhler. Frank was amazed that someone so young could have knowledge of the whole operation.

"How is it that you know so much about the operation?"

The German hesitated at first, then shrugged and said, "You will find out anyway so why not? I provided funding for the operation and used the neo-Nazi fools to carry it out. My superiors will have me killed if I go to a German jail so I want to go to America. I am an East German Stasi agent and want to defect."

Frank was shocked at this revelation and thought, 'This is way beyond my pay grade.' He stood up saying, "Hold that thought" and left the room to call LTC Garson. In about an hour, several CIA and State Department people arrived, and Frank was asked to leave after briefing them on what the German told him. As he was leaving, he wondered how General Gehlen would react to the way events turned out. Little did he know that he would find out a lot sooner than he thought.

CHAPTER 53
Wiesbaden, Germany

MG Stone and General Gehlen sat at the head of the conference table in Wiesbaden. Flanking them at the table were LTC Garson, MAJ Best, the GEEIA team, Chuck, Soaring Eagle, Mary Wright and Fritz Brenner of the German BND.

MG Stone opened the meeting, "I want to congratulate the U.S. and German teams on pulling off a joint operation to recover one of the warheads. The President and the German Chancellor are obviously very concerned but have agreed to keep it from the public for now. Where are we at in trying to locate the second one?"

LTC Garson said, "Based on the story that Airmen Logan extracted from the East German Stasi agent captured at the warehouse in Kaiserslautern, we believe that Henri Deveraux, the Frenchman who was sent to Sembach to locate the tunnel, drove away to an undisclosed location with the second warhead. We also believe that he was accompanied by Jean Monsate, confidante to COL LaCroix."

General Gehlen interrupted, "I must apologize for my men losing contact with Jean Monsate. We were not aware that he had left his residence until one of the Watchers saw him returning on foot. Monsate was in disguise but the Watcher recognized his odd gait. He was coming from the direction of the train station, so we checked the video cameras there. It was fortunate that the Nazis installed cameras and a reel-to-reel tape system during the war to record video at border crossings along the Rhine or we would not have detected Monsate in disguise. We confirmed that he did catch a train to Kaiserslautern. We could alert the French SDECE that he is a person to put under surveillance. But based on the mess they made with Langevin, we think it is best if we keep our Watchers in place for now. I am pleased to report, however, that most of the individuals named by the Stasi agent have been rounded up and are being interrogated. We also picked up the taxi driver, Hans Glick, from Ramstein although we do not think he knew of the plot to detonate the warhead at the air show."

MG Stone said, "Excellent." He then turned to Frank and smiled, "Airman Dunn, do you know how the Stasi agent's pants were ripped up to the crouch?"

Frank nervously answered, "I think it might have happened when I tied him to the chair."

"Good answer. Stick to that story."

General Gehlen smiled and said to Frank, "You would make a good BND operator. Getting back to the location of the second warhead, we have confirmed that Jean Monsate arrived in Strasbourg on the train from Karlsruhe based on the time that my men saw him returned to his house. We then showed the photo we took of Monsate to ticket agents in Karlsruhe. One of them remembered him from the horribly fitting wig that Monsate wore. He said Monsate was with another man who did not buy a ticket. My men showed him a photo of Henri Deveraux and the ticket agent identified him. We asked every employee at the *bahnhof* if they recognized the photo and were told by a rental car employee that Deveraux had returned a car shortly after Monsate bought his ticket to Strasbourg but the name on the contract was Hans Lieppman, obviously a false identity. My men then checked the parking garage and scanned the list of vehicle departures that the garage lists by license number. They discovered that a car with French license plates left the garage 25 minutes after Deveraux turned in his rental car. The car belongs to Deveraux. We are now looking at footage from cameras located at intervals on *autobahns* leaving Karlsruhe in hopes of detecting his car."

Frank recalled seeing a car with Karlsruhe license plates at the farmhouse in Sembach where the warheads were stolen. "Do you have the license number of the rental car in your notes?"

General Gehlen looked at his notes and told Frank the number. Frank said, "That car was at the farmhouse when Soaring Eagle and I were looking for Deveraux."

MG Stone said, "That puts one more nail in the coffin for Deveraux." He looked at General Gehlen, "Do you have any info on where Deveraux may be now?"

"Unfortunately, no, but the timeline from when Deveraux left Kaiserslautern to when he dropped Monsate off, helps us restrict the area that we are searching now. Deveraux had to drop off the truck somewhere between Kaiserslautern and

Karlsruhe to take Monsate to the train. However, that still covers a lot of territory."

There was a knock on the conference room door and a message passed to Fritz Brenner. He read it and looked up at the group. "A truck matching the description of the one found in Kaiserslautern has just been observed being driven into the Rhine River."

Fritz Brenner said, "The truck entered the Rhine in a remote area near the town of Frankenthal. It would probably not have been noticed but for a lone fisherman on the far bank. Efforts to recover the truck have been hampered by the river's current. It was not known if the warhead was in the truck or if it was armed." He laid a map on the conference table. He had already established grids on it between Kaiserslautern and Frankenthal and adjacent areas. "U.S. and German forces are searching for Deveraux's car and anything else suspicious. I propose we focus our two teams around Kaiserslautern since we know they already targeted the air base."

Sembach is also between Kaiserslautern and Karlsruhe.

Frank said, "Sembach may also be a target."

LTC Garson nodded, "Agree. I would like you and Soaring Eagle to work with the BND to cover the area around Sembach since you are already familiar with it. Chuck and Billy will do the same to cover the Kaiserslautern and Ramstein area."

Frank and Soaring Eagle left Wiesbaden and drove their car as fast as it would go down the *autobahn* toward Sembach. Frank flashed his lights at cars in the left lane and, as was the custom in Germany, slower cars immediately got out of the way. Frank was thinking it would be nice if drivers in American adopted this custom.

Sembach, Germany

They entered Sembach AB and called on WO4 Woodson, "Chief, Soaring Eagle and I have been assigned to help search for the missing warhead. Have you had any updates on the missing arming device?"

"No and MAJ Burns is still blaming me for ruining his career. I don't think he cares that 1LT Alexander was murdered. He's all about himself."

"Do you have any walkie-talkies we can use to keep in touch with you as we search in and around Sembach?"

WO4 Woodson came back with them, "Fully charged and good for about four kilometers range."

"Thanks, we will be on our way."

They got back in the car and passed an Air Force truck stopped at the gate. Frank glanced over and saw an Air policeman looking in the back of the truck. The driver of the truck was looking in the side mirror at the Air policeman. They continued driving into the town and Frank was thinking of contacting Nils Haupmann, the *Jagermeister,* to see if he noticed anything unusual.

Look in that truck.

This was getting spooky, but Frank knew better than to ignore the voice. He made a U-turn.

"Where are we going?" asked Soaring Eagle.

"I want to check with the Air Police on what was in the back of the truck."

They pulled up to the gate, "Hi, can you tell me what was in the back of that truck that just passed through?"

"Please pull to the side. You are blocking traffic."

They pulled to the side and Frank walked back to the gate and asked the same question. The Air Policeman looked at him and said, "Who are you and why are you so interested in what was in that truck?"

Frank noticed that the Air Policeman's hand was on the holster of his sidearm. "We are working with WO4 Woodson to look for anything unusual."

"Oh yeah, well I don't know anything about that. Wait here and I will call him." He went back into the guard shack and came out with an M-16 pointed at Frank. "Get down on your knees and lock your hands behind your head."

Frank complied and heard sirens coming towards them. He looked back at their car and saw Soaring Eagle pick up their walkie-talkie. Two police cars skidded to a stop in front of their car and Air policemen got out pointing their weapons at

Soaring Eagle. He put the walkie-talkie down and raised his hands. The policemen were yelling instructions that seemed contradictory with each other until the ranking policeman yelled at the others to shut up and told Soaring Eagle, "Get out of the car." Handcuffs were put on Frank and Soaring Eagle. They were shoved into the back seat of a police car and taken to their headquarters building.

About twenty minutes later, WO4 Woodson arrived at the police headquarters. He calmed the police down and vouched for Frank and Soaring Eagle. The ranking Air Policeman explained to WO4 Woodson that his orders were to treat any suspicious activities as hostile until it could be proven otherwise. The Air Policeman asked Frank, "What did you do to warrant your arrest?"

Frank explained, "I asked the guard at the gate what he was looking at in the back of a truck that he had stopped to inspect when all hell broke loose."

The policeman shook his head, "I don't understand. Why would you even ask him that question? It was none of your business what he was looking at. No wonder he took the action he did."

WO4 Woodson didn't want to tell him about a missing nuke so instead, said, "They are conducting an intelligence operation exercise and should have informed the guard that it was an exercise."

Frank looked at WO4 Woodson and thought that was an excellent response. It didn't place blame on the guard and using the word intelligence usually made policemen more cooperative.

The policemen huddled for some time, examining the identification papers that Frank and Soaring Eagle surrendered. The ranking policeman walked over to them and removed the handcuffs. "See to it that you coordinate better with base security to avoid mishaps like this. You all can go."

After the policeman left, WO4 Woodson asked Frank, "What did you see that made you ask what was in the truck."

"Nothing really, I was thinking that a truck would be required to move the warhead and the guard was looking at something in the back of the truck."

WO4 Woodson walked over to the policeman, "Excuse me but to close the loop, what was in the back of the truck?"

"A water tank...a very large water tank and the driver had a valid work order signed by MAJ Burns."

"Thank you", WO4 Woodson said and walked back to Frank and Soaring Eagle, "It was a water tank in the back of the truck, but I am not aware that we needed one and the work order was signed by MAJ Burns. Get in your car and let's see if we can locate the truck."

CHAPTER 54

Sembach, Germany

Henri Deveraux looked in his rear-view mirror as he pulled away from the gate. He saw a car pull up to the gate and two men talking to the guard. He was stopped at a traffic light that just turned red. He saw the guard motion the car to the side and a man approach the guard. After a short conversation the guard went back into the guard shack and emerged with a rifle pointed at the two men. The traffic light turned green and almost in a panic, Henri had to control himself not to speed away. Henri looked again at the map in the passenger seat and headed to the warehouse he was told would be his destination. The door to the warehouse was open and Henri drove in and stopped the engine. As he emerged from the truck, he saw the door to the warehouse door closing.

MAJ Burns approached Henri and asked, "Did everything go as planned?"

"Yes, but there was a commotion at the gate behind me that gave me concern. I don't know what it was about, but no one gave chase so it must have been something not relevant to us."

"Good. I will put the block and tackle into place while you unpack the warhead from the water tank."

The warhead was slid out of the truck and lowered into a

cradle attached to a forklift truck. Henri saw a mobile MACE missile was also in the warehouse and was pointed toward the rear door to the warehouse.

MAJ Burns smiled, "Officers usually do not do this work, but I have made it my business to learn all there is to know about loading a warhead into a MACE. The men were glad to see an officer take so much interest in actually doing work. Man, will they be surprised and shocked."

He expertly moved the forklift into place and asked Henri to help him install the warhead into the MACE. Once that was completed, he retrieved the arming device that he told the CIA/GEEIA team was issued to 1LT Alexander for training. He did not want to kill 1LT Alexander but when MG Stone called and told him that two nukes were stolen from the bunker, he panicked. He couldn't fathom how MG Stone knew so quickly! He thought that the Air Force would want to remove the arming devices from his safe so concocted a story that 1LT Alexander had checked one out for training. 1LT Alexander would of course deny it so he had to be killed. Ironically, the Air Force did not remove the devices from his control, so he did not have to concoct the story about 1LT Alexander had one for training purposes and therefore did not have to be killed. He regretted that since 1LT Alexander was his friend but rationalized it as collateral damage.

He asked Henri to confirm the coordinates of the target and entered them into the arming device.

"Are you sure he will be at the residence today?"

Henri responded, "Yes, I confirmed it today before I drove the truck here."

MAJ Burns smiled. He was a Soviet mole and a devout communist. He has been recruited by the KGB when he was still in college. He had to admire the clever plan his masters put together. It was a twofold plan…one with the French communist party and the other with the neo-Nazis. The beauty of it was that the Soviets were not involved in the actual theft so had reasonable deniability. The reason they stole two warheads and gave one to the neo-Nazis was a diversion. The Americans and the BND would eventually locate the one warhead but without the arming device, the Ramstein air show was not really in danger. His Soviet masters thought that detonating a nuclear weapon at Ramstein AB would possibly provoke the United States into possibly attacking the Soviet Union before they discovered that it was the neo-Nazis who were to blame. They would think the neo-Nazis stole both and would waste their time mounting a search for the other one among known neo-Nazis. The Soviets were really working with the French Communist Party since they were being persecuted by de Gaulle and losing popular support in France rapidly.

MAJ Burns thoughts were interrupted when Henri asked, "How long before we launch the MACE?"

"We should be ready in about ten minutes. Can you open the door so I can move the launcher into place?"

MAJ Burns rechecked the coordinates to be sure they were correct. The target was Colombey-les-Deux-Eglises, the private residence of Charles de Gaulle and he would be there with his closest advisors and family for a week's vacation. A vacation with unexpected fireworks. He smiled at his little joke.

He laughed when he thought that the plan will kill two birds with one launch. They would kill de Gaulle and the world would think the Americans did it since the missile was theirs and launched from an American base. The Soviets saw it as an opportunity to split NATO and to have the FCP fill the vacuum upon de Gaulle's death.

CHAPTER 55
Sembach, Germany

WO4 Woodson was headed to MAJ Burns office to ask him about the water tank. Frank and Soaring Eagle followed in their car. WO4 Woodson noticed the doors to a large warehouse open and a MACE being moved into place. He then saw the tow vehicle was being operated by MAJ Burns. He picked up his walkie-talkie and radioed Frank, "Something is wrong. Do you see the MACE being moved out of the warehouse on your right side?"

"Yes, what about it?"

"Get your weapons ready. There is no scheduled training today and certainly not with MAJ Burns driving the tow vehicle."

Frank got the two MP-5's from the back seat. He inserted magazines in both and picked up two canvas bags containing additional magazines. He handed an MP5 and a canvas bag to Soaring Eagle and they both followed WO4 Woodson to the warehouse. They saw MAJ Burns lower the jack stands on the launcher and turn toward them with a look of shock on his face. He hurried back into the warehouse as WO4 Woodson pulled up to the side door of the warehouse. Henri emerged from the side door and shot WO4 Woodson with his PPK pistol. He was about thirty yards away from Woodson and his shots were not accurate so only managed to hit him in the leg. Frank and Soaring Eagle returned fire hitting Henri several times while he was trying to load another magazine into the PPK. Frank ran up to Henri to kick the PPK away and started to bind his hands with cable wraps when he noticed that Henri was dead. Soaring Eagle checked on WO4 Woodson who said, "I'm OK. Stop Burns from launching the MACE. Shoot at one of the wings before he launches it."

Frank nodded but said, "What if we hit the nuke?"

"The nuke won't arm until it reaches a certain altitude. You need to cripple the missile before they launch it."

As he said that a roar could be heard from the missile. Frank and Soaring Eagle emptied their MP-5 magazines at the right wing since they couldn't see the left wing. They reloaded and managed to hit it again as the missile launched. They saw it rise in horror and as it accelerated, the skin began peeling off the right wing causing it to veer to the left and lose altitude. It augured into the ground about three kilometers away in a farmer's field. The missile flew into pieces upon impact and Frank was waiting for a brilliant light followed by a shock wave and tremendous heat associated with a nuclear detonation. Nothing happened though. Frank looked at Soaring Eagle, "Are we dead yet and just don't know it?"

Soaring Eagle was in shock and didn't answer. WO4 Woodson laughed and said, "We're not dead but I am bleeding and would really like you guys to take me to the infirmary."

Frank and Soaring Eagle wrapped WO4 Woodson's leg in a tee

shirt they pulled form their luggage and helped him into the back seat of his car.

Go after the traitor.

Frank told Soaring Eagle, "Take him to the hospital. I'm going after MAJ Burns."

Frank ran into the warehouse. Everything was scorched or burning inside but no sign of MAJ Burns. The sprinkler system had gone off, and the fires were under control. He looked around and saw the back door to the warehouse was open so surmised that MAJ Burns had escaped that way. He went through the door and saw the arming device lying on the ground where MAJ Burns must have discarded it. He retrieved it and went back to his car.

He tried to put himself in MAJ Burns shoes to figure out where he might have gone. He picked up the walkie-talkie and keyed it. He was surprised to hear WO4 Woodson's voice.

"Are you in the hospital?"

"We are on the way. Did you find MAJ Burns?"

"No, he ran out the back and after throwing the arming device away, disappeared. Any idea where he might be going?"

Woodson said, "Try his house first." Woodson gave him directions and stayed on the radio until Frank meandered through base housing towards the Bachelor Officers Quarters.

"What kind of car does he drive?"

WO4 Woodson told Frank, "An older yellow Mercedes. Be careful. He is desperate now."

Frank saw MAJ Burns run out of the Bachelor Officers Quarters with a suitcase and an M-16 rifle. MAJ Burns did not see him until Frank's car was pulling in behind him. MAJ Burns turned and with eyes wide, pointed the M-16 at him but forgot to charge it so Frank drove into him, hitting him in the knees with the front bumper. MAJ Burns collapsed and screamed in pain. Frank jumped out of the car as MAJ Burns was struggling to charge his weapon. Frank kicked it out of his hands and drove his knee into MAJ Burns stomach. MAJ Burns was gasping for air as Frank turned him face down and secured his hands with the cable wraps. "Stay there."

Frank went back to his car and got the radio. He got Soaring Eagle this time. "I got MAJ Burns, but he needs some medical attention."

Soaring Eagle laughed, "I think you're getting the hang of this. I am still at the infirmary so will get an ambulance on the way."

"Tell them his kneecaps are smashed."

"Roger that."

Frank looked down at MAJ Burns, "What the hell made you turn traitor?"

Burns sneered, "You stopped me but there are many others who share my beliefs and they are right under your nose. We will defeat you."

"Who do you work for?" Burns turned his head and would say no more.

CHAPTER 56
Sembach, Germany

The Sembach Base Commander ordered a lock down of the whole base as a precautionary measure. He ordered the Air Commandos to secure the MACE crash site and the remaining missiles of the Tactical Missile Wing.

Frank returned the arming device to WO4 Woodson, who was on crutches but was released from the hospital. He punched in the code to disarm the warhead.

Frank said, "I didn't know who else to give this too since Burns and Alexander are dead and I'm sure the team in charge of locating the warhead would insist upon the nuke being disarmed before searching the wreckage of the MACE."

WO4 Woodson laughed, "I'm sure they would." Woodson looked up the coordinates for the target and found they were for a town called Colombey-les-Deux-Eglises but nobody knew what was there at the time.

When it was later determined that it was the residence of Charles de Gaulle was located there, the President of the United States and the German Chancellor informed President de Gaulle. They also told him that Jean Monsat was a communist and appeared to be the mastermind. Charles de Gaulle said he would have the French SDECE investigate it. He did not thank the U.S. President or the German Chancellor. They both came away with the impression that they were not believed.

The BND released Langevin back to the SDECE since there was no longer any reason to hold him. Besides, he really didn't know anything that interested the German government. One week later, Jean Monsate and Francois Langevin escaped from SDECE confinement with the help of the French Communist Party. They were provided with false identification papers and were driving through the mountains to a safe house near Mont Blanc. As they were coming down one of the mountain, the right front tire suddenly exploded and they careened over the edge of the road into a deep ravine and the car erupted into a fireball.

The Soviet sniper smiled in satisfaction. One shot took out the front tire and the second incendiary round exploded the gas tank. He was sure to receive an award for this action but did not why he was assigned to this target. No matter, it was for Mother Russia.

MAJ Burns was hospitalized with both kneecaps crushed but otherwise in good shape physically. His mental state was questionable since he babbled incessantly about his career being ruined by WO4 Woodson. When Frank heard about it, he wondered if that was a defensive mechanism to avoid answering questions about why he turned traitor. Two days later, MAJ Burns suffered a massive coronary and the autopsy revealed that air had been injected into his bloodstream. The air was likely inserted into the intravenous tube in his arm, but it could not be determined if it was accidental or a homicide. All concerned with the case were certain that he had been murdered but who? The Soviets, the Neo-Nazis or the French communists all had a reason to silence him.

The truck that was dumped in the Rhine was recovered but badly damaged by the swift river currents. The truck was examined to determine if any radioactivity was present. The residual amounts found were expected from transporting the warhead. The tires were shredded off so could not be compared to the plaster casts of the tires taken at the farmhouse near Sembach. Since both nukes were recovered, it was an anticlimactic event.

The neo-Nazis captured in the warehouse in Kaiserslautern were interrogated by the BND. They confessed to breaking into the bunker at Sembach AB and one even had the audacity to ask if he could have the tools back that they had left in the tunnel. They denied killing the couple who lived in the farmhouse and said the Frenchman did it, but they buried them in the garden as it seemed a decent thing to do. The other neo-Nazis that took part in the taking of the warhead device were arrested at the *gasthous* in Kaiserslautern. The mechanic at the German air base mentioned by the Stasi agent escaped arrest. A review of the phone records in the *gasthaus* found that a call had been made to the German air base and probably warned the mechanic to get away. Heinrich Lund aka Reinhardt Uhler was arrested in Ramstein but denied knowledge of the plot to detonate a nuclear device at the air show. He did confess to passing on information gleamed from airmen talking in taxis to gauge the awareness of authorities at Ramstein

AB. He implicated Hans Glick as a source of that information and told them of the 'accidents' he staged to hurt or kill airmen. Frank was surprised to learn that he and his friends were the first of Hans's victims.

Oleg Pavlov was turned by the BND and agreed to assist in tracking down Soviet networks in West Germany.

CHAPTER 57

Moscow, Soviet Union

Nikoli Strakova was the Director of the top secret covert operational unit of the KGB and was responsible for executing strikes against NATO that could not be walked back to the Soviet Union. OPERATION MACE should have been a devastating blow to the NATO Alliance that would have looked like a Neo-Nazi conspiracy with the French Communist Party. He was still trying to reconstruct what went wrong. It all seemed to have started when the BND discovered the *Environmental Monitoring and Analysis* office in Bremen which led them to the Helmstedt station. The subsequent raid by the BND and the documents they seized mentioned Sembach but, at the time, it should not have set off any alarm bells. The request for information was benign. He continued to review the message traffic from their Helmstedt station to try to understand what clues the BND could have gleamed from the Soviet contact with the French Communist Party to unravel the plot to kill De Gaulle and some of the top leaders of the French government.

The only saving grace was that only MAJ Burns, Ivan Kraskov, Jean Monsate and Henri Deveraux knew of the whole plan and they were eliminated. He had MAJ Burns killed by one of his assassins in the hospital after he was captured. Jean Monsate and for good measure, Francois Langevin, were killed in what was made to look like an auto accident. Henri Deveraux was killed by security forces at Sembach so could not be interrogated. He learned from his mole in the BND that Kraskov had died while being interrogated but told the BND nothing. The mole in the BND could not find out the status of Oleg Pavlov. It didn't really matter though, since Pavlov was not aware of the plot.

He concluded that it was just bad luck that someone must have discovered the dead residents of the farmhouse over the tunnel. Nothing else made sense for the BND to connect the dots to their mole MAJ Burns. Nikoli was very concerned that his political bosses would not see it as bad luck and would try to pass the blame onto him for the failure of OPERATION MACE. He knew he must concoct a story that it was the failure of Ivan Kraskov, not Nikoli. Afterall, Kraskov was not around to contradict him.

Nikoli smiled. He had several other operations in the queue that had the support of the President of the Soviet Union and did not really fear retribution. He was confident that the investigation by his political bosses would only be an annoyance for a short time.

CHAPTER 58
Ramstein, Germany

Frank arrived back at his barracks room in Ramstein and unpacked his bags. His roommates were TDY somewhere, so he had the whole room to himself. He heard a knock on the door and yelled, "It's open."

A2C George Otter and A2C Ray Burnside entered.

"Hey man, welcome back. Want to grab a beer down at the Capri bar?"

"Yeah, that would be great."

"Did you know that Johnny Holbrook is rotating back to the states?"

"No, is he OK from the accident?"

"Yeah, his three years are up so it's just his normal rotation. That means we must find another roommate or wait for one of the new guys coming in to be assigned. We talked to Tony D'Angelo about asking you if you were interested in moving and he gave his blessing. So, are you interested?"

"You bet. When can I make the move?"

"Johnny leaves next week so any time after that is good for us. You go TDY so much that we think sooner is better."

"I can move the day after Johnny leaves."

They called for a taxi and headed to the Capri bar. Heidi was tending bar and Yutta came over and sat down with them. She looked at Frank, "I haven't seen you for a while. Did you find a girlfriend in another bar?"

"No, I was TDY. Do you want a drink?"

"Of course," she turned to Heidi, "Please bring me a cognac and coke. Frank is buying."

"Do you want to be my partner in a *fussball* game against these two guys?"

She got up and said, "Let's go. By the way, did you hear what happened to the taxi driver, Hans Glick?"

Frank hoped he sounded unconcerned since she struck a nerve about somebody who tried to kill him and the two guys currently with him, "No, what happened?"

"He was arrested, along with his friend Reinhart Uhler, but nobody seems to know what they did. I heard it had to do with drugs."

Frank was surprised but when he thought about it, he could see General Gehlen's hand in spreading that story. "Drugs are getting to be bad business" he said.

The next morning, as he was leaving the barracks to go to breakfast, he saw Billy waiting for him. "Want a ride to the

GEEIA warehouse?"

"Yeah but how about I buy you breakfast first?"

Billy looked at his watch, "Sounds good. We have time for breakfast."

After breakfast, Billy told Frank, "We are going to the SCIF later to meet with SMS Oliver."

"Do we have another job coming up?"

"Something like that." Billy said cryptically.

Don Bakersfield and Gerhard Schultz were at the warehouse sitting at one of the long work benches. They got up and everyone shook hands all around. Don said, "It's good to be back. The wife made my favorite dinner last night."

Billy looked at his watch again, "Might be a short-lived stay. SMS Oliver wants to meet with us in about a half hour, so finish up what you're doing so we're not late."

They drove to the SCIF in Billy's car and Frank was surprised to see Mary Wright, LTC Garson, MAJ Best and WO4 Woodson sitting in the conference room. SMS Oliver walked in behind them and said, "You guys did good. MG Stone has been told to brief the CIA Director at Langley on the FRENCH KISS operation. He said he wanted to bring the GEEIA/CIA team with him to fill in any details that the Director may ask him, so you are all going with him. Pack a bag with the most formal uniforms you possess and civilian clothes for about a week's stay. You will have about three free days to do what you want in the states without taking leave. The General has reserved an Air Force executive jet for the trip that will pick you up at Base Operations on the Ramstein AB flight line tomorrow morning at 0900. Any questions?"

Frank asked, "Is there a cover story for us to use with whoever may be inquisitive?"

"Yes, your cover story is that you will be TDY for a training class. I will cut the orders today" said SMS Oliver.

Mary and Frank got together after the meeting, "Can you join me for lunch" Mary asked?

"Sure, we can go to the Rod and Gun."

"I was thinking more about a nice restaurant I know in Kaiserslautern. Is that OK with you?"

Frank looked at Billy who smiled, "Take the rest of the day to get ready for the trip."

After lunch, they went to Mary's hotel. "I will get you back in time to pack and get some rest but not before we pick up where we left off in Strasbourg."

CHAPTER 59
Andrews Air Force Base, Maryland

The flight took about seven hours. They landed at Andrews Air Force Base in Maryland. Because they were with MG Stone, they were provided with rooms in the Distinguished Visitors Officers Quarters (DVOQ) on Andrews. It was a nice room and Mary was only down the hall. Each room had a large bed and the furniture was made from aromatic cherry wood. A small kitchen was decorated with pictures of combat aircraft and had a coffee maker complete with packets of coffee, sugar and dried milk. He put his clothes in the closet and found an ironing board that he used to get the wrinkles out of his dress shirts and pants.

Mary knocked on the open door, "The base is providing dinner in the lobby of the DVOQ in about a half hour. It must be nice to be a General."

"I don't think the pay is great, but they do have a fair share of amenities. Is there a dress code for dinner?"

"Nope. It's come as you are." She sat down on the bed and watched him do his ironing. "You are a jack of all trades."

Frank laughed and said, "I used to iron my ties when I was in high school until they got so shiny, I had to buy more. I graduated to ironing shirts and pants when the Air Force sent me on so many TDY trips."

They joined the rest of the group in the lobby for dinner and he was pleasantly surprised to find the food cooked to perfection. He expected more of the usual fare served in the dining facility then remembered the time a Colonel showed up at Ramstein AB and Gerhardt embarrassed the cooks. Rank definitely has its privileges.

After dinner, everyone sat around for about an hour talking about the meeting in the morning. One by one, they peeled off and went back to their rooms. Frank took a shower and went to bed. About an hour later, he heard a soft knock on the door. Thinking it was Mary, he smiled and opened it to find MG Stone. "Sorry to bother you but I wanted you to know that I may be calling on you tomorrow during the briefing to the CIA Director to provide details of the operation if I am asked for them. You were more involved in stopping MAJ Burns than any of the others. Are you OK with that?"

After getting over the shock that it wasn't Mary knocking, Frank answered, "Of course General Stone. Anything I can do to help."

"I knew I could count on you. Get a good night's sleep. We may have a long day tomorrow."

After MG Stone left the room, Frank thought to himself, 'What the hell did I just agree to do? Maybe he didn't really mean it and it was only a ploy to see if Mary was in the room.'

Just then there was another soft knock on the door. Frank

thought it was probably MG Stone again. He opened the door and Mary slipped in and hugged him. "What did the General want? I almost opened my door to come to your room when I heard footsteps. I looked through the peep hole and saw him heading for your room."

"He asked me if I was ready to support him in case some questions were asked that he didn't know the details."

"Oh, well lock your door and let's see if I can *support* your weight on me" she said as she slipped her clothes off and lay back on the bed with a smile on her face.

The next morning, they were served breakfast by some airmen in the DVOQ lobby before they left for Langley. Frank was glad to see Chuck Whelan and Soaring Eagle Milligan sitting at one of the tables with MG Stone. After breakfast they all climbed into an Air Force van and left Andrews AFB and headed east on the recently built Capital Beltway, crossed the Woodrow Wilson Bridge and headed north along the Potomac River to the CIA Headquarters building.

Langley, Virginia

When they got to the gate of the Headquarters, an armed guard asked for their IDs and said, "The Director is expecting you." Their driver dropped them off in front of the building and left to park the van. They stopped in front of the visitor's desk and were all issued badges. A man in a three-piece suit approached and said, "Welcome to Langley and I hope you had a nice trip. The Director is standing by for your meeting. Please follow me."

He led them to the nicest conference room that Frank had ever seen. Air Force conference rooms were dingy in comparison. Pictures of foreign cities adorned the walls. They were steered to seats on one side of a long table. Shortly after they were seated, the Director of the CIA, along with numerous others, sat down on the other side of the table.

The Director greeted them and motioned to MG Stone to start the briefing.

"Gentlemen, as you know, a disaster has been averted which could have resulted in the assassination of the President of France, Charles de Gaulle and many French citizens. A traitor, named MAJ Ted Burns, launched a nuclear tipped MACE missile at the town of Colonbey-les-Deux-Eglises, the private residence of Charles de Gaulle. WO4 Woodson, Airman Logan and Mr. Milligan, seated at the table, disabled the missile after it launched and prevented it from reaching the intended target. The detonation would have spread a cloud of radiation across Eastern France and subsequently would drift across Germany and other nations to the east. He turned to Frank and said, "Could you please provide the details Airman Logan?"

Frank gulped, thinking that no one asked questions that MG Stone couldn't answer but was thankful for the heads-up last night, "Yes sir. The United States, in a joint effort with the German BND, learned that the French communist party in conjunction with several neo-Nazis' stole two MACE nuclear warheads from a bunker at Sembach Air Base. One was found in a warehouse in Kaiserslautern. The neo-Nazis intended to detonate it at the recent air show at Ramstein Air Base. We believe the French did not intend to provide an arming device but used the neo-Nazis as a diversion from their real intent…"

Frank was interrupted by the Deputy Director for Operation, or DDO who said, "We are aware of the overall plot but what we are interested in is the details surrounding the assault on the warehouse where the MACE was housed."

MG Stone said, "Frank, why don't you start from the time you, Mr. Milligan and Warrant Officer Woodson approached the warehouse."

Frank was getting nervous but told them, "WO4 Woodson was shot by Henri Deveraux when approaching the warehouse and Mr. Milligan and I returned fire…"

"I understand you both had MP-5 submachine guns. Who told you to arm yourselves with them?" asked the DDO.

Frank was getting irritated with the interruptions, "WO4 Woodson did, sir."

"He is not your supervisor so why would you take orders from him?"

"Number one, he outranks me and number two, when he saw the MACE being towed out of the warehouse, he knew something was very wrong, right Chief?"

WO4 Woodson nodded, "Yes, but you have to understand that we were acting as a team."

The DDO said, "I understand, but the President is going to have to explain to President de Gaulle why your team found it necessary to kill Henri Deveraux, a French citizen."

Stay calm.

Frank's brain switched gears. They were looking for an operational justification to a political problem. "Sir, we didn't know at the time that the man who shot Chief Woodson was a French citizen. Mr. Milligan and I saw an armed civilian shooting at us, and we returned fire. We would have done the same even if we knew he was a French citizen."

The DDO smiled, "Good answer, continue please."

"Chief Woodson told us to shoot at the leading edge of the wings of the MACE before it launched…"

"So, what would you have done if it didn't launch?"

"We would have secured it and arrested MAJ Burns."

"Continue."

"We fired two magazines of 9mm ammo at the right wing of the MACE that caused the skin of the wings to peel back and auger the MACE into the ground."

"Weren't you concerned that it may have detonated when it crashed?"

"Yes sir, but we were taking it a step at a time."

All laughed at this response which made Frank feel a little

giddy and slightly embarrassed.

WO4 Woodson said, "I knew the warhead would not detonate until it reached a certain altitude. It is a safety factor built-in in case of a rocket motor failure at launch."

"Then what happened?"

Frank told them that he and Soaring Eagle helped WO4 Woodson into his car and Frank went searching for MAJ Burns. He saw MAJ Burns at his residence carrying a suitcase and a weapon.

"Is that when you ran him over?"

Frank was getting pissed off, "I did not run him over! I hit him in the knees to disable him and kicked the weapon from his hands when he fell over screaming in pain."

The Director said, "Well done. I think I would have run the bastard over." All laughed again.

The rest of the meeting was cordial with questions on details that were readily answered by the team. After about two hours, they took a break and were served coffee and pastries. MG Stone took Frank aside and said, "Good job. I could see you were getting upset by the DDO but that is his way. I could see that he was impressed with your confidence but doubt that he will admit it."

The Director reconvened the meeting and said, "The only thing left is to present you all with awards that you cannot take with you but will be reflected in your CIA personal file."

He looked at the GEEIA team, "I know you are not CIA employees, but a file has been established for you. If you decide to leave the Air Force, we will have a place for you here."

They returned to Andrews AFB along the same route they took earlier. MG Stone told them that they have three days to do what they wanted to do but be back at Andrews by 1800 for the flight back to Germany.

Back in his room, Mary asked, "Are you going to go to Philly?"

"No, I am going to look up an airman by the name of Jerry Sturgis who rotated back to the states before I got to Ramstein."

Mary looked a little puzzled, "Did you know him from before being stationed at Ramstein?"

He got a little testy and explained, "No, I just want to know why a guy would profess love for a girl, get her pregnant and desert her."

"Is she a friend of yours?"

"Not really. I know her and feel bad for her. Her family and the whole town of Ramstein, except for a few close friends, think she is a whore. I don't share that opinion and want to let Sturgis know that I think he is a shit."

"Would you like some company? My family is on the west coast and three days is not enough time to fly there and back."

Frank looked at her, "I might not be such good company."

Mary smiled, "I know how to cheer you up."

CHAPTER 60
Deal, New Jersey

Jerry Sturgis's parents lived in Deal, New Jersey. Deal had been settled sometime in the 1660's and is one of the most expensive places to live in the Unites States.

Frank and Mary boarded a shuttle at Andrews AFB to go to National Airport where they rented a car. He had looked up the address of Jerry Sturgis some time ago when he was pulling Charge of Quarters, or CQ duty back at Ramstein. This duty was rotated among TDY personnel who happened to be in station and required him to man the GEEIA administration office for twelve hours from 1700-0700. GEEIA had 'ready teams' who had to provide the CQ with their location at all times in case there was an emergency. If an emergency call came in, the CQ had to alert the ready team of the nature of the emergency and wherever it was in Europe or the Middle East, inform the commander and the first sergeant to get approval to respond to the emergency and coordinate transportation for the ready team. The ready team was responsible for making sure they had all the equipment they would need to deal with the emergency. However, no one currently assigned to GEEIA had ever experienced an emergency while on CQ duty so usually it meant the hardest thing he had to do was stay awake. If found sleeping while on duty, the punishment was severe.

The trip took a little over seven hours because they took a

break for lunch and Mary's frequent requests to stop so she could take photos. Deal is situated on the Atlantic Ocean; which makes it most popular in the summer season. As it was now fall, Frank and Mary checked into an upscale hotel at a very reasonable price.

Frank asked the hotel manager, "Can you recommend a place for dinner?'

The hotel manager said, "The Jersey coast has some of the best seafood restaurants in the country but a lot of them have closed for the winter." He mentioned several that were still open, and they opted for the closest one since they were tired of driving and were hungry.

Frank ordered the seafood pasta with shrimp, scallops, mussels and lobster in a red sauce. Mary had the lump crab cakes. They split a bottle of Sauvignon Blanc wine.

"What time do you want to go looking for Jerry?" Mary asked.

"I was thinking about nine o'clock. That will give them time for breakfast but should be before they would go out for the day. We should drive past the Sturgis 'mansion' after dinner to be sure someone is home but wait until morning to confront Jerry."

They went back to the room and Mary took so long in the bathroom that Frank fell asleep before she came out. She smiled and slipped in next to him and was asleep almost immediately. The next morning, they made love before breakfast. They left the hotel and drove the virtually abandoned streets to the Sturgis 'mansion'. Frank knocked on the door and a butler opened it and said, "Can I help you?"

Frank answered, "Yes, we are looking for Jerry Sturgis."

The butler stammered a bit and just about the time he was going to respond, a woman's voice came from behind the butler, "I am Jerry's mother. Why are you looking for him?"

Frank said, "I am from the GEEIA squadron in Germany where Jerry was stationed, and I have to ask him something…in private."

She looked at Frank with a blank look. The butler started to say something, but the woman waved her arm and said to them, "Please come in. My name is Jennifer Sturgis."

Mary said, "Thank you. I am Mary Wright, and this is Airman Frank Logan."

"My husband and I are just finishing breakfast. Would you care for something to eat?"

Mary said, "No thank you. We already had breakfast."

"Then could I offer you some coffee while we talk?"

Frank was ready to say no, but Mary graciously accepted. They followed her into a fashionably decorated breakfast nook overlooking the beach and the Atlantic Ocean. A man stood up, folding a newspaper that he was obviously reading and gave his wife a puzzled look.

"Gerald, this is Mary Wright and Airman Frank Logan. They came by to talk to Jerry but apparently they were unaware of his premature passing."

Frank stared at her with his mouth hanging open, "I am so sorry, I had no idea."

"Please sit down." Jennifer said and turning to the butler who followed them, "Please ask Cook to bring two more cups of coffee."

They all sat down, and Jennifer asked Frank, "What is it that you wanted to talk to Jerry about?"

"I'm sorry. It's not important now. I think we should leave."

Gerald and Jennifer looked at each other. Gerald said, "I would like to ask you something first. Jerry wrote to us and said he was in love with a girl named Heidi from Germany and was going to start the paperwork to have her immigrate to the United States. He said the Air Force process takes too long and as soon as he was discharged, he was going to bring her here. He spent his last days in the Air Force at McGuire AFB here in New Jersey. We bought him a sports car that he took back and forth to the base. On his way home from McGuire after he was discharged, he hit a deer and veered into a tree. He was killed immediately. He was our only child."

Frank lowered his head then looked at Mary, who had tears in her eyes. He looked at Gerald and Jennifer and said, "That's what I was going to talk to Jerry about. Heidi had his son and thought he had abandoned her."

Jennifer put her hand to her mouth, "The poor girl. She gave birth to a boy?" Then she smiled, "My grandson?"

"Yes, I have not seen him but a girl I know says he looks like Jerry."

Jennifer looked at Gerald. "I want to bring her here with my grandson."

Gerald hugged her, "So do I."

"How do we get in touch with her? What is her last name?"

"I don't know but we are heading back in two days and I could get last name and how to contact her."

"Where are you staying until you leave? No matter, please stay here and tell me all about her and my grandson."

Frank and Mary accepted their invitation. He didn't want to stunt their fervor, so told them that Heidi was a waitress instead of a bartender since it sounded better and was kind of the truth.

Andrews Air Force Base, Maryland

On their flight back to Germany, Mary told Frank that she would have to report back to the consulate in Strasbourg. He nodded but was preoccupied with how he was going to approach Heidi with the news. Jennifer told Frank to call them collect after he talked to her. He knew Heidi would be overwrought upon learning that Jerry was killed in an auto accident. He didn't know if she would welcome the opportunity to raise her son in America. Heidi was a very pretty woman and would probably fall in love with another man at some time. How would Gerald and Jennifer react to that? He knew he was over thinking the issues and should take his own advice and take it one step at a time.

CHAPTER 61
Ramstein, Germany

There were three cars waiting for them at Ramstein Base Operations. One was the consulate car for Mary and the other two were being driven by Billy's wife and Don's wife. Billy offered to drop Frank off at the barracks. He hugged Mary but did not kiss her with everyone looking at them. MG Stone waved from the plane as the door closed and taxied toward the runway for the trip to Weisbaden.

Frank went into his room, dropped his bags on the floor and lay down on his bunk. Long flights tired him out and in a minute he was asleep. His roommates, Buddy and Eddie, barged into the room about two hours later.

"So, you're moving out," said Buddy in an agitated voice but with a smile on his face.

Eddie chuckled, "I don't blame you. I would move out of a room with me in it if I could."

Frank mumbled sleepily, "It's nothing personal."

Buddy and Eddie burst out laughing.

George Otter and Ray Burnside walked in the room. Ray said, "Ready to move?"

Frank didn't have much. He had a locker filled with his uniforms and civilian clothes along with some souvenirs he picked up here and there. The five of them had him moved into his new quarters in about 20 minutes.

Buddy clapped his hands, "All done. You're buying the beer for us helping you move."

"OK, is the Rod and Gun good for you guys?" Everyone nodded assent.

The dart board was open when they got there, so Frank ordered the beer as the rest of the guys started shooting a game called '301 checkout'. The object of the game is to start with a score of 301 and subtract from it to get to zero. Each player gets three darts per turn and must hit a double to start scoring and hit a double to win. If the player goes above the score needed to double out, it is considered a bust and his score reverts to that when he started to double out. The first one who gets to zero wins. They played until a queue started to form to take the board, so they quit and ordered steak dinners, the specialty of the Club.

When they were done eating, Buddy said, "Let's go the Capri bar." George bowed out which he almost always did since the time they were run off the road by Hans Glick. Buddy, Eddie, Ray and Frank called a taxi and headed to the Capri bar.

Yutta saw Frank and yelled, "You're back! How long are you staying this time?"

Frank laughed, "Who knows? The Air Force gives me little

notice."

"Buy me a drink and sit down with me." She led Frank to a table in the back and asked Heidi to bring her a cognac and coke and Frank a pilsner beer. They made small talk for about 15 minutes when Frank asked Yutta to take over bartending from Heidi and ask her to join him. "So, I am not your girlfriend anymore?"

"You are always my girlfriend, but I have something to say to Heidi that is personal."

Yutta looked at him to see if she could tell if he was lying. "OK, but you owe me another cognac and coke."

Heidi came over to his table, but he could see that she was uncomfortable. He explained to her what he had found out about Jerry Sturgis. She started crying and he held her hand.

"Heidi, his parents want you and your son to come to America to live with them. They are very rich and can get your immigration approved quickly. Your son is probably an American citizen, but the laws are complicated. His parents have a very good lawyer who said there is a precedence that he can use to make him a citizen."

"I can't leave my mother. I am her only source of income and the town looks down on her for taking care of my son while I work." She was hard to understand through her sobbing, but he got the gist of it.

She got some control back, "What is 'precedence' mean?"

"Oh, it means it was done before and approved in a similar case so should apply to this one."

She looked confused, "That is good, *ja*?"

"*Ja, das ist gut.* I will ask them if they can bring your mother to America also. I need to know though; would you be willing to go without her if it's not possible?"

Heidi smiled, "I'm not sure she would even want to go to America. Maybe I can get a job in America and send her money. In any case, I would like to raise my son in America."

"Just one thing, what is your last name?"

"Berger. I am Jewish like Jerry."

Frank smiled, "Beautiful."

Yutta came back to the table with a fresh cognac and coke and a pilsner for Frank, "You made Heidi cry and then she came back to the bar smiling. What did you say to her?"

He hefted the pilsner to his mouth and said, "You will have to ask her."

Frank called Gerald and Jennifer when he got back to the barracks. They, along with their lawyer, arrived in Frankfurt two days later. They met with Heidi, her mother and little Jerry. He didn't know the details but a month later received a letter from Gerald and Jennifer thanking him profusely and inviting him to their house at Deal anytime he was available. Gerald owned an electronics company and offered Frank a job when he decided to leave the Air Force. A picture was attached with Gerald, Jennifer, Heidi, little Jerry and a woman who he assumed was Heidi's mother.

All's well that ends well.

Frank smiled.

ACKNOWLEDGEMENTS

I would like to thank my family and friends; Lee Graff, Marie Brenner, Christe Schrenk and Shamoli Patel for providing frank assessments of the various versions of the book as I stumbled through rearranging and eliminating paragraphs that kind of rambled.

I especially valued the suggestions and insights provide by Tim Selway who despite his busy schedule, read the book at least twice and made substantial comments.

Lastly, I want to thank my lovely wife Judy. She ground through my many typos and grammatical errors and corrected them. She provided encouragement throughout the writing of the book that reflects the many things she has done for me during our marriage, to which I am eternally grateful.

Made in the USA
Columbia, SC
03 December 2020

8. Let cool slightly before serving.

Nutrition information: (per serving)
Calories: 386, Fat: 21g, Saturated Fat: 7.5g, Cholesterol: 51mg, Sodium: 213mg, Carbohydrates: 41.5g, Fiber: 3.5g, Sugar: 21g, Protein: 5.5g

9. Coconut Cake

Coconut Cake is a moist, delicious cake, loaded with shredded coconut for an extra flavor boost all the way through.
Serving: 8
Preparation Time: 15 minutes
Ready Time: 1-2 hours

Ingredients:
- 3 cups all-purpose flour
- 2 1/2 teaspoons baking powder
- 1 teaspoon salt
- 3/4 cup butter
- 2 cups granulated sugar
- 4 large eggs
- 2 teaspoons vanilla extract
- 1 cup whole milk
- 3 1/2 cups shredded sweetened coconut

Instructions:
1. Preheat oven to 350°F. Grease and flour 2 (9-inch) cake pans.
2. In a medium bowl, sift together flour, baking powder, and salt. Set aside.
3. In a large bowl, cream butter and sugar until light and fluffy.
4. Beat in eggs, one at a time, scraping down sides of the bowl as needed.
5. Beat in vanilla.
6. Alternate adding flour mixture and milk, beginning and ending with flour. Scrape down sides of the bowl and beat until just combined.
7. Fold in coconut. Divide batter evenly between prepared pans.
8. Bake for 30–35 minutes, or until a toothpick inserted in the center comes out clean. Allow to cool for 10 minutes before turning out onto a wire rack to cool completely.

Nutrition information: Calories 490, Fat 24g, Saturated fat 15g, Sodium 289mg, Carbohydrate 61g, Fiber 3g, Sugar 39g, Protein 6g

10. Apple Dumplings

Apple Dumplings are a classic dessert dish made with cored granny smith apples filled with butter, brown sugar, and spices and wrapped in a pastry dough. The combination of these flavors come together to make a delightful treat.
Serving: Makes 8 servings.
Preparation time: 25 minutes
Ready time: 35 minutes

Ingredients:
- 4 granny smith apples, cored
- 4 tablespoons butter, melted
-4 tablespoons brown sugar
- 1 teaspoon ground cinnamon
- Pinch of ground nutmeg
- 1/4 teaspoon ground ginger
- 1/2 teaspoon salt
- 2 rolls (14-ounces each) refrigerated pie crust
- 2 tablespoons cream or milk

Instructions:
1. Preheat oven to 375°F.
2. Core apples and place in a large bowl.
3. In a small bowl, combine butter, brown sugar, cinnamon, nutmeg, ginger and salt and mix together.
4. Pour mixture over apples and toss until fully coated.
5. Cut each pie crusts into 4 pieces. Place an apple in the center of each piece and wrap the crust around it, pressing to seal.
6. Place the dumplings on a baking sheet lined with parchment paper.
7. Brush each dumpling with cream or milk.
8. Bake in preheated oven for 25-35 minutes, or until golden brown.

Nutrition information: Per serving: 245 calories; 12g fat; 33g carbohydrates; 4g protein; 88mg sodium; 0.1g fiber.

11. Cornbread

Cornbread is a popular American dish that makes a tasty and hearty side to a variety of meals. It is made from a simple batter of cornmeal, eggs, butter (or oil) and milk. A perfect balance of sweet and savory, this versatile bread can be cooked in a skillet and served hot.
Serving: 10
Preparation time: 10 minutes
Ready time: 35 minutes

Ingredients:
- 2 cups cornmeal
- 2 cups all-purpose flour
- 1 tablespoon baking powder
- 1 teaspoon baking soda
- 1 teaspoon salt
- 2 eggs
- 2/3 cup vegetable oil
- 2 cups buttermilk

Instructions:
1. Preheat oven to 375°F.
2. In a large bowl, stir together cornmeal, flour, baking powder, baking soda and salt.
3. In a separate bowl, beat eggs lightly before whisking in the oil and buttermilk.
4. Pour the wet Ingredients into the dry and mix until just combined.
5. Grease a 9-inch baking pan with cooking spray.
6. Pour the batter into the pan and bake for 30-35 minutes, or until a toothpick inserted comes out clean.
7. Allow to cool before serving.

Nutrition information:
Serving size: 1 slice (approximately 2 inches in diameter)
Calories: 200

Fat: 10 g
Carbohydrates: 24 g
Sugar: 2 g
Protein: 5 g
Fiber: 2 g

12. Strawberry Shortcake

This classic strawberry shortcake is the perfect combination of light and fluffy biscuits, lots of juicy strawberries, and freshly whipped cream. It is a great summer dessert that everyone will love!
Serving: 6
Preparation time: 10 minutes
Ready time: 30 minutes

Ingredients:
- 2 1/2 cups all-purpose flour
- 3 tablespoons granulated sugar
- 4 1/2 teaspoons baking powder
- 1/2 teaspoon fine sea salt
- 10 tablespoons cold unsalted butter, cubed
- 1/2 cup cold buttermilk
- 2 pounds fresh strawberries, halved and hulled
- 2 tablespoons confectioners' sugar
- 2 cups heavy cream

Instructions:
1. Preheat oven to 425°F (220°C).
2. In a large bowl, whisk together the flour, sugar, baking powder, and salt until combined.
3. Cut in the butter with a pastry blender or two knives until it resembles a coarse meal.
4. Add the buttermilk and stir until blended.
5. On a floured surface, knead the dough once or twice, then roll it out to 1/2 inch (1 cm) thick. Cut out 12 circles with a biscuit cutter.
6. Place the circles on a parchment paper-lined baking sheet and bake for 12 minutes or until golden brown.
7. Hull and halve the strawberries and add the confectioners' sugar.

8. Whip the cream until stiff peaks form.
9. When the biscuits are cool, top each with some of the strawberries and whipped cream.

Nutrition information:
Calories: 448, Total Fat: 28.7g, Total Carbohydrates: 44.7g, Sugars: 13.3g, Protein: 4.1g, Sodium: 311mg

13. Caramel Cake

Caramel Cake is a deliciously sweet and moist sponge cake with a delicious caramel topping for the perfect indulgent dessert that everyone can enjoy.
Serving: Makes 12 servings.
Preparation time: 20 minutes.
Ready Time: 1 hour.

Ingredients:
- 1 ½ cup (190 g) all-purpose flour
- 2 teaspoons baking powder
- 1 teaspoon salt
- ½ teaspoon ground cinnamon
- ½ cup (115 g) butter, melted
- ¾ cup (150 g) firmly packed light or dark brown sugar
- 1 teaspoon pure vanilla extract
- 2 large eggs
- ½ cup (120 ml) whole milk
- 1 cup (240 ml) caramel sauce

Instructions:
1. Preheat the oven to 350°F (175°C) and butter and flour a 9-inch (23 cm) round cake pan.
2. In a medium bowl, whisk together the flour, baking powder, salt, and cinnamon.
3. In the bowl of an electric mixer, beat the butter and sugar until light and fluffy. Add the vanilla and eggs, and beat until creamy.
4. Add the dry Ingredients and the milk, and beat until just incorporated.

5. Pour the batter into the prepared pan and bake for 25-30 minutes, or until a toothpick inserted into the center comes out clean.
6. Let cool for 10 minutes before removing from the pan.
7. Once cool, top with caramel sauce and serve.

Nutrition information
Per serving: 223 calories; 11 g fat; 28 g carbohydrates; 3 g protein; 104 mg sodium; 36 mg cholesterol.

14. Lemon Bars

Lemon Bars are a delicious and easy-to-make dessert that combines a creamy and tart filling atop a delectable, buttery crust.
Serving: Makes 16 bars
Preparation time: 15 minutes
Ready time: 45 minutes

Ingredients:
- 1½ cups all-purpose flour
- ½ cup powdered sugar
- ¾ cup cold butter, diced
- 4 eggs
- 2 cups white sugar
- ¼ cup all-purpose flour
- ½ cup freshly squeezed lemon juice
- ½ teaspoon baking powder
- 2 tablespoons lemon zest

Instructions:
1. Preheat oven to 350°F (175°C). Grease an 8x8-inch square baking pan.
2. In a medium bowl, mix together 1½ cups of flour and powdered sugar, cut in butter until it resembles course meal. Press mixture into the pan.
3. Bake for 15 minutes in the preheated oven, until lightly browned.
4. In a large bowl, whisk together eggs, remaining sugar, ¼ cup flour, lemon juice, baking powder, and lemon zest until well blended.
5. Pour the filling over the crust.

6. Bake for an additional 20 to 25 minutes in the preheated oven. The bars should be golden brown, and the center should no longer be jiggly.
7. Allow bars to cool before cutting into squares.

Nutrition information: 164 calories; 7.5g fat; 25.6g carbohydrates; 2g protein

15. Southern Pecan Pralines

Southern Pecan Pralines are a classic Southern confection made with brown sugar, butter, cream, and pecans. These sweet, buttery treats are a delight for both children and adults alike.
Serving: Makes 24 pralines.
Preparation Time: 20 minutes
Ready Time: 40 minutes

Ingredients:
- 3/4 cup light brown sugar
- 2 tablespoons butter
- 1/4 teaspoon salt
- 1/2 cup heavy cream
- 2 cups shelled pecans
- 1 teaspoon vanilla extract

Instructions:
1. In a medium saucepan, combine the brown sugar, butter, salt, and cream and place over medium heat.
2. Stir continuously until the sugar is completely dissolved and the mixture begins to simmer.
3. Stir in the pecans and boil for 3 minutes, stirring frequently.
4. Remove from heat and stir in the vanilla.
5. Spoon the mixture onto parchment paper or a greased baking sheet in 1-inch circles.
6. Allow the pralines to cool until firm.

Nutrition information: Per Serving (1 Praline): 98 calories, 5.3 g fat, 9.8 g carbohydrate, 1.4 g protein, 0.6 g fiber.

16. Blueberry Cobbler

Blueberry Cobbler is a classic dessert made with a buttery, crunchy cobbler topping and tart juicy blueberries. It can be served warm or cold and can be made with fresh or frozen blueberries.
Serving: 8
Preparation Time: 15 minutes
Ready Time: 1 hours 15 minutes

Ingredients:
- 2 cups fresh blueberries
- 2/3 cup sugar
- 1/4 cup all-purpose flour
- 3 tablespoons butter, melted
- 1 teaspoon ground cinnamon
- 2/3 cup all-purpose flour
- 2 tablespoons sugar
- 2 teaspoons baking powder
- 1/4 teaspoon salt
- 1/2 cup milk

Instructions:
1. Preheat oven to 375 degrees F (190 degrees C).
2. Place blueberries in a 9 inch baking dish. In a small bowl, combine 2/3 cup sugar and 1/4 cup flour; sprinkle over the blueberries. Drizzle with melted butter and sprinkle with cinnamon.
3. In a medium bowl, combine the 2/3 cup flour, 2 tablespoons sugar, baking powder, and salt. Gradually stir in the milk until a soft dough forms. Drop dough by spoonfuls over the blueberry mixture.
4. Bake in the preheated oven for 30 minutes, or until topping is golden brown.

Nutrition information:
Calories: 228
Fat: 6 g
Carbohydrates: 41 g
Protein: 3 g
Sodium: 168 mg

Potassium: 64 mg

17. Pound Cake

This classic Pound Cake is moist, golden and fluffy. Its rich flavor is perfect for special occasions or everyday dessert.
Serving: 8
Preparation time: 10 minutes
Ready time: 1 hour

Ingredients:
- 3 cups all-purpose flour
- 1 teaspoon baking powder
- 1/2 teaspoon salt
- 2 sticks (1 cup) butter, at room temperature
- 2 cups granulated sugar
- 4 large eggs
- 1 teaspoon vanilla extract
- 1 cup milk

Instructions:
1. Preheat oven to 350°F. Grease an 8-inch loaf pan.
2. In a medium bowl, whisk together the flour, baking powder and salt.
3. In the bowl of an electric mixer, beat the butter for 2 minutes on high speed. Add the sugar and beat until light and fluffy, 2 to 3 minutes.
4. Add the eggs one at a time, beating after each addition. Beat in the vanilla.
5. Reduce mixer speed to low. Add half of the flour mixture, then the milk, then the rest of the flour mixture. Beat until just incorporated.
6. Pour the batter into the prepared pan.
7. Bake for 45 minutes, or until a toothpick inserted in the center of the cake comes out clean.
8. Let cool in the pan for 15 minutes before turning out onto a wire rack to cool completely.

Nutrition information: Per serving: 366 calories, 16 g fat, 5.5 g protein, 49 g carbohydrates, 1.5 g fiber, 14.5 g sugar, 186 mg sodium

18. Mississippi Mud Pie

Mississippi Mud Pie is an indulgent dessert adding a decadent Southern spin to the classic chocolate pie. Rich and creamy, this pie is sure to become a favorite!
Serving: 8-10
Preparation time: 20 minutes
Ready time: 3 hours

Ingredients:
- 1 ½ cups chocolate cookie crumbs (about 30 cookies)
- ½ cup (1 stick) unsalted butter, melted
- 2 tablespoons granulated sugar
- 2 tablespoons light brown sugar
- 2 ½ cups semisweet chocolate chips
- 1 (14-ounce) can sweetened condensed milk
- 2 tablespoons bourbon
- 2 teaspoons pure vanilla extract
- 1 ½ cups heavy cream
- 1/3 cup confectioners' sugar
- 1/4 teaspoon salt
- 1/2 cup chopped pecans

Instructions:
1. Preheat the oven to 350°F.
2. In a medium bowl, combine the cookie crumbs, melted butter, granulated sugar and brown sugar. Stir until evenly mixed.
3. Press the crust into an 8- or 9-inch pie plate. Bake until lightly golden, about 10 minutes. Let cool completely.
4. In a medium saucepan, melt the chocolate chips with the condensed milk. Remove from heat and stir in the bourbon and vanilla.
5. Pour the mixture into the cooled crust, spreading evenly. Refrigerate until set, about 2 hours.
6. In a medium bowl, beat together the heavy cream, confectioners' sugar and salt until soft peaks form. Spread the whipped cream over the pie and sprinkle with the pecans.

Nutrition information: 220 calories; 16g fat; 25g carbohydrates; 4g protein

19. Sausage Gravy and Biscuits

Sausage gravy and biscuits is a classic American comfort food. Rich crumbly biscuits smothered in savory sausage gravy, this quick and easy meal is sure to please.
Serving: 4-6
Preparation Time: 20 minutes
Ready Time: 45 minutes

Ingredients:
-3 sausage patties
-¼ cup butter
-4 tablespoons all-purpose flour
-2 cups whole milk
-4-6 biscuits (homemade or store-bought)

Instructions:
1. Brown sausage in a skillet over medium heat. Once cooked, remove from the heat and set aside.
2. In the same skillet, melt butter over medium heat and add in the flour. Whisk until flour is fully combined with the butter and the mixture is smooth.
3. Slowly whisk in one cup of the milk until the mixture is thick and creamy.
4. Add in the rest of the milk and bring to a simmer.
5. Crumble the cooked sausage into the gravy mixture and whisk to combine. Simmer over low heat for 10-15 minutes, stirring occasionally.
6. Gently place your biscuits in the gravy and fold with a spoon to combine. Heat everything through for an additional 5 minutes, then serve.

Nutrition information (per serving): Calories: 410, Fat: 23g, Carbohydrates: 28g, Protein: 23g, Sodium: 1000mg, Fiber: 2g.

20. Buttermilk Fried Chicken

Buttermilk fried chicken is a classic Southern dish that is full of flavor. It is simple to prepare and great for a family dinner or a special occasion.
Serving: 4
Preparation time: 30 minutes
Ready time: 1 hour

Ingredients:
- 4 chicken legs
- 2 cups of buttermilk
- 2 cups of all-purpose flour
- 2 teaspoons of garlic powder
- 1 teaspoon of paprika
- 2 teaspoons of baking powder
- Salt and pepper to taste

Instructions:
1. Start by marinating the chicken in a bowl of buttermilk and set aside.
2. Create a coating mix by combining the flour, garlic powder, paprika, baking powder, and salt and pepper in separate bowl.
3. Dip the marinated chicken pieces in the coating mix, shaking off excess.
4. Heat up a skillet and fry the chicken in batches for around 10-15minutes or until golden brown and cooked through.
5. Place chicken on a plate lined with paper towels and let the excess oil drip off.

Nutrition information (per serving):
Calories: 804 kcal
Fat: 43.6 g
Carbohydrates: 35.2 g
Protein: 57.7 g

21. Peach Upside-Down Cake

This Peach Upside-Down Cake combines fresh peaches, sweet brown sugar and lemon zest for an easy and delicious cake.

Serving: 10
Preparation Time: 15 minutes
Ready Time: 1 hour

Ingredients:
- 2 tablespoons butter
- 1/4 cup packed brown sugar
- 2 to 3 peaches, pitted and sliced
- 2 cups all-purpose flour
- 1 teaspoon baking soda
- 1/2 teaspoon salt
- 1 cup buttermilk
- 1/2 cup vegetable oil
- 2 large eggs
- 1 teaspoon vanilla extract
- Zest of 1 lemon
- 1/4 cup granulated sugar

Instructions:
1. Preheat oven to 350 degrees F. Grease a 9-inch round cake pan with butter.
2. Sprinkle brown sugar over the bottom of the pan and arrange peach slices on top.
3. In a medium bowl, mix together flour, baking soda and salt.
4. In a separate bowl, whisk together buttermilk, vegetable oil, eggs, vanilla extract and lemon zest.
5. Slowly stir the wet Ingredients into the dry Ingredients until combined.
6. Pour the batter into the prepared pan. Sprinkle the top with granulated sugar.
7. Bake for 40 to 45 minutes, or until a toothpick inserted into the center of the cake comes out clean.
8. Allow to cool for 10 minutes before inverting onto a plate. Enjoy!

Nutrition information:
Serving size: 1 slice (1/10 of the cake)
Calories: 289
Fat: 12.7g
Saturated fat: 2.5g
Carbohydrates: 38.2g
Sugar: 17.3g

Protein: 5.2g

22. Sweet Tea

This old-fashioned, Southern-style sweet tea is the perfect companion to a summer day. It's easy to make and always refreshing. Servings: 4
Preparation time: 10 minutes Ready time: 10 minutes

Ingredients:
6 cups cold water 2 family size tea bags 1 1/2 cups sugar

Instructions:
1. In a large pot, bring the cold water to a rapid boil over medium-high heat.
2. Reduce the heat and add the tea bags, stirring to dissolve the sugar.
3. Cover and simmer for 10 minutes.
4. Remove from heat and allow to cool for 10 minutes.
5. Remove the tea bags and pour the sweet tea into a pitcher.
6. Serve and enjoy.

Nutrition information: Not available

23. Chess Squares

Chess Squares are an old southern comfort food classic! A combination of a buttery crust, vanilla pudding, and plenty of sugar and butter, they are incredibly rich, creamy, and delicious.
Serving: 12
Preparation Time: 15 minutes
Ready Time: 50 minutes

Ingredients:
- 1/2 cup melted butter
- 1 (16 ounce) package of yellow cake mix
- 2 packages of instant vanilla pudding
- 1/2 cup white sugar
- 4 eggs